AUGMENTED STATES

A CYBERPUNK SAGA BOOK 5

MATTHEW A. GOODWIN

PART 1

CHAPTER 1

Moss took a deep breath, the ventilator doing most of the work, the air hissing out.

The day was bright and hot. A sheen of sweat coated him under the skin-tight Dermidos. The outfit was doing its job, camouflaging him as he squatted by the side of the road. From up close, he could see the suit shimmer a little as he moved, but he was all but invisible to the truck-mounted scanners as well as the security guards.

He squinted into the distance to see a plume of dirt getting closer. The main road to B.A. City was well-paved and wide, surrounded by a sea of crops on one side and endless solar panels on the other. Moss knew from experience that this was how most of the planet looked. Outside the dense cities, most of Earth had been clearcut and converted into resource production for sale both planetside and to the off-world colonies.

Moss knew there used to be towns and smaller cities dotting the landscape everywhere, but he couldn't picture it. He had tried but could not imagine a world so different from his own.

A little brown bird flitted by and landed on one of the tall stalks of prophet root.

1

Moss had spent so much of his life out here. More accurately, he had remotely controlled a robot who spent its time out here. Experiencing the real thing was different. It was hot and having to wear breathing apparatus was irritating if lifesaving.

He took another breath and heard the little whisper.

Getting close, Gibbs communicated neurally from his elevated position on the little hill cresting in the distance. Gibbs had grown up with Moss in the same corporate housing unit and left with him for the city what felt like an age ago. At the time, Gibbs was pudgy and weak, though he fancied himself tough. He had grown up a lot and was now a competent fighter for the revolution and a skilled marksman., as well as Moss's best friend.

Ten four, Moss responded, as did the two others waiting alongside the road.

Moss looked across the road at Issy, the woman he had loved his whole life, who had recently joined them. She met his glance and smiled. Dressed in green fatigues, she didn't blend into the environment as well as Moss did. She gave him a little thumbs up and he matched it.

He peered down the road. The massive delivery truck causing the dirt plume was getting closer. It was as enormous as a building turned on its side with wheels larger than a person. Rectangular, with four armed turrets at its corners and impenetrable glass on its front, it was the very picture of imposing. The cloud of dust kicked up in its wake began to blot out the sun as it approached.

Be ready, Ynna reminded them, as though they weren't already. She had devised the plan and the nerves were clear in her tone. Ynna had first introduced Moss to the outside world. She had helped shape him into the leader he was slowly

2

becoming. She had also started, seemingly despite herself, dating Gibbs.

The giant truck lurched toward them and the ground began to vibrate. A little at first but soon violently, sending small rocks bouncing into the air. Moss steadied himself and gripped his Kingfisher pistol.

He took one more slow breath.

Now, he heard and ducked, covering his head just before the massive explosion blasted a chunk out of the road. They knew the truck would be too thick to blast through with a simple rocket, but the massive machine crashed to a halt as the front left tire dropped into the fresh crater. The turrets began to turn as the operators fired a barrage of machine gun blasts at the spot the rocket came from.

Moss smiled. Ynna's plan was working perfectly. The rocket had been controlled remotely.

Clever girl, Gibbs said, and they heard the crack of his rifle from off in the distance. The armor-piercing bullet crashed through the metal of one of the turrets and it instantly stopped firing.

The operators in the other turrets ceased firing as well, spinning their weapons and looking for those who were attacking them. Doors at the front of the truck opened and security officers began to pour out, weapons ready.

The last officer stepped from the door and Moss saw the flash as Ynna darted into the truck just before the door slammed closed. She wore the same advanced Dermidos as he and was barely visible as she moved.

Go, he said, and he and Issy deployed their cover shields. The heavy metal devices they had buried at their positions fired quick anchors downward before telescoping into low metal walls. The two opened fire from each side of the road.

3

The exposed security officers dove for cover and shot back, their bullets denting and rattling Moss's shield.

As they reloaded, Moss popped out from behind the shield and shot an officer with a bolt, sending him crashing down on another. Issy's rifle cracked twice, felling two more in quick succession. Her years of practice at the shooting range came in handy. She was an excellent shot, cool under pressure.

Moss saw blood spray the inside of the truck's windshield as he fired more shots at the officers. The turrets wheeled and began shredding the area. The ground plumed as bullets tore into it and the shield began to give under the barrage.

Gibbs, Moss shrieked in his mind. *I'm pinned down.*

Makes two of us, Issy said, no doubt in the same position on the other side of the road.

Amid the other gunplay, they didn't hear Gibbs's shots but saw the results. One after another, the turrets stopped firing. As soon as they had, Moss and Issy peeked out and returned fire at the remaining guards. Moss had become quite a good shot and soon the poorly-trained and even worse paid security officers were all lying on the ground.

Issy stepped out from behind her smoking shield, shaken but doing all right. Moss stood and pulled off the mask of his second skin, winking at Issy. He had to leave his oxygen mask on because the air outside the city walls was toxic. The door to the truck swung open.

"Hey, doe eyes!" Ynna called accusingly at him and Issy. "Little help here. We are gonna have more security here pronto and still have a lot of shit to do."

They rolled their eyes at her, although they knew she was right.

They hustled over and moved beyond the cab of the giant vehicle to the binders that connected the front to the towed storage. How massive the vehicle truly was became clear as they came alongside. A ladder was required to get up to the roof and the joiners required to attach the parts were as big as Moss. He stared down at them.

"Well, shit," he said.

Issy stepped up beside him, pointing at the coupling. "It's magnetic," she told him with an easy laugh, patting him on the back.

"Ah," he said.

Anders, time to grab, Ynna communicated. *We are clear.*

Looking down, Moss heard a loud metallic thump and the connectors detached from one another, the pieces falling to the ground so heavily as to crack the concrete and shake the earth.

Five minutes out, Anders informed them. They had left the dropship back in the city and didn't want to put it at risk by bringing it out too soon. They had the one stolen ship and used it for most of their missions.

Moss moved into the shade provided by the truck. It was hot out and while the suit cooled his body, the temperature difference between a head exposed to the sun and artificially cooled body was jarring. He looked at Issy, who was staring at Ynna in her skin-tight Dermidos (now turned back to black to save energy for the next cloaking), smoothing the fabric over her backside. Moss knew what Issy was thinking. She had never said the word 'jealous' but had made more than one allusion to it. Ynna had been genetically designed for physical perfection, and while Moss loved the way Issy looked, she had a natural woman's body. He never knew what to say when she

5

disappeared into her mind like this so he would always say something like, "How you holding up?"

"I'll never get used to being shot at," Issy deflected as she looked up at Moss, her voice partially muffled by the breaking mask.

Moss nodded. "Probably for the best."

"At least this is the last one," Issy said, moving in beside him. The moment was quiet with just a few birds trilling in the fields. The first vulture had moved in overhead and more would soon follow. Though much of Earth's remaining wildlife had been forced into the small patches of land that had not been clear cut for use by ThutoCo, the vultures were still a fixture in the skies.

"Seriously," Moss agreed. "I'm happy the off-worlders are going to be providing us help, but for the last six months all we've done is jobs for them."

"It'll be worth it," Ynna told them as she stepped around. "With that fucking Warden who shot me at the head of Carcer, it's no fun out on the streets."

"Because this *is* fun?" Issy asked her wryly.

"Better than in the city, I promise you that," Ynna said. "I got Tak set up with his own Detritus crew — setting up outposts, taking down comm towers, bringing in allies, all the ground level shit. He's up to his ears in Carcer guns, so we should thank our lucky stars for just a few gun turrets."

"We're not complaining," Moss said. "We're just saying."

"I know what you're saying and I'm telling you to knock it off. We fucked over all our real friends when your grandmother killed Alice Carcer, and they are the ones paying the price while we do jobs for theoretical friends in the sky."

Moss had just been shot at and was not in the mood for a lecture from Ynna. "Alice Carcer was a blight and, of the two of us, *you* were the one in the room who could have stopped Sandra."

Ynna took an intentionally intimidating step toward Moss, pointing a finger. "I know what that woman was. I'm just reminding you of the cost."

"Guys." Issy stepped in to defuse the situation but sounded nervous. She put a hand on Moss to calm him.

Ynna smirked, "Listen to your ball-and-chain."

Guys, Gibbs communicated.

"You listen to yours," Moss said with smug satisfaction.

No, guys, seriously, we've got company, Gibbs warned.

"Shit," Ynna said and sprang toward the ladder. Moss and Issy were right behind, clambering up into the light. Moss shielded his eyes and squinted into the distance. Instead of the one large column of dust the truck had produced, he saw a dozen or more headed their way.

"Fucking Scubas!" Moss snarled. He had hated them his whole life. The nomadic raiders who lived outside the walls of the city had been thorns in his side even when he worked at ThutoCo. They would break into storage areas and steal supplies, pull up swaths of prophet root fields and generally cause problems.

No one had been able to find where they lived or knew much about them. They had been given the name 'Scuba' because of the large breathing apparatus they wore to keep from inhaling the deadly spores said to exist everywhere outside the city walls.

7

Moss knew their buggies and vehicles, designed to drive over undulating, rocky terrain, would move on them quickly.

Anders, he said, *hold off until we deal with some shitbags*.

The stolen dropship was one of their most valuable assets and something they couldn't afford to lose.

Copy that, Anders said, and Moss noticed a little speck in the distance turn around. Moss looked at Ynna. "Can we get into these turrets?" he asked, knowing they would make short work of the Scubas.

Ynna was examining the locked metal doors on the strong metal tubes. She shook her head. "I don't think so."

"Where's Judy when you need them?" Moss groused. Judy had been a Carcer Corp. technician before joining them and was usually able to solve problems like this.

Moss sighed, lying down on top of the transport to use the higher ground to his advantage. The metal was hot, having been cooking in the sun for hours. Issy lay down beside him and readied her weapon while Ynna hopped down and disappeared into the fields off the side of the road.

"I really hate Scubas," Moss said to Issy as he pulled his face covering back on, the material pressing the respirator uncomfortably against his mouth. He cloaked and watched the suit shimmer to match the gray of the metal container. Issy's eyes flashed, and he wished she hadn't demurred when he offered for her to wear it instead. Things had been much better between them since they had talked out their problems, but he still didn't feel he understood her.

"I know," she said. "You really always have. Gosh, I remember that one night after a Scuba took a potshot at MOSS II. I don't think I've ever seen you that mad."

"I don't think I've ever drank that much either," he said with a laugh. "Drank? Is that right? Drunk? Drunken?"

She laughed. "You certainly were drunken … I really thought you were going to make a move on me when I carried you back to your hex."

He didn't remember how that night ended but felt guilt and shame rising in him. "Really?" he asked nervously.

She looked as though she was about to answer, but Gibbs's rifle cut them off. The shot echoed and they knew the raiders were getting close. Moss readied himself, wishing he had more than a pistol. But the beam weapon was well-made, and he would be able to put up a good fight.

His stomach turned when he saw the number of vehicles pulling onto the road. They were all patched together, looking as if they were constructed of rust more than anything else. They belched black smoke that mingled with the trailing dirt and dust as they veered onto the asphalt.

In addition to the driver, each vehicle had at least three people hanging off the side like monkeys dangling from branches. They were whooping and calling out, brandishing old firearms or simple metal poles. All the vehicles had spikes, poles, bits of sheet metal and holsters soldered all over them.

"Shiiiit," Moss said, looking nervously at Issy, who faced him and returned the dismayed look.

Moss heard Gibbs's rifle once more, but this time fireworks followed. The driver of the lead car burst at the chest as he was struck with a massive bullet, his blood spraying the shocked riders. With no hands on the wheel and at such high speed, the tires spun hard to the right, flipping the buggy in an instant and sending it bouncing into the one beside it.

Metal crunched and screeched as both cars hurtled off the road, the ones behind squealing around and accelerating toward them.

I am the rocker, I am the roller, I am the out-of-controller! Gibbs communicated to them, eminently pleased with himself.

Great, kid, don't get cocky, Ynna commed back.

Moss exhaled slowly and fired, a blue beam flashing forward. It dissipated before hitting any of the cars, but one swerved at the sight of it, careening off the road and slamming into the base of a massive solar panel. But there were still more cars, so many more, and they were approaching fast.

Issy began taking shot after shot, shells clanging and hissing against the metal of the transport. Gibbs took out one more driver near the rear of the convoy and a couple of raiders here and there, but they were getting close now. The engines screamed their approach and screeched to a stop in front of the transport. Some of the raiders took shots while others hopped down and made their way towards Moss and Issy.

They ducked their heads and fell back, crawling away to cower behind raised ventilation shafts. Some of the raiders scrambled onto the roof. Moss fired, sending one shaking violently back to the ground while Issy shot another, spraying a crimson plume into the sky. As more climbed up, Moss and Issy had to continue their retreat, firing as they went, but they were quickly becoming overwhelmed by the raiders in their patched and ragged outfits, ancient ventilators and threatening body paint.

From the safety of his hex, Moss had always joked that they looked like the perfect cliché of raiders. Right now, it was not so funny. Four of them were getting close, the sounds of their breathers hissing toward Moss.

They all turned as a cry went up from the cars.

Ynna sprang from the field, stabbing one raider through the neck as she fired her machine gun into another before pulling the blade out and throwing it into the chest of a third. Another shot at her, sending a bullet into the already dead body of their friend. Ynna cast down the body and returned fire, shredding the raider and throwing down the spent gun. Her Dermidos crackled as it ran out of charge and Ynna appeared, standing on the side of the road for all to see.

A woman clad in strips of leather charged Ynna with a piece of rebar fashioned into a spear, while a burly man approached with a machete constructed of a piece of sheet metal stuck into a chunk of wood. Ynna moved toward the woman, ducking when she thrust the rebar and grabbing it, yanking the woman forward and punching her in the jaw.

The burly man screamed through his mask and ran forward just as Ynna pulled the spear free and hurled it forward. Moss expected it to sail right into the chest of the man, but Ynna was not a practiced spear hurler and it clanged to the ground as he raised the machete.

As this was happening, Moss and Issy used the distraction to attack the raiders on the transport. Moss fired four shots in quick succession, taking down all but one of the raiders. Moss's blue bolt was absorbed by a hidden dampener on the last one, who looked up from the shot and began to charge. Issy took a single shot at the raider as he moved on Moss. The brute fell backward, clutching the bullet hole.

Issy darted forward to see the spear fall to the ground and Ynna being rushed. She shot the man and he fell to his knees just in front of Ynna who turned and yelled, "I had him."

"Yeah, yeah," Issy said with a shrug. "You're welcome."

Moss stepped over to take in the scene. Bodies littered the road, now chewed up with bullet holes. The area smelled of acrid smoke, blood and the body odor of the unwashed attackers.

Anders, you're clear, Ynna told the pilot.

Copy, he said.

"I swear there were more of those buggies," Issy said, tilting her head to crack her neck.

Gibbs, you see any more? Moss asked.

And really, that was one hell of a shot, Ynna said, holding a thumbs up toward his spot on the hill.

They got no answer.

Gibbs, Moss said, turning to look up at where his friend had been.

Ynna started running before Moss could even process it, screaming, "Gibbs!" into the respirator.

CHAPTER 2

They ran up the hill, panting with fear and exhaustion.

He was gone. Tire tracks led up and down to the spot. In the confusion, none of them had noticed the buggies drive up that way. The ground was chewed where the raiders had spun the vehicles to make a quick getaway. Under a slight tree growing between the shadows of two massive solar panels, they spotted a small spot of blood. It stopped Moss's heart.

Gibbs's blood. He was hurt. He had been taken.

Moss blamed himself and knew Ynna and Issy were feeling the same way. Staring down at the small pool of crimson, Ynna screamed into her mask, the sound so loud that the surrounding birds fled in terror. She punched the little tree with her cybernetic hand, splintering it into pieces.

"We have to get him!" she shrieked at Moss and Issy.

Their heads turned as the dropship approached, the colossal magnet Judy had added to its base vibrating as it neared the back of the truck. The side of the ship opened, and they all watched as Sandra hopped out of the side and onto the roof of the truck before dropping to the ground. She made her way toward them as they ran to her.

Moss's grandmother was fit for her age and as threatening as she had ever been. The war veteran wore old military boots with jeans tucked in, a leather vest over a fading red and black checkered shirt, aging brimmed hat and rifle slung over her back. She was the perfect picture of an aging warrior.

"What's up?" her voice hissed out of the respirator.

"They fucking took him!" Ynna shouted, pointing in the direction of the tire treads.

"Shit," Sandra said, her eyes flickering with thought for a moment. "We can get this shipment to the colonists and then comb the landscape looking for the raiders' camp."

Sandra turned toward the ship.

"Like hell we will," Ynna shouted, running up behind the older woman. "I'm taking the van and going after him."

Sandra spun and pointed a finger. "You ain't going into a fight half-cocked just because some fucking Scubas interrupted your double-date. We go finish what we started and we will come back for Gibbs," Sandra said and, reading the room, added, "I promise."

Moss couldn't believe what he was hearing. He knew it might be the right thing to do — finish the job, get help, get ready and look for Gibbs — but it felt wrong. His friend had been taken and he needed to go help him.

"I'll go with her now," Moss announced, and he could see the disappointment in his grandmother's eyes.

"Me too," Issy added.

Sandra shook her head. "Y'all are going to get killed because you can't wait a moment. Think that's what Gibbs wants?"

"Pretty sure Gibbs wants to be rescued," Ynna snarled, starting to walk down toward the road, eyeing the buggies. Moss followed her as the magnet clanged and sucked the transport into position.

We good to go? Anders asked from the cockpit.

No, Sandra told him. *Damned fools mean to run off.*

To save Gibbs! Ynna justified.

There was a pause. *Do what you need to do and good luck, but I have to get this to Captain Patel now.*

Understood, Moss said. *Stay safe out there.*

You too, Anders agreed.

Moss turned to his grandmother. "You coming with us?"

Sandra shook her head. "Wanna see this job through. You survive this, we'll come out to pick you up once the drop is seen to."

"Okay," he said, nodding her way.

"Come on," Ynna called to him from the driver's seat of one of the buggies. It was little more than a metal frame, roughly soldered together atop large tires perfect for traversing rough terrain. The driver's seat was patched together with fraying duct tape and the back was little more than a piece of advertising billboard laid flat for passengers to stand on.

He uneasily joined Issy on the back, gripping a part of the frame for dear life. Before hopping in, Ynna had gathered all the nearby weapons and they were jammed in a heap behind her seat. The engine roared to life and they took off down the road, as Anders lifted the stolen goods upward into the sky.

Moss felt the contents of his stomach rise the moment Ynna gunned it, making the buggy swing before tearing down the road. The tracks leading from where Gibbs had been were clear, leaving long dirt stains in the road; but they quickly faded. Moss knew that Ynna would use her cybernetic eye to track the Scubas.

He had often wondered about them and why ThutoCo allowed them to operate. The company had massive security measures and it had always seemed that they could have stamped the raiders out whenever they wanted to. But they didn't.

They fought the raiders, to be sure. Made an effort to look like they were making an effort but never really took any serious action. That had puzzled Moss to the point that he had gone to the office of Mr. Greene, his ThutoCo mentor, and asked about it.

The older man had considered his words and looked around the office nervously.

"I can tell you that I don't know," Mr. Greene had said, running his hand down his mouth. "And that would be the truth."

"But?" Moss asked.

"But I have always felt that there was more to it." He tapped his perfectly polished fingernails on his immaculately clean desk. "This is not the kind of question I am allowed to ask, and we should definitely not be having this conversation — and aren't, if you take my meaning."

Moss nodded. He had been so young and naïve at the time, an unexperienced child; but even then, he could still see the cracks in the world.

"We have depots with military-grade mechs that could track down and eliminate these targets within a day. But we don't," Mr. Greene observed, putting words to Moss's thoughts. "I have never understood it either, and I know you are on to something."

A conspiratorial look crossed his face and he leaned in, deactivating his drudge personal assistant. "Have you ever tried to track a Scuba?"

"No," Moss admitted. "Though I don't think it would be too difficult."

"Exactly," Mr. Greene agreed, spreading his hands in confusion. "They don't even try to cover their literal tracks."

He lowered his voice to an almost inaudible whisper. "Try it."

Moss had. The next day, he saw a solar panel smoking in the distance. What was odd was that no official work order had been put in. He scrolled through all the available jobs and all of them were further out than the panel in need of immediate repair. Just to be sure, he even opened up the tab for ALL JOBS, displaying in red the ones above his pay grade or only available to specialists.

Nothing.

He had turned his bike and drove toward the smoke.

"Please alter your current course and select an available job," MOSS II, the computerized drudge that Moss remotely controlled, had told him.

"Stay on course," Moss said, but he could feel resistance. He controlled the unit neurally from his home and things that happened out in the world sent dulled versions of the feeling to his brain. As a result, he could feel the tug as the drudge tried to untether itself from its master's control.

The smoke was getting closer, the acrid black beginning to blot the sun.

The tug got worse.

Moss used all his mental strength to keep the machine going forward. As they approached, he could see the telltale signs of a Scuba attack. The panel ripped open, the parts mangled and hauled away. He tried to zoom the computer's camera in on the wreckage.

No.

Moss felt his real body jerk as he was almost knocked out of his seat.

"This course of action is unsafe for this unit, manual control overridden, automated control established," MOSS II informed him before the AI personality added, "Sorry."

17

Moss had not been mad but fascinated. The whole experience had piqued his interest.

The moment his shift was over, he dashed from his hex back to Mr. Greene's office; but as soon as he burst in, he could tell things were different.

Mr. Greene was distant and aloof and his drudge stood in the corner, staring at them with electronic eyes. Moss knew better than to bring it up again. He pretended there was some other business he needed to discuss and talked for just a few moments before leaving the office. Mr. Greene had lied effectively, but Moss could see the strain on his mentor's face.

It was one of the first times Moss had an inkling that things at the company were not all they seemed. At the time, he had not known that they had altered his memory of his parents and had nothing but unwavering faith in the company.

But the look on Mr. Greene's face had changed that. MOSS II altering course was a start but something about the fear, the clear intimidation that Mr. Greene must have faced, shook Moss to his core. Over time, he had put it out of his mind, but all the memories came flooding back as they bounced along the road to save Gibbs.

The vehicle shook violently as they moved, the world blurring by them. Issy reached out and clutched Moss's arm, not for her benefit but for his. He smiled. She always seemed to anticipate his needs. Having her around had become such a comfort. Gibbs and Ynna had been there for him since his arrival in the city, but it was different with Issy. She made him feel safe in a way that the others could not. Even his own family, for as tough as his grandmother was, Sandra never made him feel safe except in a gun battle.

They kept going for what seemed like an endless amount of time. The fields never ended. Moss knew this. He had spent his whole life out here and understood that most of the planet was just this. A sea of the same. The company had always said it was a necessity. In order to feed both the world and the colonies, the planet needed to be one massive farm. Moss no longer believed that. He knew there had to be an alternative.

Eventually, Ynna slowed to a stop. She jumped down quickly and Moss took a moment to calm his body down. Issy rubbed his back.

Ynna ran to the side of the road toward some prophet root. She hacked at the plants with the long knife she had grabbed and, as chunks of the root came loose, revealed a hidden wall.

"Sons of bitches," she exclaimed and waved for the others to come over. They did as Ynna ran her hands along the thick row of plants. She found a spot where there seemed to be the edge of a door. They all began pulling, Moss leveraging his robotic legs and Ynna her metal hand.

The door was obviously metal and immovable.

"Moss," Ynna said frantically. "Use the program, hack the door."

He shook his head, feeling sick. Issy hustled away from them. "I can't," he told her. "You know I can't. I'm taking the dampeners."

She knew he was taking the drugs to keep the program in his mind at bay. He had recently learned how powerful the program was, that he could hack systems with his mind. But he had also learned the program was unstable and ThutoCo was trying to hack it to gain access to his mind.

Patchwork, the team's breaker, had installed strong defenses and taught Moss more about the program, but they had all agreed it was too dangerous to let function all the time. Moss had started to take digital inhibitors to help. He was happy to know there was no chance the company could break into his

19

mind, but he was miserable in moments like this when a quick hack could solve their problems.

"But Moss," Ynna wailed, the pain so evident in her voice that it physically hurt him. "Please," she said, as though there was anything he could do.

He closed his eyes, knowing it couldn't work, but willing to try for her, for his best friend, and for Ynna.

He reached out with his mind, feeling nothing. It was like trying to go into a dream while awake. The pills were working too well.

Desperately, he tried again and was shocked when he heard the door begin to groan. His eyes shot open, and he watched as the plants began to turn and the giant door rolled aside. The ground shook and Ynna vibrated with elation, turning to wrap Moss up in a hug of pure gratitude.

"What are you hugging him for?" Issy hollered from the buggy, a remote control in her hand. "This was on their car."

Ynna pushed Moss away. "Issy, you're a genius!"

Issy gave a little salute. They ran over to the car, Ynna patting Issy on the ass before getting in the driver's seat.

"I got your back," Issy told her as they began to move once again.

The circular entrance was wide enough for two cars to pass one another and tall enough for a medium sized truck. The path did not lead straight in, but rather wound in a circle downward into the ground. Moss did not understand what this place was as they descended the concrete corkscrew.

"Parking garage," Ynna called back to them. Moss nodded, feeling foolish. He had driven a little since leaving the burb for the city, but didn't know about things like that. He sometimes wished he had been able to spend a little time learning about the world. Since arriving, they had always been on a mission. And while there was certainly down time, he mostly spent it sleeping or trying to get better at things that would help him on the next mission.

Ynna slowed once again, the buggy skidding to a stop before the end of another loop.

"What's up?" Issy asked.

Ynna pulled her weapons. "We walk from here."

"Thinking we can negotiate?" Moss asked hopefully.

Ynna nodded.

"Let me do the talking," Moss suggested. "Think you are a little too upset."

"Well, aren't you?" Ynna snarled defensively.

"Of course," Moss said, and was about to speak when Ynna threw up her hands.

"Okay, fine," she said. "Whatever. If you think it gives us a better chance, I'm game."

He could hear in her voice that she was more scared than anything else. She loved Gibbs and she could not stand the idea of anything happening to him. Moss could relate completely, but unlike her, he wouldn't allow his anger to cloud his judgment.

Ynna began to pull weapons from the car and check them. Moss moved away from her and toward Issy.

"Keep an eye on her," he warned, knowing Ynna would be more than willing to kill everyone if she thought it could help Gibbs.

Moss saw Ynna cock an eye but didn't care if she heard. He almost wanted her to.

She tossed them more weapons pilfered from the truck's guards. The Scubas' firearms looked about as useful as rusty pipes.

"Wait," Issy said, looking at Moss. "Why don't *I* do the talking?"

21

Moss and Ynna both looked at her in puzzlement until she reached out and pulled at the digital fabric on Moss's sleeve.

He grinned.

CHAPTER 3

"We mean you no harm," Issy said as they approached the front gate at the bottom of the ramp.

It was a wall of corrugated metal pressed up against parked cars and soldered together. The wall stretched to both sides and reached the cement roof with only little slats cut in for the Scubas to look out.

Moss knew his suit had enough power to stay cloaked for a little while but not exactly how long. He also didn't know if there would be any weakness in the wall though he was happy to try to find one.

"Lots of guns for no harm," a voice called from behind the wall and one of the panels swung open. A young man with wild eyes, a toothless grin and patchy blond hair pointed a rifle down at them. "Whatchu want?"

"We are just here for our friend," Issy told him, and Moss noticed that he was not wearing any sort of breathing apparatus. He wondered if whatever the contagion was didn't travel to these depths or if he had missed a detoxifying mister at the surface.

Pressing himself against the wall and being careful not to rattle it or draw any attention, he kept looking for anything he could use to breach the wall. He could hear people whispering and moving around on the other side and he wondered how many there were.

He kept moving, slowly.

"Put those weapons down," the Scuba demanded.

Ynna and Issy exchanged looks but Issy slowly lowered her weapon. Moss had expected this to happen, but it terrified him. Gibbs was captured and now Issy and Ynna would be defenseless and at the mercy of the Scubas.

"We are lowering our weapons," Issy told him as Moss continued to move away from them, looking for a break, a gap, anything.

"How do I know you isn't hiding more?" the Scuba hollered down to them, his voice echoing through the enclosed cement space. Moss was far enough away that the response was difficult to hear, but he figured things were okay if there wasn't gunfire.

While parts of the wall were rusted out and others ripped or cracked, none of the gaps were large enough for a person to get through without making a lot of noise. He kept moving, surprised by how long the wall was. He couldn't imagine needing this many parking spaces layered for as many floors as they had dropped- though he did know that there was a time before flighted and self-driving cars when all people drove themselves and left their cars parked all around cities.

Then he saw it.

It would have been impossible to spot from afar, but from as close as he was the cut line was clear. It was a small square, just big enough for a person to crawl through. He got closer, running his finger over it.

It was some kind of passage.

The ground beneath was worn down, the asphalt dipping slightly and turning to pebbles. He reached for his gun but thought better of it, knowing that if he loosed it from its holster it would no longer be cloaked. He reached out, pushing on the door. He expected resistance, but the panel swung open on well-lubed hinges.

He sighed, then pushed his way though, the smell of fur filling his nose in an instant, even through the filter. He felt his heart stop as he realized he had crawled into a kennel. Matted blankets lay all around the small boxed-in space with a little opening at a far end.

His eyes darted around looking for a guard dog, but he couldn't see much in the dim light and didn't want to use his suit's battery on infrared. So he waited a moment, his hand ready to pull his gun.

He heard nothing and his eyes began to adjust. He saw the rounded opening at the far side of a wood-framed room with scrap walls of cardboard and billboard, more for show than anything else.

A shape in the far corner shifted and Moss squinted, just able to make out an ancient-looking mastiff lying on a flattened dog bed devoid of stuffing. Gray hairs coated its face and its skin hung loosely. Moss inched forward, keeping his eyes on the animal that did not move.

He kept crawling, careful to move as quietly as possible. He didn't know how many people were in this camp, but if this dog started barking, he and all his friends would be dead in an instant. Gibbs was already captured and Ynna and Issy were weaponless at the front gate with unknown numbers of guns pointed at them. He didn't dare breathe; he just kept creeping forward. He was invisible, but that would not protect him from an animal for whom smell was the primary sense.

As he neared the exit, the animal stirred, making a noise from deep inside its throat before shaking its head lazily. Moss moved quickly. He just wanted to get out of there, knowing he would have felt safer if it had been an armed guard.

He pulled himself through the door on the inside of the camp and sucked in air, the ventilator hissing quietly — though it sounded like a sonic boom to Moss. He looked around the camp. It was different than he had expected. From the look of the raiders in their shabby, patched attire and scavenged buggies, he had anticipated ramshackle homes of found materials. Instead, he saw pristine, small white domes with automatic doors and windows, small porches and umbrella lights on top.

Moss couldn't believe his eyes. It was the exact opposite of what it should be. The rows of homes were separated by well-tended faux grass paths illuminated by smart streetlights that glowed to life as people approached. The rows of homes seemed to stretch toward a central plaza where Moss could make out figures milling about in gray coveralls.

He shook his head, unsure what to make of any of it. Moving forward, he pressed himself up against one of the domes and peered down the street, seeing a larger dome on the far side. He had no idea if that was where they had taken Gibbs, but it seemed as good a place as any to start. There were people moving between the buildings and up the streets, so Moss made his way to the farthest side, up against the wall of the parking lot.

He felt something brush against him and had his weapon drawn in an instant, his heart nearly pounding through his chest.

The dog looked slowly up at him. Moss didn't know if it smelled him or heard his breath or what, but there it was. Its jowls hung down off its cheeks and the red inner skin showed around its eyes. It didn't bark, just moved in to nuzzle an invisible leg.

Moss knew what he should do, what his grandmother would do, but when he held up the Kingfisher he couldn't do it. Even a non-lethal stun could seriously injure the ancient animal and Moss couldn't abide that. Instead, he kept moving with the dog plodding along behind.

He had to stop dead when a kid came running out of a dome and disappeared down a street. Eventually, Moss neared the largest dome, the mouth of which opened into a little round park with benches and some old but well-maintained statuary. There were very few people around. Moss had seen a lot of backs when he moved away from the wall and realized most of the community was watching the interaction with Issy. He looked both ways as he moved out from between two domes, checked his weapon and darted to the large dome.

"Who are you with?" an older man in torn pants asked, wiping war paint off his face with a wet rag before handing it to a kid at his side. Gibbs sat blindfolded and strapped to a chair, a large person dressed in raider garb on either side of him.

Moss knew he should take the measured approach, listen and wait, learn what he could. It was the smart thing to do. But the sight of his friend with a bruise on the side of his head, strapped to a chair with his eyes covered was too much, and all planning went out the window. The man asking the questions was obviously some kind of leader here and Moss dashed up behind him, hooking his arm around the man's neck and pressing the Kingfisher to his temple, decloaking as he moved.

"Keep fucking quiet, untie him and then back up," Moss demanded of the two raiders who looked so shocked and terrified that it took them a moment to move. It was odd.

Dressed as they were, Moss thought they would behave like savages as they had out on the road. But they didn't.

They moved to untie Gibbs as Moss asked, "You okay?"

"Been better," Gibbs said hoarsely, the words cutting Moss. They had not been apart for very long, but Moss knew his friend must have been scared the whole time.

"Okay, asshole," Moss threatened, pressing the weapon hard against the older man, the metal pulling his skin. "You are going to let me and my friends go," he said.

"But first," the old man cut in. "You have some questions.

It took Moss by surprise once again. "Yes," he said, as Gibbs took the blindfold off and looked around the room. He seemed equally shocked. Rather than a derelict dump, they were in a modern structure with folding chairs stacked against a wall, a water cooler against another and a pull-down projector screen on the far side. It was obviously some kind of meeting place for the locals.

"What is going on here?" Gibbs asked, looking at the two people whose raider garb clashed entirely with the look of the place.

The old man sighed. "I imagine you won't, but you can put the gun down. I think it is time we talked."

Moss shook his head. "Not putting this down until I get some answers."

"All right," the man said. He turned to the trembling kid who moved to cower in the corner when Moss made himself visible. "Tell our people to stand down and allow their friends in. They have seen." The kid did not move.

"It's okay," the man soothed. "I'll be okay."

28

"He will," Moss assured the kid. He would have said anything if it meant that Issy and Ynna would be allowed in. The child was well-groomed, wearing khaki linens reminiscent of those Moss had worn in the burbs. He had big, scared green eyes and a fashionable haircut. He wasn't dirty or vicious looking but more like a kid from the burbs.

As he ran out to fetch their friends, Moss reiterated Gibbs's question. "What the hell is going on here?"

"Would it surprise you to learn it's an elaborate ruse?" the man asked, his body beginning to tremble. Not, it seemed, from nerves but rather from being held in an uncomfortable position.

Gibbs walked over, examining the man. Shaking his head, he answered, "I don't think anything would surprise us anymore."

Moss was having to hold the man up. He turned to the two raiders, still looking at them with fear.

"Move that chair to the far side of the room," he ordered, and they did so. Moss dragged the man to the chair and set him down, staying behind him with his gun trained and his own back to the wall.

"Thank you," the man said, panting in the chair, his skin glistening, curly white back hairs matted down. He looked old. The two raiders had moved toward the door. They were not armed and seemed overwhelmed by the whole situation.

After a while, Issy and Ynna entered, looking a little disheveled as they pulled their outfits back into position and gripped their weapons cautiously.

"What the hell is going on here?" Issy asked, but the moment was interrupted by Ynna running across the room to embrace Gibbs.

"Did they hurt you?" she whispered, her eyes darting around the room, calculating how to kill everyone.

"My pride more than anything," he whispered back and kissed her on the cheek.

She gave a small, sincere smile. "I didn't even know you had pride."

He smiled back.

A crowd had gathered outside the building. Some people were dressed in the ragged raider getups while most others were clothed in the drab khaki. The four outsiders looked at the older man in the chair with utter confusion.

"So, one more time," Moss began, making a show of holding the Kingfisher to the man's temple. "What the hell is going on here?"

"Let me begin with introductions," the old man said.

The kid who had been holding the rag earlier peeked through the door, holding aloft a tan shirt, and Moss nodded for him to enter. He didn't have any idea what was happening but did not feel unsafe. The people here looked as confused as he and his friends were, and although they had been shooting at one another just moments before, they seemed peaceable.

"My name is Josiah, and I am the shepherd of this flock," he explained as the kid handed him the shirt and he pulled it laboriously over his head. The people stared at the strangers and Moss couldn't help but watch them watch him as he loomed over their leader. "We are a people who have lived in the uninhabitable zone since the time of the Great Pandemic. As people of belief, our ancestors were forced from the city walls. They were deemed too dangerous and were persecuted by the heathens within.

"Our people were cast out of B.A. City just as so many were from so many cities," he continued, and the people all listened with rapt attention as though this was the first time they were hearing this. The children sat down and leaned in, and a few people even gathered up the folding chairs and made themselves comfortable.

It was the strangest standoff Moss had ever been a part of.

"Those of us with faith were thought to have abandoned science and were therefore abandoned by society. In times of great fear, great evil can be committed. The Carcer Corporation enacted the will of the people and pushed our forefathers out." He grew quiet, pensive.. "Most died," he said gravely. "So few at the time knew they needed filtered air. They wandered the land until it consumed them or they, each other. Those who did survive attempted to establish roots while trying to stay hidden."

"Why not just flee to the Refuge of the Saved?" Ynna asked. "I thought that was the whole point of that city, to give people like you a safe place to live and practice?"

Josiah narrowed one eye at Ynna, seemingly impressed that she knew of the place. "Many did try and some even succeeded, so it is said. But for most, with many children and little hope, the journey was too perilous. Instead, as I said, they settled down. Hid and tried to keep themselves safe.

"Those who the plague spared, ThutoCo destroyed," he continued. "The company bought up all the land from the crumbling national government and local owners who needed the money to start a life within the cities, and they killed our people. Outlawed by Carcer within the walls and outlawed by ThutoCo without, most survivors died a grim and unjust death."

Moss was not surprised to hear any of this. He had learned long ago that the version of history he had been taught in the burbs was nothing but one long company line. There was so much ugliness he seemed to be learning piecemeal. A tidbit

31

here, a little information there. It was becoming apparent there was so much more that he needed to learn. ThutoCo had been the cause of and solution to the Great Pandemic, as this man called it, but they also seemed to benefit from it more directly than any other company. They had polluted the planet, forced the remaining people into the cities, and then bought up all the land for their farms.

He was happy to be gaining one more piece of the puzzle, though he did not fully understand why this man was telling them this information.

"Some managed to hide," continued Josiah. "Found a tucked away place here, a hidden cave there. They persisted. They found ways to filter the air. Found ways to feed themselves and survive in a world that had tried time and again to kill them. They kept the faith and kept themselves alive."

He said the last words with a finality and the mood of the room was such that Moss expected the assembled crowd to burst into applause. They did not. Moss cocked his head.

"While fascinating," Moss said, "I don't know what any of this has to do with anything."

"Ah," Josiah said knowingly. "It has to do with everything. For you, like us, are criminals."

Moss wanted to press the weapon against the man's head harder for the accusation but realized it would only make his point for him. Rather, he let the weapon fall to his side as he said, "We are not criminals."

Josiah turned in his chair to smile up at Moss, looking at him with eyes of crystalline blue. "To us, no you are not," he said kindly. "But to others, you are the terrorist Moss, are you not?"

That stopped his heart. He was no longer cloaked, but he was covered from head to toe in a suit with a breather that altered his voice. How did these people know who he was? Moss didn't believe Gibbs had told them anything but he also hadn't been in their custody long enough to have been coerced into giving up antyhing.

Confused, he pulled the mask off and ventilator out. The people here were not wearing them and Gibbs had not been, so he was happy to be done with it.

A collective gasp went up around the room as he admitted, "Yes."

"I know," Josiah said, gesturing for his people to calm down. And somehow, Moss knew that the man had known. "We have been told about you. To look out for you."

"By whom?" Issy asked, taking a step forward. Her eyes were fixed on the man.

The calm way he spoke, his deep voice and understated confidence gave him a commanding presence that impressed Moss. Sandra was the opposite, leading with harsh words and harsher deeds. Moss knew there was something to be learned from this man who could keep everyone's attention while sitting calmly and quietly in a chair.

"Why, your employer," he said to Moss. "Of course."

"ThutoCo warned you?" Moss said, and now he felt the pieces falling into place. The protection of the Scubas, the domes, the warning: all of it was connected somehow.

"Yes," Josiah said plainly. "Though you have nothing to fear from us with them."

"Good," Moss sighed.

"Wait, what the fuck?" Ynna burst out. "You all work with ThutoCo?"

A murmur rose in the room and Josiah tapped his fingers on his knee. It was an odd thing to see the man in half a uniform which perfectly suited him and half a raider outfit.

33

Everything Moss had known about the outside world was coming apart.

"As I mentioned," Josiah said in a tone that implied he was going to continue his story, "some found refuge. Those that did survived for years, generations. They were forced to interpret the good book in a way that worked, were forced to act according to a new understanding, but they made do and they survived.

"Eventually, they learned the ways of the world, learned something that people may not have wanted them to learn. This became the key to the life you see before you.

"Our people discovered some truths that ThutoCo would rather they hadn't and a bargain was struck."

Ynna smirked and whispered, "That's a negotiation I would have wanted to see."

Josiah smiled. "Me as well. Suffice to say, a deal was made for the mutual benefit of both parties."

"Let me guess," Moss said. "One side got the better end of the bargain?"

Josiah seemed to consider his words. "Yes, in part, but we were given a life that we would never have otherwise been afforded. This camp, these buildings, lights, power, all of it."

"In exchange for?" Moss asked.

"In exchange for keeping our secret and . . . " he let the sentence die, waiting for someone to inquire.

"For?" Gibbs asked.

"Becoming this," he said, pulling in disgust at the stained blue raider pants he wore.

"Becoming the Scubas?" Moss asked. He couldn't help but be surprised. He had always thought of the Scubas as being monsters who loved to mess with ThutoCo.

"Yes," Josiah said, and the word came out merely as a breath.

"It fit their narrative to have us attack them and they provided the incentive," he admitted. "We complied. We had already been forced to raid, but now we became the Scubas and would attack their supplies.

"We did so and we got to live like this."

"Why?" Moss said, excited to finally know some answers. "Why did they want you to do this? What was the narrative?"

"Ah," Josiah said, and he turned fully around to face Moss. "That is part of the secret, part of what we know that they wish we did not."

Ynna groaned. "And here it is," she said. "Here comes the offer."

Josiah nodded. "Quite," he said. "We know something that we believe will benefit you. And you have the ability to help us."

Moss felt his shoulders fall. He wanted to know, but he did not want to jump through any more hoops. They had only just finished getting supplies for the off-worlders in exchange for their help and now this man wanted more.

"Fine," Moss said, sounding exactly as unenthusiastic as he was. "What can we do for you? What do you want?"

"Hold up," Ynna said, stepping forward, her hands up. "How do we even know you have this information?"

"Look around you," Josiah said. "Could we have all this if we didn't work with them, if we didn't have something they wanted? Do we look like raiders? Do we seem like the people they make us pretend to be?"

He was so unfazed by everything that Moss couldn't help but be impressed by the man.

MATTHEW A. GOODWIN

"More to the point," he added. "Would we have sent so many of our brothers and sisters to heaven this morning if it were not important to us to meet you?"

He looked right at Moss once more.

"You came this morning just for us?" Moss asked.

"Yes," Josiah told him. "Since the moment ThutoCo said to be on the lookout for you and that there was a reward for your capture, we knew that we had to meet with you. We have sent our people out as often as we could. We prayed that one day our paths would cross, and He has finally answered us."

"You," Moss said quietly, finally holstering his weapon. "You let all those people of yours die just to capture Gibbs and get us here? Why not just try to flag us down?"

"Would you have stopped to chat?" Josiah asked incredulously. "Would she?" he pointed to Ynna. "And . . ." he began.

"ThutoCo could have been watching," Issy filled in.

"Correct," he agreed. "Though if they had been, we would all be with the Father now."

"Okay," Moss said, meeting the man's gaze. "You did all this, you got us here. What is it that you want?"

PART 2

CHAPTER 4

T he ride back to the city had been unlike anything Moss had ever experienced. After dressing in the raider garb, they had been given use of the buggy once more and sent back the way they had come. Anders was still busy, so they paid for passage back into the city through a tunnel Moss knew of under the wall.

Garbed as Scubas, they now understood that ThutoCo would not try to stop them. Nor, it seemed, would anyone else outside the walls. Looking down as they drove through the endless fields, Moss couldn't help but feel a strange sense that this was the true death of the ThutoCo engineer he had been.

He had done so much to fight the company that raised him, so much to bring them low and stop them from doing more harm. But there was something about becoming a Scuba, the one group of people he still hated from his ThutoCo days, that seemed to solidify his transformation. It was a small thing and he knew it, but it was still meaningful to him.

He turned to look at Issy. She was as beautiful as ever to him. In a tattered yellow tank top, patched pink pants with orange suspenders and a crude breathing device, she looked nothing like the woman he had grown up knowing. But when she turned her big, chestnut eyes on him, she was everything he had always loved. Her eyes smiled at him and he felt his mouth smile back. Reaching out, he grabbed her hand in his and gave it a squeeze.

Back at the safehouse, the mood was tense. Sandra and Anders were still out making the delivery when the four of them returned. Moss and Ynna helped Gibbs over to a couch. He was not too badly injured with just a bruise on the head, but he was tired from the ordeal. He groaned heavily as Ynna turned to Issy and said, "Take care of him for a minute."

Issy nodded and Ynna grabbed Moss by the arm. "We need to talk."

She pulled him into his room and shut the door. "You know I love her," she began, her eyes fierce. "But that was some fucked up shit."

Moss was not surprised to hear this. Ynna and Sandra had often been at odds, but Moss knew Ynna had a grudging respect for his grandmother in spite of it all. This time though, Moss was worried Sandra had gone too far.

"Leaving us like that," Ynna growled. "Not giving a shit if we got to Gibbs on time. Moss, this is seriously fucked."

Moss agreed with her philosophically and was pissed too, but he needed to calm her down for the good of the team. They would confront Sandra, but not while Ynna was so mad she couldn't make a good argument.

"I know," he said, trying to soothe her. "It was not great, but we had to get those drudges to the colonists and their ship couldn't stay hidden for very long."

Ynna narrowed her eyes at him. "Are you kidding me? That was *your* best friend they took and you're going to give me this shit? Sure, the off-worlders didn't have all day, but we needed Sandra more than Anders did. And if nothing else, we needed her support. Seriously, Moss, you cannot possibly be arguing with me about this."

"I'm not," he said. "I mean, I am. I mean, not that I am, I'm just trying to say that we need to stop and breathe. We got him out; we even learned some new intel. This is a net positive."

"Yes," Ynna said. "Because of us! Because of you and me and *in spite of* her. Sandra means more to me than I like to admit, but I also am not as clouded as you. I see her for what she is."

"And what's that?" he asked, his blood starting to boil. He didn't like her accusation of being blind to Sandra's behavior.

"She is a broken thing," Ynna said. "Her passion for this cause has been overridden by a hatred of Carcer and their allies."

"She has every right to hate them!" Moss whispered angrily. Even though he had these exact thoughts himself, he didn't like hearing them spoken by someone else. He wanted to defend the only family member he had. "They took her and tortured her for years! What did you expect would happen?"

Ynna shook her head. "That's exactly my point," she sighed. "She was brutalized, and of course she has every right to be pissed. We all would be, but it makes her dangerous, affects her judgement. She is so singularly focused on the job that she sometimes loses sight of everything else."

Moss took a deep breath and Ynna continued. "I know you were pissed about that one guy," she said, thinking. "The one who helped you breach the comm tower; what was it, Ned?"

"Neil," Moss corrected.

"Right, Neil," she nodded. "He helped you, and Sandra had you kill him without warning you."

Moss tried to shake off the memory of it. "Yeah," he said, not sure what else to say. The memory of the man plummeting off the side of the tower was seared into his memory.

"I know that haunts you, and I know you're pissed even if you haven't said anything," she said, and she was right. He had been pissed about that and it had made him question his grandmother. Ynna was wrong that he hadn't said anything, though; he had talked to Issy about it. She had told him that he needed to confront Sandra but he had demurred, preferring to just let it go.

"You're right," he admitted. There was no point in lying. He hated to speak of Sandra this way, but he couldn't hold back any longer. Ynna's intense eyes were cutting right into him. "She is making decisions that worry me," he admitted. "I know she wants to do what she thinks is best for all of us, but I sometimes also fear that the hatred has just overwhelmed everything else."

"Good," Ynna sighed. "Not good that it's happening, but good that you are admitting it."

"Right," Moss said in defeat. "So, what do we do?"

"Honestly, I don't know. I actually don't even think we say anything."

"Oh? What was the point of this, then?"

Ynna shook her head and sighed as though he was a prize idiot. "To make sure we were on the same page. People look to us for guidance, and I needed to make sure that you and I were seeing eye to eye in case some new shit comes up."

"Sure," Moss said. Now that they were discussing it openly, he wished there was more of a plan. He realized in that moment that when it came to his grandmother, his feelings were frighteningly complex. "I'll keep an eye out."

"You keep two eyes out," she said seriously, before one corner of her mouth turned up and she gave him a pat on the cheek. "Now, let's go see if your dumbfuck friend is doing okay," she added, turning to leave.

"Your dumbfuck boyfriend," he muttered under his breath, following her out the door.

As they stepped through the door, Moss saw something he had been waiting for but had not expected in this exact moment. The main room was empty except for Gibbs standing at its center. The peeling wallpaper, ripped sofas, electrical cabling and small countertop stacked with unwashed dishes were illuminated by a dozen small electric candles. Gibbs was dressed in the suit that Issy had let him hide in her room. The buttons on the shirt were not aligned and his shoulders were a little wet with the water he had hastily splashed on his hair, but Moss had to admit his friend looked good.

Despite his bravado, Gibbs had been so pudgy and childlike when they had left the burbs. Now, just a few years later, he was a different person. The baby weight had turned mostly to lean muscle, though he would always be larger than Moss. His orange mop of hair had been cut and styled even though he rarely took the time to properly groom it, and his boyish, freckled face held green eyes that were now slightly wizened and displayed an understanding of the world.

Gibbs was a boy no longer, and though he would still quote movies from a long-forgotten age and make an occasional flat joke, he was about to grow up even more.

"Ynna," he said, and she stopped moving.

Moss couldn't help but watch her face register the moment. When he had met her, she was nothing but defense mechanisms. All the things she had seen and people she had lost made her exterior almost impenetrable.

45

Almost.

Somehow, with his kind heart and ridiculous nature, Gibbs had helped her open up. Over time, the two had helped one another grow. He had helped her cope with all her loss and become comfortable loving someone again without the desperate fear of loss that had always haunted her. She had helped him grow up and not be crushed under the weight of fear, doubt and regret. She had helped him learn to act and process those actions.

As unlikely a couple as they were, Moss looked to them as an example of what could be. Two people who came together to make one another better, to help the other grow and be their best selves. It was what he hoped he and Issy could be.

He smiled as he watched Ynna's unaugmented eye well before she blinked, and one small tear roll down her sculpted cheek. The corner of her lip turned up ever so slightly. She was not the type to let emotion (except anger) overwhelm her, but she was unable to hold back in this moment. Her body began to tremble as she stepped toward Gibbs.

Tears now forming in his eyes too, he knelt on one knee. The antiquated rite caused Ynna to let out an overwhelmed laugh.

"My fearless fighter with a flawless face, my perfect love, my . . ." he was going to continue but Ynna rolled her hand in a hurry-it-up motion. He laughed, his face overcome with elation. "I have been in love with you from the first time you called me a name. You have helped me survive and thrive when I thought I was going to be crushed by the weight of the world. You have protected me, literally all the time, like even today and . . ." he paused a moment, holding back a torrent of emotion.

"Spit it out, man," Ynna said, though her normal ball-busting tone was replaced with an almost desperate need for him to say it.

"Will you marry me?" he asked, and Moss couldn't remember a time when he had smiled more widely.

Ynna sprang forward, almost knocking Gibbs over as she pressed her hands on the sides of his face and kissed him. She continued to kiss him until he backed his face off hers.

"You didn't really answer," he said with an ecstatic smile.

She laughed, jumping onto him and wrapping her legs around his waist. "Yeah, yeah, I'll marry your dumb ass."

At that, Patchwork, Steampuck, Zip Thud, Belle, Judy and Issy all came pouring out of their rooms, cheering and blowing on paper horns. It was a rare moment of pure revelry and was exactly what Moss needed. There had been so much work recently that it was nice to take a break and enjoy a moment for their friends.

Champagne bottles began popping and plastic stemmed glasses bought for the occasion were produced. Belle, the android girlfriend of their newest member who went only by his online name, Zip Thud, turned on some music. Electronic thrumming began in an instant and everyone crowded around Ynna as she showed off the ring.

Marriage as an institution was largely meaningless these days, but people still loved it culturally. The industry was huge and there were entire streaming channels dedicated to wedding obsession. Moss knew that Ynna was not the type to spend her days thinking about her dream wedding, but he also knew that growing up wealthy, she had spent a good deal of her childhood dwelling on it. Despite the person she had developed into, there was going to be some wish fulfilment in getting married.

Moss happily watched Patchwork walk over holding out some champagne. The young breaker had his dreadlocks pulled into several LED hair ties that pulsated in time with the music. One of his cybernetic eyes was black, meaning that he was also doing something online while attending the party. He wore intentionally ripped pants with dripping seams that flared at the bottom while being tight at the top. His shirt said something in Japanese written in white on geometric patterns. As he always did now, Patchwork wore at his side the Samurai sword Moss and Sandra had rescued for him.

Taking a sip, Moss smiled at Patch.

"Happy for them," Patch observed genuinely.

"Me too."

"Need to get me some of that," Patch said, pointing at the happy couple.

Moss smiled. "Good looking guy like you, shouldn't be a problem."

Patchwork did a little dance in place. "Got that right, but it's not like we are hitting up the clubs these days, you know? My socks are starting to look like porcelain statuary."

Moss did an imitation of throwing up in his mouth and Patch laughed. "You could hack Belle, go a couple of rounds with her," Moss joked.

Patchwork looked across the room at the pretty robot gushing over the ring as Ynna vamped and posed. "Not really my thing, for a lot of reasons," he said quietly.

"Gotcha," Moss nodded.

"Plus," Patchwork added, "it'd kill Zip. Kid's in love in a way I never seen before."

Moss had to admit that it was true. Zip Thud was young — Moss estimated around sixteen — and obsessed with his robot companion. He doted on her and bought her an endless supply of clothes so, in her words, she could 'Always look like a princess.' On the day he had chosen for her birthday, he had made them hijack a D2E truck so they could steal her branded princess attire. It was the kind of sickeningly sweet affection that only a person so young could possess.

"Yeah," Moss agreed. "That kid loves Belle something fierce."

They both took a sip as they watched Zip stare adoringly at Belle. Patchwork turned to Moss. "How you feeling? The pills working still?"

"Yes," Moss said. The two had not had a single conversation where the topic didn't come up. Since he had been helping Moss with the corrupting program in his mind, Patchwork was always checking in about it. He had put several safeguards in place to keep the program from leaking into Moss's mind, but he had made it clear that the program was too advanced to be held back forever.

"Good," he sighed. "You let me know if anything happens."

"I will," Moss said as he always did.

Patchwork lowered his head and looked at Moss seriously. "Anything," he repeated, as he always did.

"I'll let you know," Moss assured him, and he meant it. He had learned recently how powerful the program could be but was also terrified of it. It could be hacked, and though Patchwork had put protections in place, Moss did not want to know what would happen if someone was able to actually penetrate it.

"Feel like I should go ooh and ah," Patchwork said, and Moss nodded. He would wait to congratulate them. He wanted to do it in private rather than like this.

Patchwork stepped away and joined the gathered crew. Everyone was drinking and chatting happily. Everyone except Judy, who stood against the wall with a pained smile. Moss knew how hard this would be for them and he made his way over, sliding up beside them.

"Hey," he said.

"Hey," they replied, looking up and letting their face fall. Wearing gray coveralls with sleeves rolled to three quarters, Judy was dressed the way they normally were these days.

"You don't have to say it," Moss said quietly, not that anyone could hear them over the music even if they were trying.

"I know," Judy said, putting a bottle to their lips and taking a pull. "I really *am* happy for them, you know?"

"I know."

They looked away, eyes lost in some far-off memory. "It's just, it should have been me too."

"I know."

"My story should always have ended in a wedding," Judy said, tears forming in the corner of their eyes. They bit their lip to hold back the feelings, knowing it was not the time to burst into tears.

"I'm a little surprised to hear that," Moss said, and it was true. He had known Stan and Judy shared a love for the ages, but he was stunned to hear them say they wanted a wedding. Judy was a hard person who had shown no interest in pageantry.

"Yeah, well, there's a lot you don't know about me," they said and clearly, that was to be the end of their moment.

"I hope to change that," Moss said and reached up to put a hand on their back before thinking better of it.

"I'm getting there," Judy said, and Moss was happy with that answer.

The talking ended and all eyes turned as the door opened and Anders walked in followed by Sandra.

"Off-worlders got their goods," she said triumphantly before seeing everyone gathered. "The hell's going on here?"

CHAPTER 5

"Congratulations!"

Anders's eyes went wide with delight, and he charged across the room to scoop up Gibbs into a big bear hug. Gibbs winced. Things had never been quite right between the two since Anders had slept with Ynna. Gibbs had always hated that fact. Once it had become clear that Ynna wanted to be with Gibbs, the situation had calmed; but it was never quite right, though Anders bore Gibbs no ill will whatsoever.

Seeing Anders with the crew made Moss feel that he had never taken enough time to get to know the man. The former space pirate had joined them quickly after helping them with a job, but Moss never took the time to really get to know him. They'd had a few deep conversations, but they were few and far between. With so few true allies in the world, Moss wanted to remedy that.

Sandra sidled up beside her grandson and snatched the drink from his hand, downing what was left. "Good for them," she said.

Moss nodded. He loved his grandmother, but his feelings for her at the moment were muddy. "It is," he agreed. "I think it will be good for the crew too. Something positive to focus on."

"I agree. Need a break from the relentless grim shit."

"That we do," Moss said, still watching Anders.

"Hey," Sandra said, drawing his attention. He turned to look into the old eyes of his grandmother. "I'm sorry about what I had to do back there. I hope you understand."

"I do," he said, and in part, he did.

"We needed to get that shipment out and finalize the deal," she reminded him. "Everything we are working toward depends on that."

"I know." Moss sighed.

Sandra gave a dissatisfied exhalation. "Anyway, looks like you got him back in one piece and no worse for wear."

Moss nodded again. "We did."

"And the blushing bride. She want to put me through a wall?"

Moss considered his answer before speaking. He did not like to lie to her nor to any of them, but he also didn't want to change the mood or create any strife. "She wasn't thrilled, but once we got him back safe and sound, she cooled," he offered, knowing Sandra wouldn't believe him if he had simply told her Ynna had been fine with it. He added for good measure, "Pretty sure it's going to be the last thing on her mind now."

"Probably right about that," Sandra said. "Pretty princess finally gets her ring."

Moss shook his head and snorted. "Go congratulate them and don't be an asshole," he told her with a little smirk.

She chuckled and tousled his hair like he was a child. "You're right."

She stepped toward the group and Moss made his way to the bottles sitting on a chipped pink tile counter with grout that Moss presumed had once been white but was now an off-putting green. He poured himself another little cup and felt a pinch on the ass before a kiss on the cheek hit him.

"Anders, I told you I don't like that," he joked as he turned. "Oh, Issy, it's you."

"Har, har, har," she said with a smile, taking the cup from his hands. "Can you believe it?"

He grabbed his third in as many minutes and poured one more, looking around a moment to see who was going to swoop in and snag this one. She had changed from her Scuba cover into normal street clothes, and it reminded Moss that he wanted to do the same.

"Not really," Moss said honestly. "If you had told me that year he was obsessed with Spurs and Holsters to the point that he started wearing a cowboy hat to school, that that kid was going to get married to a badass street samurai, I'd have laughed in your face."

Issy let out a laugh. "I had forgotten that game! Gah, he was such a dweeb."

"Right, because you and I were the pinnacle of cool," he joked.

"Speak for yourself!" she said, shoving his shoulder. "I was invited to the Butlers' sweet sixteen!" Moss bowed in admission of her victory. She lowered her voice and said in a conspiratorial tone, "You know they made out at that party?"

Moss couldn't believe it and at the words, he was sixteen again. "Really?"

She rolled her eyes and laughed in his face, "Ew, Moss, no! For one, they are sisters, and two: they are *sisters*!"

"Right," Moss said as he felt his face flush with embarrassment.

"You really need to work on that gullibility," Issy said.

"Don't you like that I trust you?" he cooed, trying to make her feel bad for messing with him.

55

She shook her head. "I'd rather you knew me well enough to know when I am fucking with you."

"Fair," Moss admitted, turning to Gibbs and Ynna who were now dancing to a Sinatra song. "Look at them," he said happily.

"I know," Issy said, joining his gaze as she slid up next to him and laced her fingers into his. "I'm really so happy for them."

Moss thought about their future. He had no idea what it would hold. They had a plan to take on the companies but it seemed like such a lofty ambition. It was more likely to succeed now that they had the off-worlder's help, but there was still such a long way to go.

Even if they were successful, changing the world would not be easy and the transition would be difficult. What would that mean for the people standing in the room, he wondered. Would Gibbs and Ynna be able to settle down? Would Patchwork find someone to share his life with? Would Judy be able to move on from Stan, if they even should? Would Sandra live long enough to see the change? All those questions flooded his mind until he turned to look at Issy as she watched their friends. What was their future?

"Do you want kids?" he blurted, shocking even himself that the words left his lips.

Issy was so surprised by the question that she took a step back and stared at him a moment. "What?"

"Sorry," Moss stammered. "I was just thinking out loud."

"Do you?" she asked, clearly trying to recover.

"Yes," he said simply.

She seemed even more astonished by the quick answer. "Oh," she murmured. "Me too."

Moss felt his heart swell. They had not talked much about the future. It always seemed like such a foreign concept, considering they were being shot at all the time, but Moss was happy to know that they were pulling in the same direction. He gave her hand a little squeeze.

"What made you think of that?" she asked softly.

He shrugged. "Just thinking about everything, I guess. And meeting Mr. Greene's daughter, I suppose, got me considering things as well."

"Well, she *is* pretty cute," Issy said, smiling.

"Yeah, but you know it's more than that."

"Of course. There's more to everything."

Moss couldn't help but laugh at the true simplicity of the statement. "Yep."

"Something to think about, I suppose," she said, and he wasn't sure which aspect of the conversation she was referring to but decided not to press it. "I love you, Moss," she said, staring right into his heart.

He knew she loved him and he had loved her for a decade, but hearing the words, hearing them in that moment, meant more to him than he could ever express to her. His face flushed and his hands went numb as he said, "I love you, too."

They kissed, and for a moment everything was right with the world.

It was dark in the room when Moss awoke, a little hungover.

Dark, but not pitch black. It was never pitch black. Between screens, clocks, streetlamps, ads, headlights and little LED lights on everything, there was never actual darkness. He knew it was early morning and, for a change, it was hot. B.A. City was almost always foggy, wet and cool, or cold. There

57

were few warm days and even fewer hot days. For the one week a year in September when it was hot, the people spent the first two days reveling in it and the remainder complaining about the heat.

The warmth had set a lovely mood the previous night when everyone made their way to the roof to drink, eat and dance in light layers rather than the usual hooded sweatshirts. It had been nice, but now, the drink wearing off and the blanket coated in a sheen of sweat, it was uncomfortable.

As he pulled the sheets aside, Issy shifted, rolling onto her stomach and in the low light, Moss allowed himself to do something he normally wouldn't; just take her all in — her entire naked form. She was a beautiful sight. To him, perfection.

The small dimples on her lower back made him mad for her. Before her, he had only slept with machines. Even when he thought he was having sex with Irene, it had turned out to be another relief aide. They had all been designed for pleasure, created and crafted to be the ideal of perfection; but to him, the perfection was in the flaws. A stretch mark, a mole, a hair too long; all the things that Issy would hate about herself and want to change were the things that Moss loved.

He looked down at his own legs. Above the knees they were human with flaws and below a synthetic masterwork. They were indistinguishable from afar but looking closely he could see the seam. See where his body became something else.

In that moment in the dark, he couldn't help but realize that his mind was the same. Half his own and half a program. Even if he had dampened his ability to access it, it was there.

Issy stirred and snorted before beginning to snore softly.

He stared at her a bit longer, lost in thought, before standing and dressing himself- — an act he enjoyed. For his whole life, machine arms had dressed him. Because it was the way he had grown up, he had never thought about it; it was just a way of life. Since leaving the burbs, he had come to realize what an absurdity it was. There was no reason for it, and the arms actually took longer than doing it oneself.

Over time, he had come to understand it was just another way ThutoCo made their employees complacent. Sure, they incentivized them to exercise, but they never allowed their employees to do enough for themselves to become truly competent.

It hadn't been until he left the burbs that Moss realized his parents had raised him slightly differently. Until they had been taken away by the company and killed, they had encouraged Moss to think for himself and to do activities that other kids did not. When Moss was five, his father had set up a climbing wall in the hex and a small obstacle course with things he brought home from his lab.

Moss had thought it was just fun, but when he was older he came to understand that his father had been trying to prepare him for life outside. It was another small thing his parents had done for him that he would never be able to thank them for.

"Couldn't sleep?" Issy asked as Moss pulled a tight shirt over his toned chest.

"Only just got up," he told her. "Unless you want to go another round?"

He cocked an eyebrow at her, but she grimaced. "Too hot for that shit. I'm still all sticky from last night."

Moss chuckled. "I sometimes worry that being friends our whole lives has diminished the romance."

"Oh, yeah?" she asked, rolling onto her side to expose her full nude form to him in the blue light. Moss could feel himself getting hard immediately.

"I said romance, not . . ." he began, but she pulled him toward the bed.

He really did love her.

As Moss unscrewed the cap of the plastic tub on the kitchen floor and scooped himself a bowl of bran flakes with fruit-like flavored chunks, Ynna walked in groggily in a tank top and tight little shorts that did nothing to hide her form. She walked over to the counter and took a swig from one of the half-full champagne bottles.

Moss set the bowl down and clasped his hands behind his back, thrusting one hip sideways and affecting a cutesy voice. "When's the big day?"

Ynna produced a cigarette from a pack on the counter, lit it, looked at him flatly and said, "Soon. Figure we should do the thing since every day is one step closer to an early grave."

"Pretty sure I read that quote on the cover of Beautiful Bride Monthly," he joked.

She cracked a smile. "Funny."

"I try," Moss said, pouring the Sitta' Butta' brand root milk on his cereal and sitting at the table. As he began to eat, Gibbs joined them, wearing almost the same clothes as Ynna — a tight wifebeater and small shorts that left nothing to the imagination. Moss coughed up his cereal.

Gibbs laughed. "At this point in your life, if you haven't seen a buldge, well, I just feel sorry for you."

"You tell 'em, babe," Ynna laughed.

She groaned as she stood over the sink, turning on the water. Patchwork had hacked the usage tracker so they could run water without alerting the billing department, but they still had to use very little so it didn't set off any alarms at HydroSell.

"Does anyone ever do the dishes in this fucking place?" she groused, sliding a tie off her wrist to pull her hair up.

"I feel like I just did," Moss said, thinking back.

"That was two weeks ago," Steampuck informed him as he strode into the room. The South African throwback to the Victorian age sat down at the table with a cup of tea he had brewed in his own room.

"Really?" Moss asked, honestly feeling it had been more recent than that.

"Really," Puck informed him as he set his tea down on a saucer he had also brought with him.

Both cup and dish were white with blue painting all about the rims. The formal cup matched the formal attire he wore even in casual moments. Moss had seen him in his fine pajama set, but even this early in the morning and in the heat, he was dressed in tailored black-and-white striped pants, a ruffled shirt that protruded out of a meticulously stitched vest, and tall, polished leather boots.

"I felt for a time as though dishes were my only purpose here," Puck continued, "but since I have been tasked with spreading our word, I ceased washing the dishes and left them to you lot. I have watched the deterioration ever since."

"I appreciate the part where you told us you were doing that shit," Ynna said with considerable snark. "Oh, wait…"

"Didn't hear you complaining when I did not inform you that I *was* doing the dishes," Puck said with a clever smile.

"Funny how that works," Ynna said, scratching her nose with her middle finger.

Moss cleared his throat to change the topic as Ynna washed one bowl for herself and shut the water off to Gibbs's clear annoyance. "So, Puck, how is the word-spreading going?"

"Ah, quite well, thank you for asking," Puck said, enunciating every word and speaking too loudly for that time in the morning. "Since young Patchwork has been disseminating my messages, more and more people are awakening to the truth of our world. It is quite lovely, though I would prefer a larger platform or perhaps a more significant assignment. Though I am happy to be utilized for more than sanitization, I would prefer something which aligns more closely with my particular set of skills."

Moss nodded. Puck had mentioned this before, and Moss knew that the man was getting impatient though he had no idea what a good fit would be.

"We are working on it," Moss told him as the front door opened and Judy walked in with two boxes of Rolling Pin donuts and a carton of Keelhaul Coffee. The smell of coffee and sugar filled the room and Gibbs ran over to Judy.

"Oh, see, I thought it was Ynna but it's really you I love," he said, kissing them on the cheek and bringing one of the boxes to the table.

"You just love me for my treats," Judy said with a smile, and Moss smiled too. After their partner had been killed, Judy had disappeared into a video game for a long time, retreating from the real world. Moss was happy to know that they seemed to be fully back and beginning to recover from their loss, despite the blip the night before.

Gibbs spoke through a full mouth. "I'm a fickle, fickle man."

"That he is." Ynna laughed, stamped out her smoke and grabbed one of the coffee cups, beginning to fill it before Judy even set the carton down.

"No, that's cool," Judy joked as they struggled to hold the box steady for Ynna.

"What's all this ruckus?" Sandra asked as she entered the room, sending a wave of silence through them like a boss entering the breakroom. "Don't have to stop the fun on my account," she said, walking over and plucking up a chocolate donut. "Ah, manna from heaven."

She sat at the table besides Gibbs. "So, thinkin' we should get into it," she said seriously. "What happened with the Scubas?"

Moss shook his head. "Thought you said we didn't have to stop having fun."

His grandmother winked. "I was lying."

CHAPTER 6

"So, when all is said and done, they will give us the information they believe can take down ThutoCo in exchange for being able to safely move into the city," Moss said.

Sandra looked at him with pure incredulity. "And all we need to do is get Carcer out?"

"Right," Moss said with a smirk. "*Just* that."

"Lucky for those dust-covered motherfuckers, that's exactly what I've been working on," Sandra said, beaming with pride.

Everyone was surprised but Ynna spoke first. "You think you can destroy Carcer? How? There's no way."

Sandra stood, wearing a superior smile. "I didn't say 'destroy,' I said, 'get them out.' There's a difference."

"Not really," Ynna said. "There is no way to get them out of B.A."

"We can't," Sandra said, "but the mayor could."

This brought a chorus of laughter from around the table until everyone realized she was serious.

"A more ceremonial position there hasn't been since the king and queen," Puck observed of the mayor's office.

Sandra nodded. "Been true a long time but I mean to change that."

"How?" Moss asked in disbelief.

"We are going to have a lot of moving parts and a lot of things are going to have to go right, but there is a clear path for us. First, we are going to have to get our candidate elected. No simple thing since the same family has been in power since dirt.

"Second, and most important, we are going to need to install someone of our choosing at the head of the Carcer Corporation so we can begin to dismantle them from within once our person at the big desk decides to turn them away."

No one spoke.

"This can never work," Ynna said quietly.

"Or maybe," Gibbs said, stroking his chin, "it's just so crazy that it has to work."

Ynna shook her head, not amused by him this time. "No."

"I agree with Ynna," Moss said. "If there was a way to do either of the things you just described, we would have done it already."

"I hear you," Sandra said. "But there hadn't been a way to do these things 'til now. We've worked hard and some things are finally falling into place. All the actions we have taken, all the ways that we have shown up the companies for what they are, it's turned the will of the people. We have an opportunity to strike, and we have to take it."

"Just like that, things have changed?" Gibbs asked.

"No," Sandra said, beginning to get annoyed. "I just said that a lot of things have had to change. A few more things are going to have to change in the next few months too, if we want to see this through.

"Look, I ain't no fool. All of you in this room know that already. What I'm suggesting sounds like madness, I know. But we've been mad before. You all took ThutoCo down a peg, broke out of one of the more secure locations in the land and killed the head of the world's largest security companies. These were no small fish. We made bold strokes and we are about to make our boldest.

"If we want things to change on a massive scale, we need to take massive action. Sure, we are gonna assume some big risk, but we strike while the iron is hot or call it quits," she said, folding her arms across her chest.

"No one is calling it quits," Ynna piped up. "It just seems like getting a sympathetic mayor elected *and* somehow taking over Carcer at the same time is unrealistic."

"Even for *us*," Gibbs said with false bravado.

"Let's say we get our candidate elected," Moss said. He had been considering his grandmother's words. As crazed as she may have become, she was no fool; and if she believed they could do these things, Moss believed it too. "How do we install someone in Carcer?"

"Now you're asking the right questions," Sandra said, pointing a gnarled finger with skin so thin as to be almost translucent. "I have a plan for that. Detritus Three was able to flip a Carcer board member and we learned who the next CEO will become in the event of the death of Warden Ninety-Nine. So, we replace this person, off the prick who shot our lovely Ynna and begin to burn down the establishment from the inside."

"Replace?" Moss asked.

"Yessir," Sandra said. "But all of this comes later."

Again, no one spoke, so Sandra continued. "Moss, I'll want you to meet with our contact who will take you to our candidate. Listen to what they have to say. We will have to help them in any way we can."

MATTHEW A. GOODWIN

"I can do that," Moss said, and turned to Issy. "Want to join me?"

She gritted her teeth as the corners of her mouth pulled down guiltily. "Actually, Belle, Judy and I were going to take Ynna dress shopping."

"Oh," Moss said and turned. "Well, then, gents, shall we?"

"Actually," Puck said. "I have rather a lot to do."

Zip Thud and Patchwork nodded, and Moss turned to Anders. "Don't want to," he said bluntly.

"Ooookay," Moss said, sounding more dejected than he had expected.

Standing from the table, Gibbs happily offered, "I'll go."

Moss smiled. "Great," he said, looking at his friend. "Throw some pants on and we can do this thing."

"Oh, we can do this thing," Gibbs said, turning to leave before smacking himself on the ass cheek. "But I never agreed to pants."

"Right," Ynna said, standing as well. "Now that Moss is done getting picked last in dodgeball, we can be on our way too."

Issy stepped over to him and gave him a peck on the cheek. "Love you," she whispered apologetically before skipping off to her room.

Sandra closed in on him. "Were you picked last in dodgeball?"

Moss examined his feet. "Yeah."

"You clean up good," Gibbs said, looking at Moss in his black suit.

The cab they had picked up a good distance from the safe house was flying smoothly over the city. Sandra wanted to set the tone for the day and had ordered them a nice cab with leather interior, multiple screens and a drink fabricator. It was sleek black on the outside with tinted windows and, unlike almost all vehicles in the city, there were no digital advertising displays anywhere on the exterior.

Moss looked at his friend in a blue pinstripe suit with salmon shirt. He looked good also. "Not as good as you."

"Nah, baby, you're money," Gibbs said with a smile.

Moss laughed and shook his head. "It ever bother her?"

"What?" Gibbs asked, sincerely confused.

"All the quotes, your obsession with this bygone era?" Moss asked. Gibbs's face dropped and grew serious.

"Yeah," he admitted. "It does. I know she sometimes finds it endearing, but when I use it as a defense mechanism or try to cover my feelings with some joke from a movie she's never heard of, let alone seen, it pisses her off."

"Sorry," Moss said, and he meant it. "Can't stop?"

Gibbs chuckled sadly at his own expense. "Been trying to. Or at least tone it down some. But it's hard. You know, you think you are one thing for your whole life, and then everything changes and you have to change along with it. It's not easy."

"Believe me, I know," Moss said. Gibbs didn't answer. "Sorry, this wasn't about me."

"It's fine Moss," Gibbs said. "Ever since Ynna showed up at your door, you've been the star of this show."

Moss didn't say anything. He knew Gibbs well enough to know that he would keep talking.

"I guess that's why I was happy Ynna chose me," he said. "Not even chose me, but saw me, you know? The second

69

we landed in the city, I felt like a tag-along or even like I just didn't belong. I see that in Puck sometimes now, too.

"But with Ynna, it's so different. I know she thought I was a putz at first, but it didn't take long for us to realize that on some fundamental level, we are cut from the same cloth."

Moss smiled. "What cloth is that?"

"Felt," Gibbs joked. "She's helping me to grow and change, but I guess it's a little weird feeling like I don't know what I'm going to grow into. Sorry, I'm rambling. Maybe this doesn't make any sense."

Moss put a hand on his friend's shoulder. "It makes sense. And I know I have told you this already, but for what it's worth, you are an amazing man. Don't make me remind you again that you saved my life."

Gibbs smiled but he was still lost in thought.

"She's lucky to have you too," Moss added, and Gibbs looked up at him, his brows pinched. "It's true, man. I know you think that she is stooping or whatever, but it's not true. She may bust your balls or mock your quotes but deep down, she needs you. She was a lost soul and you've helped her, too. Don't forget that."

"I guess that's one of those things that my logical brain knows but I can't allow myself to think," Gibbs said. "It's hard because…"

"Don't say it." Moss shook his head.

"Because she's so hot," Gibbs said, smirking.

"Aaaand, moment ruined." Moss laughed. After a beat he said, "I'm really happy it's just us."

"Me too," Gibbs agreed. "Like old times."

"Nothing like old times," Moss noted, and Gibbs chuckled.

As they neared downtown, the cab began to lift. They were leaving behind the world they knew and entering that of the elites. In this part of the city, skyscrapers were joined by massive platforms to create streets quite different from those below. They were thick and sturdy, so you would never know you were hundreds of meters off the ground unless you walked to the edge where viewing platforms, edgeside bars and infinity pools gave a view over the city. Storefronts flanked all sides, selling fine watches, personal use relief aides, crystal accessories, flighted cars, and clothes more valuable than the combined paychecks of one thousand ThutoCo employees. This elevated district was the opposite of the street below.

Here, the streets were quiet, with just a few people in their superb attire walking to the shops or heading to a meeting at one of the three-star restaurants. Between the walking paths with glass bottoms, well-manicured trees and shrubs grew in precisely laid brick planters. Rather than oppressive neon signs, dancing holograms and flashing billboards, the ads here were subtle. Attractive models were pictured in stills using the various products.

Even the speed of things was different up here. People not only moved more slowly but also comfortably. They didn't seem scared that someone would try to rob them at any moment or that they might be run over by a rickshaw. Nobody was smoking, sucking down a quick coffee or wolfing a street bite. A couple strolled hand-in-hand, the women stopping for a moment to chat with an older man walking his dog, a small fecal collection bot trailing their steps.

After transmitting access codes, the cab touched down and the door swung open. Moss and Gibbs stepped out. It even smelled better here. Unlike the odor of chemicals and cooking vatmeat of questionable origin, the air smelled clean here. The sun shone and some birds chased one another between trees, singing as they went.

"Man," Gibbs uttered breathlessly. "Maybe *we're* the dumb ones."

Looking at how lovely it was here, Moss couldn't help but agree for a moment before shaking the thought. "Think about the people below us."

"Pretty sure the people here would say 'beneath us,' you know?" Gibbs joked with a sad smile.

"Exactly," Moss said. "The Market Street Undermarket is down there."

"Right." Gibbs nodded his head. "Ynna won't go there."

"Even my grandma doesn't go there."

Gibbs grimaced. "A place Sandra won't go is a place I don't even want to think about."

"But that's the point, right?" Moss said as they moved from the landing pad onto High Market Street. "Those people down there are suffering. That neighborhood may have a bad reputation, but it's because the wealthy elites built this palace right on top of them. They quite literally blocked out the sun for the already poor and then judged them for not being able to make a life for themselves. It's fucked.

"I've heard that the runoff from all these platform businesses just drops down and the retractable shades over High M. funnel the water down, so it's constantly damp down there."

"Yikes," Gibbs said, and they turned left to begin walking toward the small mall abutting one of the buildings. A shopping aide drudge robot stepped off a charging pad and began making its way toward them, its metallic forearm opening and dropping a silk pouch for carrying goods. Moss and Gibbs shook their head no in unison. "And don't get me wrong," Gibbs said almost sheepishly. "It's not like I have forgotten what we are fighting for. It's just that I can understand why people would want to live this way."

He made a sweeping gesture with his hand.

Moss chuckled. "You're saying you don't love living in squalor!?"

"Hard to believe, right?" Gibbs smiled. They stepped into the shadow of the nearest building, its glass front rising before them into the clouds. "Where we meeting the contact?"

"BiblioFoam Café," Moss said, pointing to the glass double doors of the Fogrise Mall.

Gibbs followed Moss into the mall, its interior as nice as the street they had just left. Small streams burbled along the main path toward a circular center. Little footbridges led to each store, where young people forced by wealthy parents to 'get a job' sat behind counters staring at palmscreens.

Gibbs stared at one such youth before turning to Moss and remarking, "I can't believe Ynna used to be like that."

Moss laughed. "Me neither," he said. "Hard to believe we were kinda like that."

"Would you go back?" Gibbs asked almost absentmindedly as they looked for the café.

"What?"

"To the burbs," Gibbs continued. "If you could forget all of this, forget the fight, not have to deal with the program and being shot, would you go back to your old life?"

Moss had to think for a moment. "No," he said finally. "I wouldn't change it. You?"

"You kidding me?" Gibbs laughed. "I would never have landed a girl like Ynna in the burbs."

Moss laughed.

"I figured you might go back," Gibbs said.

Moss turned to him in surprise. "Really?"

"Yeah," Gibbs said with a clever smile. "So that you could earn enough Productivity Points to finally change MOSS II's name."

He punched Moss on the arm as he laughed at his own joke. Moss rolled his eyes, though he was truly happy to be doing this with his friend. Even in a completely foreign environment, doing something strange and new, it was comforting to be beside Gibbs. They had been friends for so long and been through so much, it made him breathe a little easier when they were together.

"There," Gibbs said, pointing to the café where a woman stood tapping furiously on her palmscreen.

"Okay," Moss said, straightening his tie. "Ready to meet the next mayor?"

CHAPTER 7

The café was not like anything Moss had ever seen. There was a bar at the back made of a dark wood with books set into it. The floor was also wood, or at least designed to look like wood, and all the walls, which curved into the ceiling, were bookshelves.

The entire space had a spherical design and Moss found himself murmuring, "It's like a fishbowl of books." He looked in astonishment at the space.

"They must be glued on the ceiling," he said, tilting his head to look up at the curving shelves. There were a few circular wooden tables with stools. Set in the middle of the tables were black metal lanterns with candles burning inside.

Another young person with dyed white hair styled into spiked long triangles stood behind the counter wearing an apron. Beside the door stood a stylish young woman in smart business attire.

As they approached, Gibbs remarked, "That might be the best-looking woman I've ever seen."

Moss shook his head.

"And that's coming from somebody whose fiancé was genetically designed to be pretty," Gibbs added for effect.

"Right, and what do you think your fiancée would say to your comment?" Moss asked.

Gibbs laughed. "Oh, Grandpa, she appreciates human beauty as much as I do and has no interest in us suppressing our appreciation or inborn human desires. Much healthier to talk about our feelings than pretend we don't have them."

"Oh." Moss was astonished. "I didn't realize you guys were so modern."

Gibbs laughed. "We aren't," he said. "What you didn't realize was how antiquated burb society is."

Moss didn't have a comeback for that.

He turned to look at the woman with her hourglass figure, perfectly styled umber hair, thick rimmed glasses over large brown eyes and full lips. He felt guilty that he agreed with Gibbs. "Just don't tell her that," Moss warned.

"Of course not."

"Mister Che, Mister Floyd," the woman greeted them as they approached, using the false names they had provided. "I'm Sofia Juarez, personal aide to mayoral candidate Persimmon LeBeau."

"Good to meet you," Moss said, extending a hand. Moss resented Gibbs for saying something about her looks because as she shook his hand and looked into his eyes, he couldn't help but notice her beauty.

To Moss's great consternation, Gibbs seemed totally fine when he shook her hand. For the first time, Moss wondered if it was Gibbs who had grown up more since leaving the burbs. He quickly laughed off the thought.

"You two represent," Sofia said, looking down at her palm for a dramatic pause, "a coalition of concerned citizens who are interested in providing assistance to the campaign over the next few months, is that correct?"

"Yes," Moss said, unsure how much this aide knew about them.

"Okay," she said. "I was told to set up this meeting but not precisely what it was about. Can you help me so that I may update Mix LeBeau's schedule?"

Now he knew. She was fishing.

"No," Moss said, sounding more nervous than he expected. "I think it's best if we discuss it with them personally."

A micro expression of annoyance flashed on her face before the politician in training took over and she smiled. "No problem."

"Sorry," Gibbs offered kindly.

"It's no problem. I'm just trying to help the candidate," she said in a way intended to make them feel guilty.

"Right," Moss said, and she raised her eyebrows expectantly.

"If you could please take us to Mix LeBeau now," Gibbs said.

Sofia turned in frustration and Moss watched Gibbs stare as she guided them a little further before turning down a long narrow hallway that looked like a service area. It was unadorned, pale stucco under fluorescent lights for what seemed to go on forever.

They stopped at a wet-paint sign sitting in front of a metal stanchion. The floor glistened behind the sign, but Sofia simply moved the barricade and continued to walk, her tall heels clicking as she did. Moss and Gibbs shared a look and followed her.

Around a bend, there was a floor-to-ceiling screen showing an advertisement for the Bay Aquarium. Sofia produced a metallic card from her pocket and waved it over the wall to the right of the poster. The piece of wall flashed green, and the ad shimmered like rippling water.

Sofia stepped through with Moss and Gibbs right behind.

Moss instantly recognized the smell of synthesized ocean air; it was the scent he had chosen to wake up to every morning in his hex. It was dark through the door, and it took Moss a moment to see the stairs illuminated in a low blue.

"This is B.A. City's hottest club, Wadyd," Sofia told them as Moss groped for a handrail. The tiled floor beneath his feet was slick with water and he felt uneasy in the fancy, polished and unworn shoes now on his feet. They followed her uneasily down the curving stairs to a small room coated in navy velvet with a square opening on one side. A strikingly handsome shirtless man sat there, checking coats.

Two armed drudges stood beside the door that opened into the club. They had been modified to fit the aquatic theme — coated in shiny blue and green paint with shimmering low lights emanating from within. Instead of head-shaped tops usually found on robots, the two had gold tridents protruding from their shoulders.

Moss tried not to laugh at the absurd unnecessary nature of it all.

"Right this way," Sofia said as the drudges stepped aside.

Moss expected flashing lights and thrumming music when the doors opened, but what he saw was quite the opposite. The large circular room was at least ten meters high and walled with acrylic fish tanks connected all the way around. What lay inside made his jaw drop. He had never seen anything like it in his whole life. Schools of brightly-colored fish darted in unison, flashing through the water. Rays displaced plumes of sand as they shimmied up and back into position at the base of the tank. Moss's eyes went wide as he watched a hammerhead shark lurk in a slowly dancing forest of kelp.

"Oh," he heard himself say before the air was sucked out of his lungs. His body propelled itself toward the tank as he stared in amazement at a fish bigger than a car. White on the bottom and spotted on top, Moss had read about the whale shark as a child and became so enamored that he did a presentation on the supposedly extinct animal for a class.

So awestruck by the massive animal, Moss didn't even see Sofia look up from her palmscreen or say, "What's with him?"

Gibbs laughed. "He loves animals."

Sofia snorted. "So it would seem."

Moss watched the shark effortlessly glide through the water as small remora dragged behind like leaves in the breeze. Moss knew the others made fun of the way he would get when he stumbled upon any wildlife and that most people he met didn't understand it, but he didn't care. In that moment, just for a moment, the whale shark was the only thing in the world.

Sofia broke his concentration, tapping him on the arm. "If you want, my friend Sydney can get you a deal on a HomeClone replica of that thing," she said, gesturing toward the shark.

Moss didn't even turn his head to say, "I can't imagine anything worse."

Sofia scoffed. "Just trying to be nice."

"Don't mind him," Gibbs said and pinched Moss hard just under the rib.

It jolted him back to the real world. He looked around the room itself. Illuminated in the shifting light from the tank, the seating area circled around a central bar made of printed coral, flat on top for drinks but bumpy and jagged all along the edge. Holoprojected fish darted in and out of the holes in the surface or appeared to feed on the sides.

The tables, made of the same coral with thin pedestals and flat tops, were surrounded by plush chairs occupied by customers consuming glowing drinks and plates of sushi. The symbolism of the affluent clientele eating the majestic animals that surrounded them was not lost on Moss, and he grimaced at the stone slab plates of rolls.

Behind the bar, aged sushi chefs crafted precise meals beside young, attractive bartenders creating cocktails. The dichotomy exactly represented what the people wanted to see: practiced cooks hunched from years of preparation alongside sex appeal and novelty in their drinks. Moss found himself laughing at the predictability of the elites, who were more concerned about the correct look of their servants than the amazing and diverse wildlife contained around them.

A waitress sashayed over, slinking between pillars of fish tanks that joined floor and ceiling. She wore a skintight bodysuit of scales, and her hair was microdyed so it would shimmer and shift as though underwater. She wordlessly held forward a metal tray with sunken sections. Fresh drinks still smoking dramatically, a few pieces of immaculate sushi and tiny vials of powders were on offer. No prices were listed, and Moss assumed patrons just synched their wallets to the bar and were charged without ever having to think about it.

He knew better than to take anything off the tray, but Gibbs had popped a roll in his mouth before Moss could stop him.

"Oh, my," he groaned in ecstasy. "Mo — Che, you have to try this."

Moss's eyes shot daggers at him. "I'm good."

"Safe to assume you won't be dining at a place like this again any time soon," Sofia said smugly, and nodded at a silver plaque mounted on a red square with three stars printed into its face.

Moss sighed and grabbed one of the rolls, placing it delicately in his mouth. As the perfection of the bite swirled in his mouth, he couldn't help but wonder whose bank account had been connected to them and how much they were just charged for that delicious morsel. Guilt prevented him from looking back at the tank for a moment and he turned to Sofia.

She nodded for the waitress to excuse herself and guided them around the bar to a roped-off area which Moss at first took to be empty. Sofia winked to the drudge standing beside the velvet rope and it turned its trident slightly before unclipping one end.

On the other side lay four bulbous portholes sunk into the floor with round cranks on top. Sofia pointed to number three and then stared at Moss until he walked over and began to turn the wheel. It looked as though it would take a lot of effort but it moved as smoothly as butter, and he was able to pull open the door with ease.

They followed her down a ladder to another hallway and finally a sliding Amado door. When it opened, Moss was amazed once more. The all-glass room jutted out from the side of the building and gave the impression of being above the exposed city below. Moss's feet stopped moving immediately and he felt his pulse in his head. Even though he knew it was safe, the sensation of looking that far down through the walls and floors made him feel as though he was going to pass out.

"You alright?" Sofia asked, and Moss pulled himself together.

"Yeah," he said. Blinking, he looked down to see two young children staring at him with worry from a translucent hot

81

tub. They appeared to be about four and seven years old, but Moss was not a good judge of age.

"Boys," a soft voice said from the far side of the room. "Please go with Sofia."

The kids in the tub groaned. "But —" they began, but were cut off.

"Boys," Sofia said in a stern but caring voice as she grabbed two plush towels from beside the tub. She ushered them away quickly and Moss and Gibbs turned as Persimmon stood from a clear chair at a clear table.

"Greetings," they said, stepping forward and extending a hand. "I am Persimmon LeBeau."

Persimmon was tall and dressed sharply in a well-tailored green suit with gold and red stitching. They had dark skin and small eyes set in a sharply featured face. Their head was shaved along one side with a cascade of platinum hair swooping down the other. One eye was augmented and permanently black; Moss assumed they were constantly monitoring the news feeds. They wore light makeup and a kind smile that clearly masked a sharp intellect.

"Hi," Moss said. "I'm —"

"No need," Persimmon cut him off. "The noms de plume are of no interest to me. Please, join me."

They sat.

"I'm quite a busy person so I will cut to the chase — unless you would prefer to lather one another up a bit first?" Persimmon asked, smiling amiably at Moss and Gibbs.

They sat and Moss marveled at how the chair, which appeared to be of hard plastic, was actually soft and comfortable. "Straight to business is good for us," Moss agreed, happy for a politician who didn't want to engage in theatrics.

"I called this meeting because our goals are aligned. We both would like to see me elected mayor and break the endless chain of succession. We want the Carcer Corporation out of the city for good, we want the other large companies to be held accountable, and we want to give power back to the citizenry. Do you agree?"

"Yes," Moss said, and Gibbs nodded silently.

"I know that there is much work to be done to see these goals accomplished and I will speak frankly with you," they said. "First, to get me elected, there will need to be bloodshed," they said without emotion. "I believe this is not something to which you are unaccustomed."

"Was that a quadruple negative?" Gibbs asked with a smile and when no one laughed, he flushed.

"We have been known to find grime under our fingernails," Moss said, feeling clever.

"Good," Persimmon said, stroking their chin thoughtfully. "Your hands will be undoubtedly dirtier by the end of this."

"It'll be worth it," Moss said. "For them," he said, and pointed down at the city below.

Persimmon smiled genuinely for the first time. "We are aligned in that," they said. "I grew up here and love this city. I believe we owe it to the people to give it back to them. I will not allow my sons to grow up to be corporate slaves. They will know a world better than the one I have known."

Moss narrowed his eyes in philosophical confusion.

"Loving a place and believing it needs to be improved are not mutually exclusive," Persimmon said in answer to his unspoken question. "This city gave me everything, but the learning curve was steep for me and the path hard. I see it for the corporatocracy that it is. I see the oppression. The inequality. I see it all. I mean to change it.

"But don't misunderstand my words. None of that means that I have anything but love for the city. I love the hills. I love the artists, the creators. I love the music. The food. The teams. I love the history. All the things that make the city what it truly is. What gives it its beating heart.

"All the things that have been taken by the kinds of people who come to a place like this." They laid their hand flat and gestured to the room around them. "I will play this part. I will play it better than most if it means I can give the city back to its inhabitants."

Moss smiled. He liked Persimmon and hoped he could help get them elected.

"What can we do?" he asked.

"You two are from the burbs, is that correct?" they asked.

Moss and Gibbs exchanged looks. "We are," Moss said.

"And thank you for not calling us bubs," Gibbs added.

Persimmon let out a light laugh. "I'm half Black, half Asian, and nonbinary. You think I traffic in slurs?"

"I suppose not." Gibbs smiled.

"You suppose right," they said. "As to your question; I'll be blunt. I need you to kill a man."

CHAPTER 8

Moss had expected that. He did not think of himself as an assassin by any stretch, but he had become comfortable with doing what was necessary to see this goal achieved.

"This city has been run by a hereditary line for time out of mind," Persimmon explained. "One family has been elected — if it can be called that — since the national government fell. They have done it by taking every company cock in every orifice and begging for more. They have sold out every citizen in every generation. What is left of the laws that used to govern this land is now little more than kindling.

"The government shows up for tax season and the occasional war. The mayor's office is a sham. A disgrace to the principles of democracy."

Despite their promise of cutting to the chase, Moss noticed that Persimmon couldn't help but wax philosophical. Moss said nothing and simply looked at Persimmon. Their one human eye met his.

"You need to kill Duke Doland VII," they said. "His father's final term is up and it is time for him to take up the job. The job he was born to have and never deserved. The job that should go to someone who is deserving, someone who will work tirelessly to help those who need it most. A person who will stand up for what's right and not kowtow to the companies and their fat wallets.

"You put a stop to DD Seven and I will help you help me," they said with a devious smile.

"What makes you think you'll be elected if he dies?" Gibbs asked. "Also, won't you be the most likely suspect?"

"Of course I will be, but they won't be able to prove a thing," Persimmon said. "They will try. They may even try to have me killed too. But neither will come to anything. Because I am different from them. I have lived my whole life with a target on my back. Scraped my way from the street just down there," they said, pointing. "I have fought and I have survived. They can send people at me, but they won't touch me.

"The people love me. The people will have my back and protect me as I protect them. I have fought for them and will fight for them.

"And what makes me think that I will be elected? I know this city and I know the people will vote for me so long as there isn't a Doland willing to pay for their votes. The family will scramble to put a candidate on the ticket, but it will be too little, too late."

"Okay," Moss said. "Tell me a little about the younger Duke."

"You don't watch the news?" Persimmon asked.

"No, we spend our time *making* news."

"Clever boy," they smirked. "I should get you on my speech writing staff."

"I'll stick to cold-blooded murder for now," Moss said with a grim determination that caused Gibbs's breath to come out ragged for a moment.

"Don't think of it as murder," Persimmon said. "Think of it as justice."

"Little Duke is not a good person?" Moss asked, even though he knew the answer.

"That is correct." Persimmon took a slow sip of their vermouth on the rocks. "He is a bad man."

"Tell us," Gibbs said, clearly interested.

Persimmon leaned in, steepling their fingers. "He has been known to…" they paused for dramatic effect. "Take up two parking spots at once."

Moss nearly choked on his laughter. The joke had been so unexpected that it landed perfectly.

Persimmon smiled. "I am not all doom and gloom."

"Right." Moss smiled.

"But really," Persimmon said flatly, "he hurts children."

"Fuck!" Moss exclaimed in disgust.

Gibbs blinked, nonplussed. "Kinda buried the lead, there."

"It is important for you to understand what kind of people we are dealing with," Persimmon said, all levity gone from their voice. "They believe themselves to be kings. They think they are born and raised to be rulers. Everything they learn is based on an inherent understanding of their place in the world — a place at the top.

"This belief does not lead them to learn the importance of justice or of righteous governance. It does not lead them down a path of altruism or selflessness.

"It teaches them instead that the world is theirs and that they may treat it accordingly. They are entitled, self-righteous, self-important and self-aggrandizing. They believe everyone owes them everything and do not even see how easy they have it, falling into self-pity or furious indignation if they don't get their way. These people are handed the world and don't even see or care that it's in their hands.

"They are given everything and care for nothing. They become uninterested and, as people like them have throughout the entirety of human history, they find solace in vice. Bored children who inflict pain to feel anything at all."

"We know the type," Moss said. "But," he warned, "they will not go silently into the night. You believe the people will protect you, believe that they can keep you safe. You are fooling yourself.

"The Doland family will do anything they can to stay in power. They will force Carcer to take action, to send clandestine agents after you. I don't think you are naïve, but I worry for you."

"Your concern is touching," they said. "Truly. But I do have plans in place. I have not come this far in politics by being a fool. I have people inside Carcer. They will warn me if things change there. They will also help us take down the company once I am elected."

"That's actually something that I have been meaning to ask," Moss said. "What do you plan to do once Carcer is out?"

Persimmon smiled serenely and traced a circle with their fingernail on the table. "That transition will be the most difficult. While we know that Carcer needs to go, the infrastructure required to replace it will be complicated and delicate. Creating a justice system on the foundation of our current bounty system is complicated and nuanced. I have a team of people in place working on the transition.

"What you must understand, young man, is that when every revolution ends, complex bureaucracy begins. You can change the world, cast out the villains, but if you do not have a plan in place, are you any better? Bringing anarchy in the place of evil consistency?

"Yes, you may be the lesser evil, but lesser is not absent. As such, I will have a plan in place for that day. We will utilize the current system of freelancers and bring them in under a mayoral umbrella as we transition to a civic police force."

Moss ran his hands down his face. "That sounds incredibly complicated," he said, trying to imagine the realities of such a change.

Persimmon bowed their head. "It certainly is. The real ugliness of revolution comes after the bloodshed."

Moss nodded slowly, considering the words.

"To my earlier point," Persimmon said. "The lesser Duke is an evil man with evil desires and would be a threat were he to become mayor. You are too young to remember the fourth Duke, and I was only a child, but evil men with too much power…" they trailed off and simply shook their head, white hair dancing around their face.

"Do the world this service and we will reconvene to discuss our continued partnership," they added after a moment.

"Okay," Moss said, standing. "It was a pleasure to meet you."

"I think this is the beginning of a beautiful friendship," Gibbs said.

Persimmon smiled as they shook hands. "Cute," they said to Gibbs. "The classics are all but forgotten now."

"Not by everyone," Gibbs said, beaming because someone had not only understood but appreciated one of his references.

Moss and Gibbs turned to leave. "Before you go," Persimmon called after them. "Do stop and have a meal upstairs on me. You should experience it once in your life. The chef here had to train for fifty years to be worthy of the Japanese cybernetic hand given to only one sushi chef a generation."

"We'll think about it," Moss said, knowing he wouldn't.

Persimmon seemed to pick up on his intention. "I knew your friend Stan, too."

That stopped Moss. He turned back, hands on the sides of the ladder. "You did?"

"I did," they said. "I know he would have wanted you to try the food."

Moss knew there was no doubting the truth of that. Before he had been killed in Carcer City, Stan had made it his personal mission to teach Moss everything he could about food appreciation.

"Really," Moss said as he began to climb. "It was a pleasure to meet you."

Persimmon smiled and gave a little wave.

After eating what Moss had to admit was the best meal of his life, Sofia guided them back out into the mall. Standing beside the wet paint sign, she handed Moss a metal business card with nothing but an address on it.

"Mix LeBeau wanted to give you both the opportunity to visit their tailor," she said. "Their treat, of course."

Moss took the card. "That's kind," he said.

"They recommend you visit before you meet with the other candidate," she said, giving Moss a peculiar look.

"Thank you," he said, but she seemed to have decided she didn't like him, and he understood why.

"I look forward to seeing you again," Gibbs said with a wink.

Sofia smiled. "Likewise." She disappeared back into the club.

"What was that?" Moss said as they began to walk.

"What?" Gibbs asked.

Moss threw his arms up. "You know what!"

"Oh, yeah," Gibbs said with a shy smile. "I don't know. I think being with Ynna has given me a weird energy that other people pick up on."

Moss shook his head, and they made their way back to the landing pad where they picked up another cab.

"You thought about what they said?" Gibbs asked as the cab lifted and began to fly to the address on the card.

"What?" Moss asked, watching the glittering world recede.

"About what comes next," Gibbs clarified.

Moss sighed. "Not as much as I should have."

"I worried that would be the answer," Gibbs said with a sad laugh. "I don't think Ynna has either."

"I hope my grandmother has," Moss said. "But really, I'm not sure how much help she will be."

"She does have a warrior's soul," Gibbs said.

Moss looked at his face in the reflection of the window, seeing her eyes in his own. "She does."

After a long pause, Gibbs asked, "Will you start to come up with a plan?"

"Yes," Moss said. "During the meal, I was thinking, remember The Conservation?"

"The place Anders took us?" Gibbs asked. "Sure, but I waited in the car, remember?"

Moss chuckled. "Right, you did. Well, I think I want to talk with the people from there about what we can do for the world when we do finally kick ThutoCo's ass."

"Sounds like a good plan to me," Gibbs said. Then they looked at one another in confusion as the cab banked and began to slow. "Expected a longer ride," Gibbs said.

Moss agreed and they both looked out the window to see the cab sliding down onto the roof of another skyscraper. They stepped out of the cab to see an unmarked door leading down into a stairwell.

Where the other shopping district had stylized awnings with small vents that heated or cooled the surrounding area, this was just a roof in the sun. Heat waves radiated off the concrete and Gibbs groaned as soon as they stepped out.

"It's hot," he groused.

Moss shrugged.

The door beeped and a small man in a fine suit stepped through. Moss had never seen a person of such diminutive height and would not have thought it possible. He stood slack-jawed for a moment until the man said "Hello" in a high-pitched voice.

"We are here to see The Tailor," Moss announced.

The small man nodded. Moss couldn't help but stare and wonder. The man's body did not quite look proportional and his face seemed almost stretched. Despite Moss's gaze, he remained placid as he asked, "Do you have an invitation?"

Moss held up the card. "I do," he said. "Mix LeBeau sent us."

"Very good," the man said, reaching into his fine, perfectly fitted charcoal suit jacket. He produced two headsets, just thin wraparounds with an earpiece, and what looked to Moss to be a micro holoprojector. As he strode toward them, Moss could see Gibbs studying him as well.

Moss noticed the small implant in his eye for recording every moment and figured The Tailor was watching. He stopped staring and smiled as he took the headset, not wanting to make a bad first impression. Moss knew he was operating in a different world from the one he was used to. This was one of money, influence and power. He wanted to use these people to help him change the world and thought it was best to ingratiate himself.

He put the headset on and inserted the bud, the soothing tone of soft violin music filling his ear. The hologram bud pressed against his other temple projected the word *test* in a light blue before his eyes, and disappeared.

"Follow me," the small man said and turned to guide them toward the metal door.

They followed him down a dim staircase with unadorned walls. At the bottom, there was nothing more than a keypad and a blank cinderblock wall that Moss took to be a door. As he entered the card Persimmon gave him into the base of the pad, his suspicions were confirmed. The wall lifted slightly and slid away, revealing a beautiful waiting room on the other side.

The floor was stunningly patterned with red, purple and gold trimmed carpets around stone carved pillars that arched upward into a beautifully mosaic ceiling. The small tiles were as intricately patterned above their heads as the stitching was delicate beneath their feet. The walls were of smooth blonde brick, set with bright, backlit stained glass cut to look like what Moss recognized as the visual representation of the Mandelbrot set.

At the rear of the room, a woman sat at a small desk with a headset similar to the one Moss now wore. He took one step forward and felt Gibbs's hand on his chest. He turned to see Gibbs point in the direction of small shoe cubbies carved into the wall on either side of the door. He nodded and took off his shoes, allowing his toes to curl into the soft rug.

"Think it's going to be a problem that my feet kinda smell?" Gibbs asked with genuine worry.

Moss didn't speak. He didn't know the answer. There was an unmistakably formal air to the place, and he thought any small thing could make them stand out — and not for the better.

They crossed the room toward the woman. As they approached her, Moss had to forcibly suppress a gasp. Her face was badly scarred and the skin around her eye was pulled down so unnaturally it stuck out slightly. Moss had seen scarring like this on Anders's back but nothing quite so gruesome as the woman's face. She smiled pleasantly as they approached, but Moss could hear Gibbs make a small sound.

"Do you have an appointment?" she asked in an accent that reminded Moss of Zip Thud's.

"No," Moss said, trying to figure out where to look.

Guilt rolled over him as he realized that he didn't know how to deal with people so different from anything he had encountered before. He didn't like himself for his reaction but could not help how he felt about it. He cursed the burbs and ThutoCo for making everything so oppressively the same. The uniformity of his upbringing had not prepared him for so many aspects of the world outside.

"But we have this," he said, holding out the card. She nodded.

"No appointment," she said, the skin contorting as her mouth moved. "Please have a seat and The Tailor will see you shortly."

Moss and Gibbs turned around, noticing there were no chairs to be found. After spinning awkwardly for a moment, they knelt on small pillows on the floor in front of her desk.

They waited. As they did, Moss could not help but notice the quiet. Unlike most waiting areas or, Moss realized, most places, there were no screens, no ads, no chatter, nothing. There was not even the ubiquitous low electronic buzz. Other than the music playing softly in his right ear, it was almost silent. Rather than finding it peaceful, it was so unusual that it put Moss ill at ease.

"He will see you now," the woman said from the desk, and a large wooden door that had been obstructed from view by pillars cracked open. Gibbs groaned as he got to his feet, but Moss was able to pop up with ease on his cybernetics. They walked toward the door and stepped through, directly into an office. It was similar in style to the waiting area except there were a few paintings of women's eyes seen through veils or hijabs, and it was lighted by hanging ornate lamps rather than the stained glass.

Seated behind a stone desk was the man they took to be The Tailor. An older man with dark skin, wise eyes, deep wrinkles, a long beard and white hair cut short on top.

He waved his hand in front of himself and Moss cocked an eyebrow before a voice crackled from the earpiece.

"Greetings," it said. "I am The Tailor."

"Thank you for seeing us," Moss said, and the man nodded just before the words he had spoken were projected above his head. Moss looked up in surprise.

"I'm deaf," said the voice in their ears.

Moss was not familiar with the term. "I'm from the burbs," he said by way of explanation.

"I understand," the man said and gestured to the seats set before his desk. "Please, sit. May I offer you some tea?"

"Certainly," Moss said, the word appearing above him again. Even he knew enough to know that he should not reject hospitality when offered. They sat in the padded chairs and the old man poured hot tea into two cups from an etched gold pot.

He sat back and began to sign again.

"Deaf means that I cannot hear," he explained. "Outside the burbs, those who have unlicensed children run the risk of congenital anomalies. I was born without the ability to hear."

"I see," Moss said.

"May I ask?" Gibbs said, unable to help himself.

"Of course," the man said. "A friend of Persimmon is a friend of mine."

"Why not get it fixed? It must be possible."

The Tailor smiled, showing yellow teeth. Moss sipped his tea, smiling at the sweet taste.

"For the same reason I do not simply put a chip in my brain. I, and all of those in my employ, are Pristiners," he said. "We believe the body is evolutionary perfection and does not require the modifications of human hubris."

"I'm not sure that's the right word," Gibbs whispered to Moss before the words were projected above his head.

Moss sighed. "It is kind of you to provide jobs to people who . . ." and he trailed off, feeling like he had put his foot in his mouth as badly as his friend.

The Tailor gave them a friendly smile. "You needn't worry so much; I take no offense. Speaking of the things that make me unique does not offend me. It is part of who I am, as are my beliefs."

Gibbs leaned forward. "If you don't believe in technology, why use all this?" he waved his hands above his head.

The man smiled. "You misunderstand. I believe in the power of technology and will use it for both work and pleasure. I do not believe in poisoning my physical form with it. Pristiners use doctors, for example, but only out of necessity and never for vanity."

Moss was beginning to understand and thought about the woman behind the desk. It all made sense. Still, he didn't feel it was important to dwell on the Pristiners' ethics. They had been sent here for a reason.

He also knew that Gibbs would ask questions all afternoon if given the chance, so he said, "Mix LeBeau said we should meet with you before we meet with their rival candidate."

The Tailor nodded and stood slowly, examining Moss and Gibbs from behind the desk. He wore a well-sewn top tailored like a shirt that stretched down to the ground. He smiled. "I think I can help you."

"Help us with what?" Gibbs asked.

"My job is to help people find just the right attire for any occasion," he told them and grinned. He pressed a button on his desk and the walls began to turn, showing them the true nature of this office.

Moss and Gibbs's eyes went wide.

The Tailor signed, "Let's get you ready for your meeting."

CHAPTER 9

Moss took a deep breath, immediately wishing he hadn't. The street smelled like garbage and piss. The heat only served to make it worse, cooking the foul combination to maximum ripeness. The people who passed by did not notice. They were all on their way somewhere and too busy looking at their screens to take note of the world around them.

It made Moss wonder about the efficiency of the advertising that oppressed the city. One couldn't walk five meters without passing a dozen commercials but people rarely looked up. The companies paid through the nose to display their goods on every building, vehicle, street and human, but most people were too consumed with the screen before them to notice.

Crossing the street was a young man wearing a shirt with a digital display advertising that night's finale of the true-crime reality competition show, New York's Next Top Serial Killer. Moss couldn't help but think it was absolutely ridiculous, but as the kid bumped into another youth sporting a Comph brand tee shirt with the company logo in bold yellow, he realized it was really no different. One of the kids was being paid to promote while the other was paying for the pleasure — deriving a sense of status from being able to afford the brand but ultimately just promoting it.

Moss laughed to himself. He took one last sip of his coffee and tried to slip the cup on top of the garbage can. It was so overflowing with refuse, he had to balance it precariously on a bag of what appeared to be human feces.

When Judy had first introduced him to coffee, he had never expected to learn to enjoy it, let alone reach a point where he could hardly get through a day without several cups. He continued down the street, catching his own reflection in the mirrored glass of Breastaurant Sports Bar and Grill.

He looked good. The Tailor had made him and Gibbs undress right there in his office, appraising both of their nude bodies for a long time before fitting them. Before dressing them, he had them groomed. They each stepped into a changing room with virtual displays from which they could choose their haircuts based on AR images. It hadn't taken Moss long to realize that the man had given them no choice; the "recommended" haircut was actually the only available one.

Running his fingers through his trimmed, shampooed, conditioned, moussed and styled hair, he had to smile at his own appearance. He was one of the most wanted men on the planet in a city that was on lockdown by a private military; but walking toward the underground club, Moss was not too concerned.

The Tailor had made him look quite different from the old employee ID photo that Carcer used. Besides, the company itself was stretched too thin: while they technically had the city under martial law, they did not have the manpower to enforce it. The edict had ultimately resulted in wardens and officers hassling the citizenry more than they usually did. Instead of waiting for bounties to be issued, they now could simply kick down a door without fear of reprisal, round up citizens without reason, and interrogate whoever they wanted.

This had worked in favor of Moss and his friends far more than Carcer. Rather than having a city quaking in fear, they had one becoming angry and increasingly ready to fight back. Every person hit with a baton, forced into a van or pushed to the ground in cuffs was another person willing to help Moss, and his crew had been taking advantage of it through social media.

On screens around the city, people were sharing images of Carcer atrocities and the troll farms were working overtime to get the images out there, making memes and creating sensational headlines. More and more, they were garnering support from every corner of the city. They had a long way to go, but Moss couldn't help but chuckle about Carcer Corporation actually helping him more than they were helping themselves.

He turned up Third Street and headed straight for the hotel, walking with confidence. The butlers nodded without question and pulled the door aside so Moss could walk through. The power of fine attire amazed him.

He strode through the ultra-modern lobby full of wealthy people sipping expensive drinks while sitting on plush leather chairs under lighting fixtures that could undoubtedly fund their rebellion for a year. Moss continued to walk like he owned the place, making his way to a fire escape guarded by a massive woman with obvious genetic modifications. Moss knew that some parents even created their children to be this way in utero, deciding their fate prior to their birth.

He stopped before the gigantic woman in a black suit and held a finger to her ear. The woman raised a biometric security reader to the lobe of his ear. Somewhere within the stitched-in mesh of the custom suit, the tiny device was proximity hacking her reader. Moss's heart thrummed as the scanner read his earlobe geometry. Like every ThutoCo employee, his identifiables were in the shared security systems. If the device The Tailor put in the suit did not work and he was positively identified, his life would end here and now. Unarmed, he was all but defenseless against the massive woman.

The device flashed green, and the woman nodded as she punched in a code and pulled the door aside.

The door closed instantly behind Moss, and he followed the staircase upward. The floor was carpeted, and the walls were moving images of smiling faces with numbers underneath. He took a deep breath, preparing for what he was about to see. He pushed the door open and heard soft violin music being played live. It was a lovely, slow piece of music that filled the large, open space with a bar glowing indigo on one side, some seating around the room and a catwalk at its center. The catwalk was lit from above with spotlights and below with glowing tiles. A large screen at its rear displayed a larger image and would no doubt show off every detail of whoever walked out.

Small clusters of mostly men stood with drinks in one hand and specialized smart devices in the other, talking in low voices. Moss scanned the room, trying to find his target. It didn't take long for him to recognize the man from the pictures he had been shown. Once he had the man in his sights, Moss walked over to the bar.

The beautiful woman behind the bar wearing nothing but a thick metal collar around her neck hurried over to him and asked submissively, "What can I get you, sir?"

"Vodka martini," Moss said, trying to sound cool and calm and like he belonged here. The young woman nodded, her blond hair falling in front of her face. She set a device on the long, frosted glass bar top.

"If this is your first time, sir, please follow the instructions on the screen," she said before bowing and turning to make his drink. Though the bar had automated arms that could make any drink ordered remotely and have it waiting when the patron arrived from across the room, the people here chose to use the naked girl to serve their drinks. It was a choice that spoke volumes about the monsters in the room.

Moss forced himself not to think about the life of the young woman. To dwell on her suffering. It was in his nature to want to help her and those like her, and he would; but he needed to focus on the mission.

He plucked up the device. It was little more than an L-shaped metal frame with projected touchscreen and finger reader.

This would be the trick. He pressed his sheathed finger against this reader and waited. He hated having to do this. He had done it once before and it always felt like it was about to go wrong.

But the reader beeped and the screen welcomed him — or rather welcomed the persona that The Tailor had attached to his genetic identification. There were the expected menus and dropdowns, but Moss couldn't stomach looking at them. Seeing prices next to images of human beings was too much for him. He had been blissfully ignorant for so long, but now the reality was staring him in the face.

"Your drink, sir," the girl said. He had to force himself not to thank her, knowing it wasn't what these people would do. Instead, he gulped down the drink in one chug. He wouldn't let himself get drunk, but it helped.

"Coming to the stage now, Lot Number ACBF-17826," a voice announced over the speaker system and the music faded away. "The bidding for this contract begins at two hundred thousand. See your bidder plate for more details."

Moss watched as a well-toned man in his late twenties made his way onto the stage. He was naked and glistened from whatever oil they had forced on him behind the scenes. He had a collar around his neck and the number combination inked on his hip. He smiled a false smile, but his eyes cried out in misery. Moss knew he couldn't shake his head or appear sickened by all this. He had to play the part of a bidder.

He took a deep breath as the voice continued. "Raised in the Toronto Autonomous Prefecture of China, Lot Number ACBF-17826 speaks three languages, has a university-level education but doesn't shy away from using his… hands…"

The disembodied voice said the last part without a trace of subtlety.

Moss had come to realize that things like this existed, that neoslavery and human trafficking were commonplace, but seeing it made him want to simply toss a grenade into the middle of the room and walk away. This very thing was why he fought, why he did everything that he did; but sometimes, he didn't want the slow process of revolution. He wanted to take action.

Destroying this room or the people in it wouldn't solve the much larger problem, but it would feel damned good. He looked at the mayor's son and smiled. At least he knew he would do some good today.

He hit the bid button but was raised instantly. This is how he would get attention.

He raised.

They raised.

He did again.

He knew it was all a distraction, all a ruse, but the fact that he was bidding on a human turned his stomach. The companies had found a clever workaround by setting up an auction for signed 'employment contracts,' but how they got people to sign them and what they signed away made it clear what this really was.

He couldn't help but think about himself as a young person. He had signed contracts that he didn't read or wouldn't have been able to understand if he had. It could easily have been him standing on that stage. It was a terrifying thought and more than enough motivation to bid one more time.

He looked up to see Duke Doland VII bid once more before finishing his drink and slamming it angrily down on the counter. Moss turned his head and waved to the waitress, taking a deep breath. She hurried over and Moss ordered two drinks before raising his bid. It took only a moment for Duke to raise again but Moss waited and watched the countdown clock.

He would stretch these moments as long as he could. Duke was a man who got everything he wanted when he wanted it, and there was something immensely satisfying about the tiny, petty torture of making the man wait half a minute to purchase a human.

Okay, he thought as the girl brought over the drinks. As she moved away from him once again, he dug a fingernail into his wrist, pushing hard. It hurt, but he felt the false skin begin to crack. He tapped the bid button again to keep the distraction going. He knew there were cameras everywhere and that he needed to be quick and subtle. No one would notice what he was doing unless he gave them a reason. Reaching into his sleeve again, he ripped the skin with great force, peeling it off. The Tailor had made him shave the spot but peeling the glue still hurt and he made sure not to wince.

Now came the hard part. His eyes scanned the room. He wanted to check it quickly and move but knew better. So he examined the people as though scoping out his competition. In one deliberate move, he grabbed his drink while simultaneously dropping a small flake in the other. It fizzed quietly, nearly inaudibly, although to Moss's ears it sounded as loud as hot tub jets.

The naked waiter sidled up beside Moss and picked up the drink without a word. Moss smiled. He had had the easy job. Dress nice and walk through the front door.

Gibbs had drawn the short straw.

"You stand like you are ashamed to be denuded," The Tailor had said to Moss after he had disrobed in the office. It was true. Moss was uncomfortable in his own skin and particularly when naked.

"You will be our inside man," The Tailor said, pointing to Gibbs, who was standing with his hands on his hips in a superhero pose.

"Naturally," Gibbs said with a smile. "I am really, really, ridiculously good looking," he said, and winked at Moss.

It was moments like that where he really envied his friend's boldness. Gibbs had never been particularly fit, but what he lacked in muscle he made up for in confidence. It was an admirable trait even if it was a defense mechanism that would often blow up in his face.

Moss stood and made his way toward the restroom, its door located in the center of a large projected human face. Moss marveled at how broken the minds of the people here were that they wanted to go to a restroom located inside a giant human mouth. Shaking his head, he stepped in, walked into one of the stalls and stood on the toilet seat.

"It's the oldest trick in the book!" Gibbs had exclaimed in pure delight as The Tailor explained the plan.

Gibbs had gone on to describe several movies and video games that had featured this particular ploy. Moss was less amused. Standing on the seat was problematic. The slit between the door and the partition felt too large, like he could be spotted through it. The toilet seat shifted every time Moss tried to get comfortable and would clonk against the rim of the toilet bowl. The whole thing was awkward and uncomfortable.

He could hear a roar of triumph through the wall as Duke finally won his bid.

It wouldn't be long now.

"The tab is made from a mild toxin distilled from a poisonous snake," The Tailor told them, holding up the translucent flap that was about the size of a thumb print.

"Venomous," Moss had said absently, watching a limo land next to a rooftop restaurant designed to look like a medieval castle complete with holographic knights battling beside the diners. Gibbs and The Tailor looked at him in confusion. "There are no poisonous snakes. Poison is ingested, *venom* is injected. Snakes have venom."

Gibbs groaned. "Sheesh, you and the animals."

But The Tailor had smiled, showing his yellow teeth. "Interesting."

Moss smiled at the memory, but his mood changed when the door crashed open.

"Just give me a fucking minute," Duke shouted as he stumbled in. Moss could see through the crack and in the reflection in the mirror mounted above the bank of gold-plated sinks.

The entire bank of stalls rattled violently as Duke burst through one of the doors and to the toilet. He dry-heaved, swearing as he gripped the porcelain. Moss didn't need to be quiet, but he still was as he stepped down and pulled the loose thread on the sleeve of his coat.

With the force of a little tug, the thread came slithering out and released a button on his right cuff. Catching the button, he was sure not to jostle it as he slid it into position in his hand. He moved out the door and into the other, looming over the man as he vomited, the sounds of the chunks splashing into the water drowning out his movement.

Moss stood a moment and waited for a pause in the action.

107

"Cocksucker," Duke groaned and spit out a few more mouthfuls as Moss hooked his arm around the man's neck. Instinctively, the man lurched back in self-defense. He clutched Moss's arm, trying to pry it from deep against his skin, unable even to gasp for air.

Moss pressed the button into the man's neck.

The drugs began to surge through Duke's system, pumping through his veins. They would destroy his body, masking his bruises by changing the color of his skin to a sickly purple. His family would know it was an assassination, but the word of his overdose would already be out by then.

He attempted to slam Moss into the sinks, but Moss expected it and shifted his weight to the side, happy to be slight of frame. Duke crashed himself into the sinks, smashing the white porcelain and trying to vomit again. There was no place for the vomit to go and Moss felt the contractions in the man's neck. With his legs, Moss forced him back into the stall as the fighting became less intense. Duke was slowing down, collapsing toward the toilet, pawing weakly at Moss's arm. The combination of the drugs and oxygen loss was overtaking him.

Moss panicked as he heard the door crack open.

"You okay in here, Boss?"

"Fuck off!" Moss demanded, trying to sound like the audio sample The Tailor had played for him on repeat.

"Fine," the voice said sullenly. "I'll go order you a water."

Moss collapsed, panting on the floor next to the very dead Duke Doland VII.

He thought he should feel guilty. It was murder. Moss had killed countless people, including huge numbers at one time, but this was close, intimate. He had felt the man's body die against his own.

But Moss did not feel remorse. He was happy to have rid the world of one more evil scumbag. He was happy that his friend was somewhere else in the building, helping a handful of people who had been coerced into signing contracts go free.

He knew he had changed. He and Gibbs both. Once naive children, they were now hardened freedom fighters. Any shred of that kid from the burbs now lay with the corpse on the bathroom floor.

His muscles ached and the smell of vomit was making him sick. Moss released his grip and more liquid burbled out of the man's mouth. The drugs had taken effect and Duke looked like so many streetside junkies who had taken one too many hits of xeitgeist.

Leaning back, Moss used the lenscreen he had been given to snap a quick photo, which he sent to Puck. Within a second, he saw the words, "BREAKING NEWS: Mayoral Candidate Found Dead of an Overdose in Downtown Slave Market." Puck would release the story as soon as Moss was clear. Multiple versions of the story were already written with different suggestive elements that would anger different political demographics. No matter the beliefs of the reader, there was a version of the story that would make them hate the Dolands.

Heading out, Moss communicated.

Copy, he heard in response from Gibbs. *Meet you in ten.*

He stood, his arms feeling like noodles. He hoped the guard had not come back but even if he had, Moss knew he could just run at this point although it would be preferable to simply walk by. He stopped a moment to splash some water on his face. As he made his way to the door, it opened.

Moss's jaw dropped as the man stepped in.

They locked eyes and both seemed to have the same moment. Seeing one another, completely out of context, obviously confused them both.

"Well, no shit," the man said, his eyes narrowing.

"Oh, shit," Moss murmured.

CHAPTER 10

Even out of his armor and in a nice suit, Warden Ninety-Nine was a big and strong man. He loomed over Moss and filled the doorway.

Then he smiled.

"Millions of people and we meet here, like this," he said with a menacing smile. There was a glimmer in the man's eye that Moss recognized instantly. It was that of a hunter who had caught his prey.

Moss felt his heart rate begin to rise. He had just killed a man with relative ease and now it seemed he would be dispatched just as easily.

Warden Ninety-Nine took one step closer to him. "Do you realize the sheer number of people looking for you? The energy and effort being spent just to find you?" he asked. It was conversational, cool and calm, but Moss knew the man was simply savoring the moment.

Help.

Moss's eyes flitted around the room, desperately looking for something he could use to defend himself. But he had been sent in with little more than the button, and there was no way he would be able to overpower the man.

The Warden took one more step, the sound of his expensive footwear echoing softly through the room.

"That's a body I see," he sneered, looking at the feet protruding out from under the stall. "You've moved on to homicide now, I see."

Moss swallowed hard. He had to stall the Warden, give Gibbs time to reach him — if he could get to him. There was no certainty that would even be possible. He was supposed to be leading a bunch of slaves out the back to freedom. He might not be able to get back in and even if he did, what could he do?

Moss took a deep breath. Even though Warden Ninety-Nine was at the top of the list of people they needed to eliminate, Moss was thinking about his own survival more than opportunity. He just needed to keep stalling the man.

Taking another step backward, bracing himself for an attack at any moment, he said, "You realize the company that you work for is evil, right? They are the source of oppression for most of the world."

"Not work for. Run." Warden Ninety-Nine smiled, taking another step toward Moss. His dark brown eyes were trained on Moss so intently that he knew the man would be ready at any moment. Years of training were visible in the way he watched Moss, waited for a reaction or a moment of weakness. "You talk of evil in a room where you have ended a life. For all your self-righteous moralizing, you are nothing more than a murderer. People like you are absurd. You want to affect change, *do* something.

"Instead of killing politicians, get into politics." He shook his head, his eyes never leaving Moss. "You claim to be helping the people, but what do you do? You murder, you blow up buildings and steal things. *That's* helping people? You are as pathetic as you are delusional."

Moss smiled and stepped to his right toward the bank of sinks. Warden Ninety-Nine moved as well, staying close. He was enjoying this dance, happy to have the most wanted man in the city trapped with no backup. Even if he didn't know Moss was alone, he seemed to sense it. To sense Moss's dread.

"And you are better?" Moss forced a smirk, but he knew his terror was apparent. He was a trapped mouse with the cat closing in. He forced more words, desperately stalling but realizing that he was going to have to solve his own problem. "You are somehow helping people?"

Warden Ninety-Nine grinned. "Yes," he boasted without a shred of doubt. "When the people of this city are in need, who do they call? When they are threatened or molested, who do they turn to?

"Us. That's who. Unlike you, I didn't grow up sheltered by some company. I wasn't handed everything or given a free ride while I worked from home in my soft pajamas. I grew up out on these streets. I saw what they did to people, saw the way they chewed them up and spit them out. *That's* why I joined Carcer. Because I wanted to be part of the solution. It's why I laced up my boots every day and why I kept getting promoted.

"Now I run the largest defense contractor in the world. Because of hard work and a desire to help people. You think you are going to free the folks outside these walls from some Big Bad, but look around. You believe that if we were gone, the people would rejoice? No. They will riot. When those unfortunate souls out there no longer have us, they will come for you. They will look to you for protection, and then what? You turn them over to the freelancers? You turn them over to the government for protection?

"Or maybe you think you can do it all yourself?" He smiled at his own comment, as though it was the most ridiculous thing in the world. "Or you think your grandmother can? You think you know that woman? You have another think coming. You don't know her at all. You don't know her mind.

"Hand this planet over to her and you will see a dictatorship the likes of which the world has never seen. Her moral compass is so long gone that every person who ever worked for a large company will be marched into an oven.

"You think you are part of a quest for good when all you are is a cog in a madwoman's quest for vengeance."

Moss swallowed hard, not wanting to think about what the man was saying but feeling his face contort. Ninety-Nine smiled. "You know that already. Perhaps you are not as foolish as I presumed."

He took another step forward and said, "Though, of course, we will never find out." He cocked his head ever so slightly and the building shook.

Moss sighed; his friends had come for him.

His heart sank when he saw Warden Ninety-Nine smile. "What, you thought you were stalling me? Those aren't your friends. They are mine."

Very faintly, Moss could hear shouting far in the distance. When the door hissed open, Moss knew he was finally captured for good. They would never let him out if they got their hands on him now. They would torture him until they could access the program in his mind and then they would use his parent's technology to further oppress the world.

Warden Ninety-Nine's eyes went wide as he turned. His body began to shake violently and crashed to the ground.

The small blond bartender stood wearing the jacket of Duke's bodyguard and holding a taser pistol in steady hands. Moss couldn't believe it and knew there had to be more to the story.

"Thank you," he said, stepping toward Ninety-Nine's unconscious body, trying to think.

The waitress shook her head, clicking her tongue in imitation of a clock. "No time for that. Carcer is in the building."

"I have to kill him," Moss said frantically, kneeling to finish the job. This man had done so much evil, hurt Moss and his friends so badly, so often.

"Dumb fucking boy," the waitress said, dashing toward Moss and pulling him by the collar. "You'll die to kill him."

She was stronger than he had suspected, though not strong enough to physically pull him away from the warden. Moss stood and followed her as she began to run. He was livid. He didn't know when he would have this opportunity again.

Their whole plan to kick Carcer out of the city depended on the death of Warden Ninety-Nine and there he was. Moss wanted to turn and run back, but he heard Carcer officers burst through the front door. He followed the girl into the empty industrial kitchen and to a small, flip-top fridge at the rear of the room. Rolling it aside, she pulled on a small latch and lifted a small square of the checkered linoleum floor.

She signaled for Moss to jump into the darkness and he did, landing much sooner than he expected. He scurried out of the way as she dropped down too, pulling the floor back into place and pressing a little lighted button to the side of the opening. Moss heard the panel magnetizing and the little fridge slammed over to cover the gap, shaking the ground.

He smiled. Even in the heat of the moment and despite his frustration, he was impressed with these little touches.

"Follow me," the waitress whispered in the darkness. "It's not far."

Moss reached out, fumbling in the blackness toward her voice. He continued to follow the sound of her shuffling until it was drowned out by the heavy vibration of footfalls above them — the unmistakable thuds of boots thumping threateningly through the building.

A yellow light flooded the crawlspace as she lifted another panel and pulled herself down. Moss crawled over and peeked through to see an elegant hotel room. He tried to scooch around before giving up and pulling himself through to fall and land heavily on his back.

The waitress was already changing into an outfit laid out on the bed, and although he had seen her naked just moments before, he averted his eyes as she dressed. When he turned back, he saw a pistol pointed at him. Not some laser weapon, but metal with bullets. The type of weapon that would blow his brains all over the room.

"Now, what the actual fuck?" she spat before groaning theatrically.

Moss raised his hands in shock and terror. He had gone from one life threatening situation to another.

"I said, what the fuck is Detritus Sixteen doing? I know you think that you are the big boys or whatever, but we were dealing with that and now you have fucked it all up."

"What?" Moss asked, shocked by so many things the woman said.

"You're Moss, right?"

"I am," he murmured as her eyes narrowed at him.

"And you just killed the mayoral candidate in a place where Detritus Eight had been working to dismantle a human trafficking ring?" Her words were angry and accusatory.

"I — I mean, I guess so," he stammered. "Look, we weren't trying to step on any toes or do anything to fuck up your work. We are all on the same team, right? We are working to get Carcer out of the city and this needed to be done."

116

She sighed with contempt, shaking her head and growling like an angry bear. "Sure, we are all on the same fucking team, but you all think you are the star players and we all have to play second fucking fiddle. Did you even check with Seti before making your move?"

"No," she answered before he could. "Because she would have told you that *we* were working on something. By coming in and killing that prick, you undid everything we have been working for. I have been a naked fucking slave for the last two months, you realize that?

"The things I've seen, the things I've done. That'll haunt me forever. But I did it because I was going to help people. I was going to shut down their entire operation from the inside. Now, instead, we just have another fucking mess *and* the locked down city will be even tighter because we attacked the head of Carcer."

Moss wanted to be mad, and he was still mad about Ninety-Nine being left alive, but he was also guilty. He hated the idea that he had destroyed their chances of taking down this operation and the fact that he had just gone straight from The Tailor to the mission. The man had made it sound so time sensitive, they both just rushed into action without thinking and planning properly.

"I'm sorry," he muttered.

"Good," she snorted. "Not that it fucking matters now. We need to get out of here and you need to talk to Half-Caff."

Moss nodded, knowing that he had fucked up and needed to cop to that.

"Come on," she said, tossing him the gun and pulling another from a bag on the bed. Wearing a red-and-black striped shirt, studded leather vest, ripped pants and large boots, she could not have looked more different than when he had met her.

117

The pistol was heavy in his hands. Always having used light beam weapons, metal ones always felt unwieldy in his hands.

Jitters to Red-Eye, I'm coming up, Moss heard her relay. His mouth fell open. The fact that he could hear her transmission meant she was former ThutoCo or, much more terrifyingly, a corporate agent. He considered confronting her right there, calling her out while she didn't have backup, but the moment quickly passed. Even if she was an agent and he caught her, he couldn't kill another Detritus member without proof and there would be none if it came to a fight.

So, instead, he followed her out the door, her head whipping back and forth to check for enemies. There were none yet.

The hotel was stunning. The halls were wide and there were artistic screens mounted into the wall so that lighted moving shapes would dance along as they walked. Black-and-white photographs of the city made B.A. look much more beautiful than it actually was.

The hall also smelled clean. Not in the chemical cleaning sort of way that the burbs had, but like freshly washed linens. It was nice.

At the bank of elevators, Jitters pressed the call button.

"All the way up," she told him.

Moss simply nodded. A door opened behind them and a drunken man fell out, laughing. He turned to see the two with their weapons out and quickly dashed back into the room.

The elevator dinged and they got in. Jitters pressed the top floor button and they rode up.

"Sorry I was such an asshole," she said quietly. "It's just, you *really* fucked us."

"I know," Moss said. "I will make it up to you."

118

"Not me," she said gravely, and Moss thought about all the people in the city who would have been helped if not for him. He felt sick. Even knowing that the wheels were now in motion, guilt flooded over him. The idea that a single person would have to be a slave a moment longer because of his actions turned his stomach.

They left the elevator and made their way toward the emergency exit. Jitters blasted open the door with her gun and they ascended the stairs to the roof. Warm air and another beautiful view of the city greeted them.

A van idled on one of the landing pads and an older man with a hangdog look waved them over from the driver's seat. He wore his black hair mohawked and his black leather jacket's copious zippers jangled as he beckoned them.

They rushed toward the van as a cloud of Carcer drones buzzed overhead. Moss and Jitters jumped in, and Moss saw several naked people trembling on the long benches in the back. Gibbs was seated near the door and looked miserably at Moss.

"Think we fucked this one up," he said.

"I think you are right."

CHAPTER 11

They were not prisoners. These people were their allies, but as Moss and Gibbs were led down the long, narrow hallway, it did not feel as though they were in friendly company.

They had landed in the parking lot of a strip mall in The 'Toe: a part of B.A. City that Moss had never been to. The more time he spent in this sprawling metropolis, the less he felt like he knew it.

He had expected to be guided into the back room of one of the businesses or behind a false wall. Instead they had stepped from the van and been walked toward the road and down into a low ditch full of garbage that stained a narrow creek. Jitters and one other of her crew had walked ahead, looking back every now and again, before reaching a large metal grate with thick cross bars. She pressed a button on her, and the grate crackled and vanished.

Red-Eyes brought up the rear of the group, brandishing a shotgun that appeared to be as old as he was. Though he was hunched and his eyes glassy, it was obvious that he knew what he was doing and had seen some things.

Between him and Moss were all the freed people, silent and clearly terrified. Wrapped in whatever they could scrounge up and behind their scared expressions, they nonetheless appeared determined and excited to be free.

Moss followed close behind Jitters, ducking down into the large drainpipe.

"I'm actually surprised it took us this long to take the sewers," Gibbs joked quietly.

He always did that. Made little jokes when he was nervous. In some ways, it relieved Moss and when Jitters didn't shush him, Moss answered. "Right? Though I am pretty sure that was the tenth fake door for my punch card."

Gibbs smiled at him in the dim light. Jitters had turned on a flashlight, but it wasn't much use behind her. "Ooh, what do you get?"

"Free sandwich," Moss smirked.

Gibbs chuckled.

"But it's only redeemable at a safehouse in New York," Moss joked.

Gibbs outright laughed and Jitters and her friend both shot angry looks over their shoulders.

"Sorry," the two whispered in unison, genuinely apologetic.

After a few more quiet steps, Gibbs reached out and touched Moss's arm. "Hey," he whispered. Moss turned and saw his friend's eyes in the dark. "I never officially asked: will you be my best man?"

Moss wanted to guffaw. He had just murdered a mayoral candidate so that they could sway an election in their favor to force the Carcer Corporation from the city and, in doing so, destroyed the hopes of one of their allies; but in this moment, Gibbs was still just thinking of his wedding.

Shaking his head, Moss smiled and said, "It would be my honor."

"Your honor?" Gibbs asked mockingly. "Well, I'm happy to have you aboard m'lord."

Jitters wheeled on them, pointing her light in their faces. "Will you two shut the fuck up! I'm happy to know this is all fun and games to you, but some of us take this shit seriously."

Moss was sorry that he had screwed up her plan, but he was also tired of being spoken to like a child by some person he didn't know.

"You think we don't?" he snarled. "Taking this seriously and always being serious are not the same thing. I said I'm sorry for interfering with your work, but we are also trying to accomplish something here. We came with you even though we didn't have to, and I don't report to you or have to behave the way you want me to."

"Oh, I'm sorry," she said sarcastically. "I'm pretty sure that I saved your life back there. That warden was going to make short work of your sorry ass and I fried him *and* got you out. But sure, bust my fucking balls."

Jitters shook her head and the girl beside her snorted. "Fucking Detritus Sixteen is exactly who we thought they were."

Moss was about to burst but Red-Eyes shouted from behind them, "Hey! These folks need our help and you have them standing still in shit-water while you bicker like childs. Keep moving and shut it."

The girls turned and continued to lead them through the pipe until a short staircase bisected the tube. Moss and Gibbs followed them up and waited while one pushed hard on an old metal door that wailed as it scraped open.

It revealed another crumbled corner of the sprawl. Overcrowded and congested, the city was riddled with derelict

MATTHEW A. GOODWIN

pockets — places where disease or crime had taken hold and people had fled.

They all trudged down a cracked street, overgrown with weeds and covered in piles of raccoon feces in various stages of decomposition, toward a huge building with a curved roof. As Jitters pushed open the large double doors, a smell Moss did not recognize but could only identify as desperation filled his nose.

What seemed like hundreds of eyes turned to them from cots and bedrolls set up in the massive room that Moss quickly understood to be an old gym. The room was set up mostly with sleeping quarters, but there was a long row of tables on one side with food, bowed boxes of clothes on another with PVC and plastic tarp changing rooms on another. The scoreboard mounted on the wall with a ladder leaned beside it had the team names crossed out and the words, 'Freedom: 1,134 – Assholes: 0' spray painted in its place.

The people throughout the room fell silent until someone walking behind Moss called out with delight and ran to embrace a man as he stood up from one of the cots. The two sobbed into one another's arms and Moss once again felt the pang of guilt. They were clearly doing important work here and while Moss knew what he was doing was also important, this kind of thing, this kind of moment made him want to be a part of all this, too.

When he turned back, Jitters was giving him a knowing look. He let his head drop as she kept walking toward a back office with boarded up windows. Jitters opened the door and Moss and Gibbs stepped through.

The room was set up with tables and screens on all sides. People sat shoulder to shoulder, working online, undoubtedly gaining intel. A large screen at the back of the room showed the city and displayed various points of interest, all relating to the movement of human victims.

124

A man who had been leaning over one of the techs turned around and glared at Moss and Gibbs. His face and body were bisected with cybernetics. His entire left side was machine. The synthetic skin was translucent and all the mechanized innerworkings were exposed. His other, human half was that of a handsome older man, with freckled, light, dark skin. His head and face were shaved and his eyes stayed fixed on Moss.

"Well, if it isn't the chosen one," he said with a wry smile.

Moss shook his head. "It isn't like that."

"Oh, yeah?" the man who Moss took to be Half-Caff said. He changed the screen to shock jock-turned-infotainment correspondent Rude Von Tude.

The aging blond who always dressed like he had just come from surfing was mid-stride when the screen turned to him. Rude shouted, "And that was before all media turned digital. The new drug of the masses is…"

Half-Caff growled in annoyance and muted the screen. "Figured he would be talking about the mayor's son right when I turned it on."

"Look," Moss said. "I know you were working your own mission."

Half-Caff held up a hand. "Don't come in here supposing you know everything. Just because you're the hot shit of the moment doesn't mean shit to me."

Moss balled his fist. The man was intimidating, but this was starting to become too much for him. He opened his mouth to speak just as the door to the office slammed open, shaking the room and causing the plastic blinds to rattle loudly. All the breakers turned to see Sandra stomp in with Anders by her side.

"The fuck is this?" she demanded.

"Just talking to your boy," Half-Caff said, holding up his hands and smiling with false friendliness.

Moss wanted to spit. Having person after person demand that he justify himself had been one thing, but having his grandmother show up like an older sibling on the playground to protect him from bullies was too humiliating for words.

"I had it covered," he said, seething.

"Adults are talking," Sandra said, not even looking at him and dousing the wound in salt.

"Oh, yeah?" Moss snarled. "Anyone else in here just kill Duke Doland?"

"Anyone else in here just fuck up years of work?" Half-Caff said without missing a beat.

"That a joke?" Sandra asked. "This whole operation is piddling shit compared to what we are working on."

Moss could tell that comment was the line for Half-Caff, who gritted his teeth and spat, "You think this is nothing? We are saving lives here. We are reuniting families, freeing slaves. Actual slaves."

Sandra shrugged. "One at a fucking time," she mocked. "What my boy is working on dwarfs all that. We intend to free the whole city."

Half-Caff shook his head. "In contrast with your rude words, I don't plan to diminish what you are working on," he sighed, obviously struggling to regain control of his emotions. "I know your crew are working on the big picture stuff, but that doesn't mean everyone else just needs to get out of your way."

"Not true, Half," Sandra said. "Y'all do need to get the fuck out the way. What we are doin' takes priority now and always."

Half-Caff let out a pitying laugh. "Revolution is a game of chess. Queen may be the strongest piece, but she can't checkmate without every other piece on the board."

Sandra opened her mouth, but Moss spoke first. "You're right."

Everyone turned to him. Anders smiled.

"Look, Grandma, we did what we needed to do, we set everything in motion for Persimmon, but we also did fuck things up for Half-Caff. I'm not in this just to do the job I set for myself. I'm in this to do good, actual good.

"We made things worse for you, so, what can we do?" Moss asked, looking Half-Caff right in the eye. The man smiled, the false skin on one side stretching over plastic teeth.

"I know you mean well, but this isn't something we can just make a move on," he said slowly. "There is a massive operation at play here in many cities and there is not one move we can make. Look, I understand that outing the mayor's son as part of this ring was part of the plan; tarnish the man while taking him out. I get it, it was smart, but it also meant that all the people involved in the ring are gonna clench up and scurry back underground. And we are going to have to start over."

Moss thought about the people embracing outside, thought about what Jitters had put herself through. He shook his head. "No," he murmured.

"He said move on," Sandra told Moss, sounding irritated that he wasn't letting the issue drop.

"No," Moss said again. "There has to be something we can do. Some way we can help. Some move you couldn't make because you didn't have the people?"

"You know what," Half-Caff said, stepping over to one of the breakers and speaking to her in hushed tones.

127

Sandra glowered at Moss. "We don't have time for some whim side-gig. I brung Anders here because you two need to take Puck home and then get back here right quick. You started these dominos falling and we got to keep up."

Moss had so many questions about why he would be going back to Africa and what was next for them, but he just shook his head again. "I want to make this right. I need to."

"We don't have time," Sandra said, hitting each word hard.

"You're being short-sighted," Moss told her, surprising himself. "We will need every team in the city to help us once this plan is in motion. We need to garner good will, get these people on our side and ready to go. We invest in their friendship now; it'll be worth it later."

She looked like she wanted to spit. "Fine, I'll send the crew, but you need to go tonight."

"I'll go as soon as it's done, but I need to be a part of this," he told her firmly.

"Why?"

"Because we are going to ask a lot of a lot of people. I am going to. I will not ask for help if I am not willing to provide it to my allies. I am not going to demand others risk their lives if I will not risk my own. I may make mistakes, but I will always pay for them. If I am to be any kind of leader, I have to act like one."

"Don't want to be the monkey as king," Anders observed.

"Right," Moss said, thinking he remembered the fable. "I'm not some 'chosen one,' so I'm going to need to earn my place."

Sandra gave him a crooked smile. "Can't argue with that," she said grudgingly. Moss felt Gibbs's hand pat his back.

He felt like a true leader for the first time.

CHAPTER 12

"Okay," Half-Caff said, bringing up a display. "This is where they are bringing people in. Well, one of the places. The people are coerced in China, packed up and shipped here to this dock. It's locked down tighter than a nun's ass because it's an XT port."

"Why would Xuegeng Technologies allow traffickers to use their ships?" Gibbs asked.

Things had calmed down and introductions had been made. They were all sitting around a center table and Jitters had joined them.

"No way of knowing if they are even aware of it," she pointed out.

Half-Caff nodded. "We haven't found any evidence that XT knows how its ships are being used."

"The best smugglers let others do their work for them," Anders said, and took a sip of the beer Half-Caff had poured into ceramic mugs.

"*You* would know," Gibbs said. The two had never really gotten along because of jealousy over Ynna's affections, but Moss had hoped that now that Gibbs was engaged, he would be over it. He clearly wasn't, even though Anders had never really seemed to care.

"You're right, I do," Anders said flatly, not taking the bait.

"Getting in won't be easy and, if I'm honest, it isn't even about numbers," Half-Caff said.

Sandra cocked her head. "What's it about, then?"

Half-Caff brought up a visual on the display. In the center of the dock, near the gate and sandwiched between two warehouses, was a concrete cube.

"This is the control room. Everything is run through here. There are no humans on-site other than the one in this room. The computers are designed with heartbeat recognizers to allow only for human users, which is why we can't just send a bot. We need to get a breaker into that room."

Moss looked around the room. "You seem to have a glut of breakers."

Half-Caff chuckled. "Sure, but they are all too big. Physically."

Moss looked at the backs of all the people around the room. They varied in size, but none were particularly large. He wondered how much they knew of their team. Zip Thud was obviously who Half-Caff needed but Moss was surprised that he even knew about the young breaker. It made him curious as to what kind of information was shared between the teams. How much Seti knew and disseminated.

"So, we need to get Zip to that building, but how does he get in?"

"Trick as old as time," Half-Caff put plainly.

Gibbs squealed. "You're going to say through the vent," he exclaimed, slapping Moss on the arm with the back of his hand. "He's going to say through the vent."

"He would be entering through the cooling and oxygenation system," Half-Caff said, but the corner of his mouth turned up ever so slightly and he looked at Gibbs.

"Or put another way?" Gibbs led.

"Through the vent." Half-Caff acquiesced with a smile.

Gibbs nearly cheered. "It's about time!"

"Once again, you two realize that lives are at stake," Jitters said in annoyance, tapping her foot on the floor.

"Everyone has their own process," Sandra said in their defense. She was always happy to give her own crew shit, but never wanted anyone else to. "Ain't nobody on Earth in the market for unsolicited opinions."

"Don't tell us how to talk in our own fucking place," Half-Caff said.

Moss was beginning to understand how complicated a proposition it was to get all the teams working together, and why they worked in tandem rather than as one big crew. He was also increasingly impressed with Seti, who somehow managed to keep everyone pulling in the same direction. ThutoCo had also recently been able to duplicate her voice and breach her network, but when Moss had asked about it, she had simply said in her Australian accent that "it was dealt with," and that she could provide proof if needed. He had not pressed for it though he knew that she had provided it to Sandra.

That kind of breach was no small thing and could jeopardize the entire operation. But when she said it was dealt with, he believed her.

"Can I ask a question?" Gibbs put in, cutting the tension.

Half-Caff nodded and pulled a tin out of his pocket, setting it down on the table before rolling himself a spliff. "What's that?"

133

"This is obviously a massive operation. You had people infiltrating, the mayor and wardens are involved, a huge company is being used as part of the operation but, like, why? Why do people want to buy other people? There are drudges that you can make do anything you want. And if you want something lifelike to kill or have sex with or whatever, there are relief aides.

"Why go through all the trouble to capture people, bring them against their will and force them to work? It makes no sense."

He was so sincere that Moss's heart broke for his friend. Gibbs had always acted worldly and confident, but deep down he was naïve and hopeful. It was sweet, but Jitters looked like she was disgusted by the very question. She leaned in and began to open her mouth, but Half-Caff held up a hand before slowly licking the rolling paper. He tapped his finger along the edge of the cigarette, the unmistakable aroma of fresh cannabis filling the room.

"Power," he said as he lit and puffed. "Owning a robot and owning a person are two very different things. People have wanted to dominate one another since we had any sense of consciousness at all. It is in our nature.

"This civilization is what is left after we dominated the one that came before and they, the one before them. Back and back. Back and back. People who wield power wield it over other people. Dominating space or nature is never enough for them. They need to know that the thing they control *knows* it's being controlled. That's the true sense of power they crave. Even a sentient robot is never going to be enough. It needs to be something that could be free *and* understands that it could be free. That's why the industry exists. Why people put so much time, money and effort into it."

Gibbs's face was pale and he seemed to have no words.

"Why hasn't it been commoditized?" Moss asked. "I mean, there are no global laws and no one to enforce them even if there were. Why hasn't some company just taken it over if there is money to be made?" It was a grim question, but he understood how the world worked well enough to know that if there was a chance to make money, some company was always there to do it.

Sandra turned to her grandson with a grave expression as the room filled with billowing smoke. "Public image. That simple. Slavery is an ugly business and doesn't bring in enough profit to justify the PR cost. So, they leave it to... enterprising individuals..."

Moss wanted to spit. This whole conversation disgusted him. This city — the whole world, really — was just one big cesspit. He had been so sheltered, and every time his eyes were opened they saw some new injustice, some new cruelty. Humans had not only destroyed the world, but had also spread destruction to other worlds while nearly eradicating themselves.

But their survival had not made them kind to their fellow humans. It had only bolstered the oppression that already existed. Thinking again about the embrace outside, Moss was happy about being a part of this. Rather than dwell on how his move had thrown a wrench in their plan, he would help them accomplish something.

"Okay," Moss said in a tone so serious that all heads turned to face him. "We will help with this, and once we get Carcer out of this city we will help you mop up the rest of this operation."

Half-Caff smiled broadly, the smoke pooled in his mouth clearly visible through the cybernetics. "All right, chosen one. Let's get to work."

"This sounds really risky," Belle said, pacing nervously.

"I'll be fine," Zip Thud told her, standing up to hold her hand. She turned and looked at him, worry plastered over her face.

In moments like this, Moss had to remind himself that she was an android.

"You do not know if you will be fine. You cannot tell me that with any certainty," she said.

"You're right, I can't; but I can tell you that I will be careful and that this is something I want to be a part of."

"Why?" Belle pulled at the sleeve of her pink sweatshirt with Steve the Gopher on the front. "Why is it important for you to leave and go do this?"

"It's hard to explain," he said, taking her other hand and guiding her to sit beside him on the bed. He was still very young, small and slight, but in serious moments he seemed much older than his sixteen years.

"Is this 'some human thing'?" Belle asked, her face falling flat.

"No," Zip said softly. "I know how you feel about me using that term and it's not like that…" he trailed off, obviously thinking about just how to say it. "I guess there is something about helping people who are victims of circumstances, of poverty, the way my family was, that speaks to me… does that make sense? Like, I want to give the help that I was never given."

His eyes began to fill and his hands shook slightly. "It's why I wanted to be a part of this. It's like, I love the macro stuff but there is something about the micro stuff that's really cool. Seeing the actual face of someone whose life you are changing is pretty powerful."

"Like when you rescued that girl's dog?" Belle asked.

Zip turned to Moss, his body language indicating embarrassment. "It was more complicated than it sounds."

Moss smiled. "I believe you," he said, but he let a whiff of doubt come with the words, mostly just to mess around with the kid. He had come to really like Zip Thud.

"No, for reals, it was a whole big thing," Zip said, desperately justifying his actions.

Moss started to chuckle. "I'm sure it was."

"Belle, tell him," he pleaded, but she just smiled too, rolling her eyes and looking at Moss.

"It was *super* cool," she said, with far too much theatrical flourish.

Moss laughed. Belle laughed.

Zip folded his arms across his chest. "You two suck."

After a moment, Moss rescued him. "Anyway, it's going to be a small operation. Just the two of us with Half-Caff's team at the ready if we need backup. It'll have to be a quick in and out, because apparently I need to get back to Cape City."

"What is in Africa?" Belle asked, her eyes wide with excitement.

Moss shrugged. "We have to get a false face from this gene editor I met so we can replace a Carcer manager who is going to —"

Before he could finish, Belle let her head drop and started snoring. "Boring."

"Har har har," Moss said, but Zip was giggling. Looking at the two of them, Moss couldn't help but smile. They were totally in love, and it didn't matter that they were tucked away in a crappy room in a crumbling safehouse in a city on lockdown by people who wanted to kill them. To those two, there was nothing but each other.

He knew the feeling. It was how he felt with Issy and how Gibbs and Ynna felt. It hurt, though, because before all of them it was how Stan and Judy had felt. After his parents, he aspired to be like them. They had the love he wanted to have. His heart broke for Judy once again.

"I have to admit," Zip told Belle, "I thought you would be more excited."

She cocked her head. "Why's that?"

"Because you get to pick my B and E mission outfit," he said, grinning, and she squealed.

Moss snickered. "Well, that's my cue. See you in a few."

"It may be longer than a few," Belle said suggestively.

"Fine, a few and a half."

Zip gave him a thumbs up, the digital eye plates he had in place of his eyes flashing into hearts.

As he stepped through the door, Moss said, "And if Ynna's dog goes missing, I know who to call."

Belle guffawed and Zip kicked the door closed behind Moss as he nearly fell out into the hallway. The place was quiet. Pretty much everyone was out on some job, and Sandra was meeting with an informant somewhere in the city.

Moss listened to the floorboards beneath his feet, the low hum of electricity. He made his way to the little kitchen and reached for the television before retracting his hand. He knew he should eat, so he made his way to the fridge and grimaced at the leftovers with beards and canned synth meals. They were all that was left. When Gibbs didn't cook, it seemed everyone just fended for themselves. He pulled out a can and grabbed a fork from the sink, running it along his pant leg before declaring it clean enough to eat with.

Sitting at the table, he pulled the pin on the can and peeled back the lid, the meal making a sucking sound as he did. As he dipped his fork into the multicolored gelatin and took a bite, he was struck by how palatable the meal was. The texture was unpleasant to him, but the spices and salt were actually quite nice.

There was something very soothing about being alone. To have a break from the ceaseless pace of his life. He didn't think about the man he had killed, the things set in motion, his confrontation with Ninety-Nine or what had come after.

His mind was blessedly blank.

His hand moved to his mouth without thought and his eyes blurred. Closing them, he took a deep breath and reached out to the program in his mind. The program that had become more and more problematic as he discovered it was becoming more and more powerful.

His mind flashed to the moment he realized how truly incredible it was when he escaped the tower with Judy. He could hack nearly anything, could hack the world, but it took a toll. The program had already been bleeding into his consciousness, but after the tower episode the two began to feel like they were one. Like fluids mixing.

He had refused to let his mind merge with that of the program, even if it had been his parents who had created it. So, he had started taking the dampener pills. They worked completely. His mind was his own, but he could no longer interface with any computer. The cost had been more than worth the price to him.

Still, he tested it all the time. He would try to grab at the program or find some crack in his mind where it would leak through. Even with the pills, he felt he was always standing at the base of some great dam whose integrity could fail at any moment. In his calmest moments, there was still a nagging fear. And even if it could be kept at bay, he was endlessly terrified that it would be hacked. He had let a computer control his body once and he couldn't imagine what would happen if Carcer or ThutoCo got hold of his brain.

All these thoughts and none of them swirled around in his head as he scraped the spoon against the bottom of the can to secure the last bite. The sound sent a chill down his spine.

"Hey, Moss," he heard from beside him, and turning, he saw Zip Thud. He was dressed entirely in black with a ski mask rolled up on his head and a backpack complete with coiled rope hanging from the side.

Moss smiled.

"Ready to go save some lives?"

CHAPTER 13

"Hey, boys," Jitters said as she slid the van door open. She was dressed as she had been when Moss last saw her, but she had dyed her hair in the interim. It was now crimson red, complemented by dark black eyeshadow, and intentionally smudged mascara and black lipstick.

The two climbed into the back and Moss said, "Jitters, this is Zip Thud." He swept a hand to introduce the semi-famous breaker.

She laughed, looking him over. "You fucking wish."

"Just ask your mom," Zip said without missing a beat. With people he didn't know, he defaulted to his old tough-guy bullshit. It was how he had acted when he first met Moss.

Jitters covered her mouth but couldn't keep from laughing in his face. She looked at least ten years older than the young hacker and she snorted before saying, "Aww, that's actually really pretty friggin' adorable."

Jitters slid the door closed and Zip rolled his eyes. "Keep dreaming, you don't have the right parts for me."

She could not remove the amused look from her face. "Not at all what I meant when I said adorable there, tough guy," she said. Turning to Moss, she added, "This kid for real?"

"Oh, I'm as real as it gets, baby," he said. Moss had almost forgotten that this version of Zip Thud even existed.

Jitters was now laughing so hard she couldn't catch her breath, "Okay, okay, okay, enough. Enough, now."

Moss and Zip strapped into their seats and Red Eyes started to drive without a word. He looked even more tired than when Moss had seen him earlier, but he had slicked back his jet black hair with exposed white roots.

"Fill him in, chosen one?" Jitters asked, the shit-eating grin still plastered on her face.

Moss closed his eyes and took a deep breath. "If we are going to work together, I should mention that I really dislike that. There is no chosen one. This is not some grand saga. People are dying. Shit, we are going right now to rescue human beings from being sold. This isn't some action movie."

"Says the asshole whose life I saved after he blew my operation," Jitters said. The laughter was gone.

"He told it differently," Zip said.

"I'll bet he did," Jitters said as the lights of the city passed beneath them.

"Do we have a problem?" Moss asked, more annoyed than angry.

Jitters shook her head. "You guys pull this off and we will be square."

"I really *am* sorry I messed up your plan," Moss said, sighing.

Jitters let out a long breath too. "I know. And I know you insisted on coming and helping us. It's cool. You didn't have to. Sounds like you've got your own shit going on in addition to the whole election fraud thing. It's just... it's just..."

"It's just that you went through a shit ton and I blew it all in an afternoon," Moss said quietly.

"I don't like people cutting me off," she said, but her words were not angry. She was quiet a moment. "But yes. Plus."

Moss knew better than to speak, but Zip opened his mouth and Moss quickly gestured for him to keep quiet.

Jitters continued after a thoughtful moment. "I know we've all been through some shit. I am sure you've lost people, watched them die. Done things you wish you could take back. But have you ever been stripped of everything, have people judge you? Price you? Judge your very being and put a price on it?"

Moss and Zip no longer wanted to speak and just sat, considering her words. She was right about it all. They had been through a lot, but they had not known that indignity.

"And that's just day one," she said so quietly that the words almost evaporated before reaching them. "That's why I am pissed. And I know you are sorry and that you didn't want for my suffering to have been a waste, but I'm still hurting and it's totally fair for me to feel that way."

She turned wet eyes on them. The stylishly streaked mascara now streaked for real.

"You have every right to be pissed," Moss said. "Even to hate me. All I can do is try to make it up to you."

"Sure," she agreed. "It's just —it had to be *you*, you know?"

He didn't, and it must have shown.

"Well, you guys must know your reputation," she said, throwing up her hands before wiping the tears away.

Moss had no contact with the other crews and had no idea what their perception of his team was. That was, until earlier. Now he felt he had a pretty good understanding. "That we are a bunch of superior asshats who think we are better than everyone else?"

Jitters gave a sad, amused exhalation. She was obviously in a deep sea of confused emotions and, like Moss

143

tended to do, was dealing with it by not dealing with it and just getting back into the action.

"Ding ding ding," she said. "It sometimes feels like you guys don't even remember there are other teams on the field. I mean, shit, do you even know that we've met before? Well, maybe not met, but sorta worked together."

Moss had no idea how that could be the case. "Really?"

She shook her head. "Exactly."

"When?" he asked, genuinely curious.

"On the roof of ThutoCo," she told him. "You guys had blown the server room, for all the good that did, and that guy I just saved you from shot the hot chick and we all saved your asses."

"Right," Moss said, thinking back. "Thank you." He paused a moment. "You're right. I was going through my own moment; I didn't even really think about all the people who pulled us out of the mess we were in. I took it for granted, really."

"Huh," she snorted.

"What?" Moss asked.

"You're not really what I was expecting."

"What were you expecting?" Moss asked in amusement.

"I dunno. A douche, I guess. Some dude who thought he was an action star — not a nice guy who gets all introspective every time I make a good point."

Moss chuckled. "Sorry to disappoint."

"Nah," Jitters said. "Actually, it makes sense. You don't come as far as you have by being a dick. Or maybe you do; I don't know. But you seem all right."

Moss couldn't help but smile. "Thanks. Now I just need to convince all the crews of that. You know we intend to get Carcer out of the city, and we are going to need help."

She nodded. "Helping us is a good start," she said before adding, "and working with you will also inspire confidence."

"Thanks, that's nice to hear."

"Has the benefit of being true," she told him. Pausing a moment, she laughed and shook her head. "Between this and what happened at Atsuko AndroiTech on Tuesday, it's a bad week to be in robotics."

"Seriously," Zip agreed with a grin. Moss gave them a puzzled look. "You haven't heard?" Zip asked in utter surprise.

"I don't really follow the news," Moss admitted by way of excuse.

Zip's mouth fell open. "But this isn't just news; this is pretty relevant for us. Someone is helping do our job."

"I kinda can't believe *you* hadn't heard," Jitters said, staring at Moss with a mix of surprise and judgement.

"Maybe if both of you could stop being shocked for one second and just tell me," Moss snarled.

The two smirked at once. "Some guy went through and friggin' ninja'd half the company — all the way up."

In an instant, Moss understood why they had been so surprised. This was the kind of thing he *should* have known. Even if it were never reported by traditional media sources, it was the kind of thing someone would have told him. Any hit on any of the major companies was good news for them and helped to weaken the foothold of the AIC.

"Whoa," Moss said, wanting to know much more. "Who was it and why? Was it one of ours? Do we have people out there?"

MATTHEW A. GOODWIN

Jitters laughed. "We do have people in Japan, and they are looking for who did it, but it wasn't one of ours and we know almost nothing."

"Oh," Moss said, disappointed they had made such a big deal of something they could tell him so little about.

After a while, Moss turned to Jitters. "So," he said, feeling like they were finally beginning to have a rapport. "How did you get into all this?"

She shot him a clever little smile. "Saved by the bell," she said, and she pointed toward the tinted rear windows as the van banked and brought the docks into view.

Large cranes were moving massive metal shipping containers, offloading armies' worth of drudges. The mechanical servants did all the jobs humans didn't want to pay someone to do. The introduction of the robots had only served to increase the growing poverty problem, but it had not stopped their numbers from increasing. Everyone who could afford a drudge had one to help around the house. Any business that could replace a flesh and blood employee, had- or made a point that they hadn't. Some companies chose to take a stand against purchasing the machines but the business they gained from those who were politically aligned with them usually did not offset the cost to compete with the mechanized companies. It was said there was now one drudge for every person on Earth, and that number seemed to be increasing.

It certainly looked that way to Moss as he watched container after container being offloaded. A stream of trucks, transport drones and flighted carriers were constantly taking off from the warehouses lining the dock. Large lights bathed the entire area in a white glow casting long shadows. Moss's heart rate increased as he began to take in the scope of this thing.

Getting to the security box would be hard. Getting Zip in and taking over would be really hard. Finding the smuggled

146

humans and getting them out seemed like an impossibility. But that was the point and Moss knew it. He had to prove himself to the other crews, and in many ways, to himself.

The van tilted and began to lower slowly between two office buildings adjacent to the dock. This entire corner of the city was owned by Xuegeng Technologies was crammed with offices and large apartment complexes; small parks and shops were nestled between them. All were designed in a modern Chinese style, or rather what had been modern thirty years earlier. They all looked slightly dated to Moss.

They set down in a dark spot between two buildings where the light mounted on the building to illuminate the alley was burnt out.

"You two clear on the plan?" Jitters asked, and though she didn't seem to mean any offense, Zip's face scrunched in annoyance.

"Yep," Moss said.

Jitters nodded and smiled at them. "Good luck," she said sincerely. "We are here if you need us."

Moss nodded, knowing that her people were ready to spring into action at a moment's notice. "If we end up needing you," he began, but she shook her head.

"Don't even think like that," she said. "You won't need us, but just know we are here."

Zip slid the door open. "We won't," he said with an overconfident certainty that worried Moss as much as it impressed him.

She looked as if she was about to say something but decided against it. She simply nodded at Moss, who nodded back. Sliding the door closed behind him, he stepped away from the van as it lifted away.

It had been strange that the day was so nice; it was even more unusual that the night was warm. The fog rolled in every night, blanketing the city in a cold, wet blanket; but not this evening. Tonight, it was lovely.

Moss pulled out a pack of cigarettes and offered one to Zip, who was pressed up against the wall. "Shit's gross. I don't smoke," he said in whispered offense. "And what are you doing?"

Moss chuckled. He had been this kid not long ago. He had been terrified and thought he knew what he was doing. Seeing Zip pressed against a wall because he thought that was what a person did on a nighttime operation, he realized how foolish he must have looked. What he wouldn't give to go back and ask Burn what he thought of himself and Gibbs on that first night in the city. How he could possibly have taken these two bubs, these kids with no idea about the world, at all seriously. But he realized now that Burn hadn't.

"Just take one and walk, you know, like a person," Moss told him.

Zip shook his head cautiously.

"Take one of these and we can walk normally," Moss told him. "Just two guys out from one of these apartments for a smoke. Normalcy is a better cover than hiding. One person who sees you creeping like that is more likely to raise an alarm than a dozen people who walk right past two guys out smoking on a nice night."

Zip's eye plates flashed large 8-bit eyes and he tapped the side of his temple. "Gotcha."

He reluctantly took the cigarette and lighter and couldn't even inhale once without choking and coughing, the sound echoing through between the buildings. He looked mortified but Moss smiled. "It's okay," he said. "You can just hold it now."

They started walking. "It stinks and tastes like ass."

"I know," Moss agreed.

It was quiet as they stepped out to a small open plaza between some of the buildings. There was a little grassy area with a pagoda surrounded by a small creek with red and white wooden footbridges. The area was illuminated by plastic lights designed to look like paper lanterns. All of the apartment complexes had little businesses on the ground floors with their store fronts pointing toward the plaza. Most were shuttered for the evening, but a small bar and a little noodle shop were open. The drudge servers were in standby mode, waiting for someone to approach.

An old man sitting on a balcony with a pipe waved and Moss extended a salute while Zip looked like he wanted to dart behind the blue wisteria growing nearby.

"It's all good," Moss told him.

Zip rasped out a laugh. "Every time we run together you almost get me killed."

Moss put a hand on the young man's back. "I promise I won't get you killed."

Zip Thud shook the hand off his back and whispered accusatorily, "That's exactly what someone says right before they *do* get someone else killed!"

Moss couldn't help but chuckle as they neared the docks and slipped between two buildings. "You know, you remind me of Gibbs in a lot of ways."

"Nice," Zip said. "He's good people."

"So are you," Moss said, even though he wasn't quite sure why. It simply felt good to encourage the kid before they broke into a secure facility guarded by killer robots.

CHAPTER 14

"Ready?" Moss asked.

Moss knew Zip was nervous, even though the kid didn't have human eyes to emote with. This was not the kind of thing he wanted to do. Despite what he had told Belle, Zip was much more comfortable behind a screen.

"Almost," Zip said in terror, looking over Moss's shoulder at the chain link fence and warehouses beyond. "We are going to be okay, right?"

Moss smiled. "Yeah," Moss reassured. "Come on, you've been in way tougher scrapes than this. Remember the mansion and that crazy firefight?"

"Sure," Zip said.

"Or that situation with the dog?" Moss said with a kind smile.

Zip let out a guffaw. "Oh, fuck off," he said but Moss saw that the moment to breathe was helping.

"Seriously Zip, this is going to be nothing," Moss said. "A quick in and out. And as you told Belle, we are doing some real good."

Zip was trying to calm down, but Moss knew he wasn't quite there yet. He tried another approach. "Think you'll marry Belle?"

Zip let out a ragged breath and shook his head as if he could not process that question in this moment. Moss had come to understand that different people needed different ways to calm themselves before a mission, and he wondered if Zip was the type for whom distraction was key.

"Oh, um, yeah, probably," Zip said, looking back at the docks before turning back to Moss. "I mean, she's all over my ass now with Gibbs and Ynna, you know?"

"I'll bet," Moss said.

"I mean, it wouldn't mean much except to her, but that alone would be worth it," Zip said.

Moss nodded. Marrying an android did not change anything about the relationship, but Moss had come to know Belle well enough to know it would make her really happy.

"I'm sure she'll shove everyone out of the way to get that bouquet," Zip added with a little laugh.

"Right," Moss said, chuckling.

"Think you'll marry Issy?" Zip asked.

The distraction had worked too well. Moss grimaced. "It's so complicated with us. With me, really.People around me… they end up hurt — or worse. I would love to settle down with Issy and go work in her dad's restaurant when this is all over, but I just don't think that's in the cards for me."

"Could be," Zip suggested hopefully.

Moss felt the ghost of a smile cross his lips. "Maybe."

They were silent for another moment and Moss nodded in the direction of the docks. Zip's eye plates went black as he began to access the security systems.

"Let's do this," Zip said, and, crouching, they made their way toward the fence. As they neared, Zip held up a hand. They had reached the westernmost side of the facility where empty shipping containers were stored before being taken into the city. There, they were loaded with goods before going back to China where all the drudges were manufactured.

There were fewer lights, no buildings and only one patrol drudge in this sector. But that did not mean it was going to be easy to get in here; just easier. Moss pulled the pack off his back and grabbed a thick blanket. The fence was not very high but had three fierce-looking layers of barbed wire mounted at the top. The sensor grid began above the wire. That was going to be the real problem. The fence was a visual barrier, but the grid was a real one.

Any heat signature, unexpected movement or noise could trip the sensors and bring an army of drudges marching over. These drudges were not the standard human-shaped machines; they were designed for defense. Using that same scanner technology, they could find life signatures with ease and had swiveling turrets mounted on their heads. Moss remembered the first time they had seen the robots; Gibbs had scoffed and couldn't stop laughing at "how stupid they looked."

"May look stupid to your dumb ass," Sandra had snorted. "But tell me a better spot for field of fire. Three hundred and sixty degrees from there. Like to see how hard you're laughing when it puts ten new assholes in ya."

Those words resonated as Moss considered how many of drudges might be patrolling the grounds. He had tried to calm Zip by making it seem like this was no big deal, but if they alerted the sentries, they would be dead before Jitters and company even laced up their boots.

"Here we go," Zip said, nervous again as the number ninety appeared on both his eye plates. Moss nodded and the countdown began. Zip was an excellent breaker, but a company like Xuegeng Technologies which relied on mechanized defenses was not foolish. In addition to all the usual countermeasures, the system also reset every ninety seconds.

Zip was going to have to repeatedly hack the system as they went.

The countdown began on Zip's plates and Moss leapt into action, throwing the blanket over the barbed wire and helping Zip up. Though he was little, he was not in good shape. He moved awkwardly and uneasily over the fence, falling backward on the other side. He sputtered quietly; the wind had obviously been knocked out of him and he looked around in terror. Moss knew he had to hurry. He scrambled up the fence and hopped over it as quickly as he could.

His sleeve caught on one uncovered barb and hooked him, slicing his arm and causing him to wince as he fell to the ground. Moving quickly and seeing that they didn't have much time, Moss pulled at the loose fabric and quickly tied it over the wound.

It was not a bad cut, but it hurt. The small accident, combined with the two of them being so inelegant simply getting over the fence, made his confidence in the whole operation waver. He wondered if he should not have brought Zip before remembering that he was the only reason they were running this mission at all.

Panting already, Zip moved toward a tower of shipping containers. The labyrinth of stacked rectangles seemed to stretch on forever. They would run for a minute and stop while Zip did his work. Again and again. Every time they had to stop and crouch, Moss's heart rate skyrocketed. There was nothing worse than the waiting, feeling that at any moment they could be discovered. While they were moving, he was ready and confident; but each time they stopped, it was as if time was standing still.

Zip held up a hand and they stopped once again.

"Here's the real test of my skills," he whispered, the words sending a chill down Moss's spine.

"You got this," Moss assured him, but his words betrayed his fear and he quietly pulled the weapon at his side. The modified Kingfisher BotBugger XL had only five rounds, which fired magnetized bolts that could overcharge electronics on impact. Designed to keep your neighbor's drone off your property, Judy had reconfigured the bolts to be powerful enough to take down a full-sized drudge — or so they claimed.

His hand shook as Zip disappeared entirely into his work. It was silent except for the distant sound of machinery . . . and then, the sound of heavy metal footfalls. Moss swallowed hard and hurried around Zip to crouch between the young man and the drudge. The machine was imposing as it stepped out from the side of one of the containers.

These drudges were much more advanced than the ones sold in shops around the city. It was sleek with no exposed wiring or machinery. Rather than being coated in the usual flat matte, its entire form was painted with the blue and yellow of XI's corporate logo. A neon glow emanated from the gaps between the metal plates and the machine gun mounted on the top of its head spun slowly, just waiting for a target. The ghostly sight stopped.

If Moss hadn't already been sweating, he would be now. The machine turned its head down the row of containers and, while it made no logical sense, Moss was happy they had stopped in the dark between two floodlights crudely clamped into holes on the containers. His hand shook as it pressed the weapon at his hip, though he knew he could not outdraw a targeting computer.

He swallowed hard, waiting to see the gun spin toward them. But he heard a soft exhalation from behind him and the drudge kept walking a moment before disappearing behind another wall of metal.

"Fucking life or death frogger," Zip Thud wheezed as another countdown began.

Moss shook his head. "I'm sure Gibbs would get that reference," Moss said, too terrified to sugar coat anything.

As they kept moving, their chance of survival should they set off any alarms decreased. They moved around one more box and peeked their heads around the corner. Zip breathed a loud sigh of relief as they saw the security bunker.

They had made it.

Now for the hard part.

The concrete box was in the middle of an open plaza with the docks at its rear, the warehouses to the left, office complexes in front and container storage to the right. Six drudges walked in perfect lockstep in a circle around the box. It had one small slit carved into its front, allowing the operator inside to look out and see the real world — just in case all the systems were hacked. Several drones buzzed overhead, moving in time with the drudges below. Every machine was armed.

Zip turned and looked at Moss. "Sure you're not going to get me killed?"

In that moment, Moss was pretty sure he *was* going to get them both killed. He had wanted to make it up to Jitters and Half-Caff, to set himself up for what came next, but now he felt like he had been set up by the other crew. As if they wanted to prove that he was just another jerkoff who thought too much of himself. Either he would do the impossible and save the people or he would die and show everyone that he was nothing.

He cursed himself for accepting this mission, for asking for it.

Gritting his teeth, he said, "I'm fucking positive."

The 8-bit eyes registered surprise and Zip smiled. Moss pulled off the backpack and handed it to Zip, who pulled out the microbot and tablet. He handed the tablet to Moss and brought up a screen that was synched to what he was running in his plates.

"Okay," he said as quietly as he possibly could, the timers beginning to run again. "I know you have, like, legit no skills so I made it super easy. Just hit this spinning arrow before the timer runs down to start the hack again. It should keep the systems in check while I go do the hero stuff inside that bunker."

Moss nodded. "I got you."

"Okay," Zip said, sounding nervous. "Remember, if you start the process before you get within five seconds, it could trip alarms from the previous iteration, and if this stops working for any reason," he paused. "Well…"

"We're fucked," Moss filled in.

"Right," Zip agreed. "I won't be able to communicate from in there and you'll be all alone out here."

"Zip, I get it," he said, holding up a hand and looking at all of the weapons arrayed around the pillbox. Zip didn't say anything; he simply turned back and set down the small robot that looked like a six-legged spider with its front legs raised. It began skittering across the concrete toward the small building. Moss watched as the timer counted down and as soon as it hit five, he reset it again.

The microbot moved in to the side of the building and pressed itself against the metal vent. From his vantage point, it looked to Moss as though it would be too small for a person to squeeze through, but Half-Caff had calculated it and said it would work.

The little arms reached up, gripping the screws and turning them rapidly without letting them fall to the ground. The two watched and Zip turned back.

"Good luck out here," he said with a quavering voice.

Moss smiled. "Good luck," he told the young man and put a reassuring hand on his shoulder. "See you in a bit."

"Right," Zip said, and waited for another moment until Moss reactivated hack. He nodded and ran out into the open. Surrounded by machines that could tear him to shreds as easily as take a step, he made his way toward the unadorned cement square. The microbot pulled the cover free, rearing up on its hind legs.

Moss watched the moment of truth as Zip sucked in his slight stomach and began to squeeze through. He held his breath, unable to look away until he realized he had to look down and saw two seconds remaining. He quickly tapped to reactivate the hack, reminding himself not to get distracted.

A small breath escaped his lips as Zip's feet disappeared into the vent. He couldn't help but smile; it was so much like many of the video games he had played. But something was tickling the back of his mind. As he stared at the vent, he felt like there was something he was missing; but he couldn't put his finger on what it was.

Tapping the pad again, he looked back over his shoulder, thinking about the patrol drudge, Zip going in… He furrowed his brows.

As he thought, he knew Zip was creeping in, subduing the human within and beginning to break into the system. He knew it would take time. Zip had made that clear. Overriding the drudges of a drudge manufacturer was complicated enough without having to take over the entire system of a distribution line.

It still amazed Moss what these people were capable of. Zip was little more than a child, but he had learned how to hack better than most breakers who had spent their whole lives perfecting the skill. The young people around him were some of the best professionals in the world, capable of unimaginable things. It was truly remarkable, and he felt proud to be in their company.

He tapped the button one more time and idly glanced down at the backpack he had been carrying for them.

His eyes went wide.

He looked back, trying to calculate how long it had been since they passed the drudge.

"Shit," he muttered as he took off running.

CHAPTER 15

Moss's eyes flashed between the screen and the endless containers before him. He tried to remember where they had turned, what rows they had ducked into.

Even with the security hacked, he was terrified of being spotted. If a human operator caught a glimpse of Moss bolting at full tilt through the facility, he knew what would happen.

He skidded to a stop and pressed himself against a box, the metal still warm from the heat of the day. He peered around and saw the drudge.

Shit.

He would have to wait. The tablet program may have made him invisible to the mounted sensors, but he knew Zip had done something different to break the drudge. As he watched the machine walk, scanning as it went, he saw what he had feared. Dangling on the fence was the blanket.

All their work, all the advanced hacking and careful (if quick) planning would be for naught if the robot strode over and scanned the material. Something that out of place would raise the alarms and activate an army of counterbreakers that could easily outsmart Zip and have the two of them killed.

The drudge kept walking, moving slowly toward the rear fence.

It was a straight shot and the deadly machine was between Moss and the blanket. He didn't know what to do. He could call Jitters, see if she could get to it in time. But there was no way now. There would have been no way even if he had thought to call when he first realized their mistake.

Sighing, he pulled out the pistol. Zip had warned him that all the drudges were connected and disabling one would probably activate the countermeasures, but it was a risk Moss had to take. If it scanned the blanket, it was all over.

Perhaps knocking out the unit would only activate a maintenance team? Or maybe nothing would happen? He didn't know, but as the drudge took one step closer to the fence line, he knew he had to find out.

Leveling the weapon, he took one deep breath. He had promised Zip that he would not get him killed but now he was not so sure.

His finger moved to the trigger.

He pulled it away.

The drudge stopped moving. Moss cocked his head. Had it registered the blanket?

He stared, ready to fire at a moment's notice.

A warm breeze danced between the containers and was enough to send the drudge crashing to the ground. In his imagination, he could hear Gibbs saying, "You did it. The crazy son of a bitch. You did it."

A massive metallic clang reverberated through the space, shaking the ground, and Moss tilted his head to see one of the cranes coming to life. He wanted to jump for joy, to run and grab Zip and tell him what an amazing job he had done. But they were not out of the woods yet.

The crane, soaring hundreds of meters in the air, began to turn and the spreader lowered toward a massive open hole in the dock filled with containers stacked ten deep. Moss watched in awe but realized he had to move. He ran, already out of breath by the time he neared the open area where the chassis would be loaded with the container.

He darted out as the container was lifted with jerky motions. Zip had never done anything like this before and Moss pitied the people inside the metal box as it bounced and jolted upward in the grip of the giant orange crane. Moss no longer had to press the repeating hack as Zip was now in control of the whole system. He pressed the tablet against driver's side door of the truck's cab.

The program activated and unlocked the door.

Moss pulled himself up and into the cab. The seat was covered in hard wooden beads and a picture of a middle-aged man and his family was taped to the horn. Moss wondered if the driver used his children's face to keep from blasting the horn. Most shipments were done on computerized routes and operated by the self-driving vehicles, but Moss had heard that truckers sometimes took manual control of their vehicles. The interior had a strong aroma, and Moss turned to see a half-eaten Arguello Market turkey sandwich on the passenger seat and a steaming cup of Teotl Coffee in the cup holder.

He was surprised that a driver would just abandon half a sandwich and leave, but it was the middle of the night and there was no reason for drivers to be on site unless they were part of the trafficking.

Moss turned and his suspicions were confirmed as the man from the photograph came running toward him. Moss hopped down and turned to face the man. He was large with a heavy gut and thick arms. He did not look muscular but he did look powerful.

163

"Who the fuck are you?" he shouted as he came within earshot. The massive man slowed but did not stop moving toward Moss. He knew Jitters wouldn't be able to save his ass this time.

"B.A. City Trucking Inspection Department," Moss said with a friendly smile.

The man grinned, his ugly combover lifting as the wind picked it up. "No such thing."

Moss moved toward the man. "I'm sorry, sir, but I am going to need you to answer a few questions."

The driver balled his fists as he came closer.

Moss ducked as the first punch came. He had been in enough fights to know what to do. From his lower position, he struck the man hard in the side but his tiny fist didn't do much to slow the man. He looked down with the wild eyes of someone who either didn't get enough sleep or took uppers to stay awake.

He brought a massive fist crashing downward but Moss sprang out of the way.

The shipping container came into view from above and began to lower toward them, the sounds of the machinery filling their ears. The man reached for Moss, who moved to avoid him, but a fingertip caught his shirt. He grabbed at the fabric and pulled Moss in, landing a solid punch with his left hand.

Seeing white, Moss kicked. His cybernetic leg blasted forward and made contact with the man's groin.

During a training session one afternoon, Stan had looked at Moss and smirked. "Think the guy who killed you cares that he did it with a cheap shot? No. Do whatever you have to do to win the fight."

The man squealed as he released Moss. Getting kicked in the balls was bad enough without getting kicked in the balls by a metal leg. Gasping, he groped toward Moss who easily maneuvered around the flailing arms.

The container continued to move as Zip tried to place it correctly. It jerked up twice then down and left, then right and back and forth. It swayed overhead, the sound drowning out the second set of feet. Moss felt the blow to the back of his head and was knocked to his knees before he realized what was happening.

"Dad!" called a burly teen with a patchy beard, denim vest, red baseball cap and bandaged fresh tattoo. He was pudgy and thick like his father.

None of the drudges moved as Moss staggered to get up while the big kid moved past them to help his father.

"No, Buck," his dad said, regaining his power of speech but still gripping his testicles. "Grab him."

Buck wheeled around and charged Moss, who was too slow to dodge him and took the full force of a shoulder, slamming him to the open concrete. Bits of the rocky topcoat slurry applied to grip the massive tires cracked against Moss's head as it hit the ground.

He sucked in air and had just enough time to raise his hands to deflect an oncoming blow. The kid kept trying to hit him but he was no fighter — just an angry young man who seemed happy to be beating a stranger.

Moss struggled against the weight pressing down on his chest as Buck continued to pound him like a gorilla. Needing a breath, the teen paused just long enough for Moss to bring the heel of his bent hand crashing against the base of his nose. The loud crack and scream were followed by an explosion of blood that poured from his nose as he sputtered.

This brought his father charging at Moss, who wasted no time pulling the modified pistol and firing it. The bolt blasted out, sinking magnetized hooks into the man's forehead before sending an electric current strong enough to stop a large machine through his body. He collapsed to the ground as he cooked from the inside,

165

blood-infused crimson smoke seeping out of his mouth and hanging in the air as he collapsed.

Moss grimaced. He couldn't help but think the man smelled like rotisserie chicken. He wiped the blood from his face as he ran back toward the truck, just as the container slammed down on the truck's bed. Moss heard the magnetization as the bed gripped the box.

Behind him, the young man continued to moan and cry out for help. Moss felt bad until he heard a faint, muffled sound from the container. Remembering all the people trapped in that box on their way to be sold, he stomped over to Buck.

His face was swelling and his eyes rolling from blood loss. His hands were clamped onto his nose. Moss grabbed the collar of his stained vest.

"Where were you taking these people?" he growled.

Buck blinked, his eyes working to focus. "I don't know."

Moss slapped him across the face. "Wrong answer."

"I don't," he wailed.

Moss produced the gun again, pushing Buck to the ground and looming over him. "You're learning the ropes from dear old dead dad," he said. "You know what he's up to and if you want to survive this night, you're going to tell me everything."

Buck coughed, winced and began to weep, but he told Moss everything he knew.

"Holy shit," Zip said as he came trotting over. "And what did you do to the big one?"

"Killed him," Moss said.

Zip looked sick and scared but said simply, "Blunt."

"Yeah," Moss said.

"We gotta go," Zip urged.

Moss turned back to the pathetic pile of pleading Buck and raised the BotBugger.

"Please," Buck wailed. "I told you what I know."

Zip began to walk back toward the truck as Moss said, "What you did was admit that you are part of a fucking slavery ring. If you think that giving me some answers makes your life worth anything, you're wrong."

The now familiar rotisserie smell filled his nostrils as he strode back toward the idling truck.

"Great job," Moss told Zip as he pulled himself up into the passenger seat, pushing the sandwich onto the floor. "Sorry you had to see that."

Zip shook his head. "I've spent my whole life online. You think I haven't seen way worse than that?"

"Not in real life.".

Zip shook his head as he plugged coordinates into the truck and it rumbled to life. "The internet *is* real life. The digital, and whatever this is, are not binary the way you think. Things in there can be real out here. I know you spent time in the Mass Illusion and so you know the way some people play that. So, while I have lived behind a screen, I still have the experience."

"I take your point and I understand what you are saying," Moss said as the truck began to pull away. He was so distracted by the conversation, he wasn't thinking about the fact that they were fleeing a very dangerous situation that could still turn at any moment. "I helped take down the Troll Killer but seeing a recording of some gruesome shit and seeing that asshole fry just now is not the same."

"I mean, shit. My eyes are cameras that feed digital information from the lenses to my brain. How is *that* different than seeing something fed from elsewhere to my brain?"

Moss pondered that a moment as the truck rolled toward the gate where a deactivated drudge stood watch. Zip's eye plate went black as he hacked the gatehouse with ease and the fence rolled open.

"I guess you've got me there," Moss admitted. "Still, I feel a little bad about you having to see that."

Zip smiled, plucking up the Styrofoam coffee cup and taking a sip of a dead man's drink. "I'm not as delicate as you think," he said as they pulled away from the dock complex.

Moss smiled at the kid even though he didn't think sharing a stranger's coffee was as badass as Zip seemed to think.

Summertime started blaring out of the speakers and Zip's face stretched into a big grin.

Moss felt the truck shake as an explosion erupted from the docks. His mouth fell open as he spun around and stuck his head out the window to see the drudges fire their weapons at the buildings. The drones sprayed rockets at the cranes and crates with such precision that buildings began to crumble and cranes topple. Before his eyes, as much of the docks as he could see crashed into ruins.

"I'm, like, a really good breaker," Zip beamed.

Moss couldn't help but be impressed. "No kidding."

"And like you said to that groveling asshole, it's the cost of being a party to slavery," he said.

Moss stared in astonishment at this child who just hacked one of the world's largest companies and got it to destroy part of itself. "You are amazing, Zip."

The kid smiled the way Moss knew he had when Burn had praised him. It felt good and Moss just shook his head in awe of their success. His face was swelling and he was covered in blood, but they had saved some lives, hit a mega corporation where it hurt and gained intel that would solidify their bond with another crew.

"You are, too," Zip said before smiling mischievously. "Chosen One."

CHAPTER 16

"It's like, we were watching and chblooom," Jitters said, waving her hands in simulation of an explosion as the crew gathered around Zip and Moss in the large, abandoned warehouse. A woman ran around the back of the truck with bolt cutters.

"All the kid," Moss said, hooking a thumb.

"Raddio-oh-oh," Jitters said as Half-Caff stepped around a corner with Sandra.

"Boys did good," Moss's grandmother said before looking at Moss and adding, "Anders is on his way to take you to Africa."

Moss nodded. In his excitement, he had nearly forgotten that they were in the middle of a much larger plan with its wheels already in motion.

"You impressed my whole team," Half-Caff told Zip and the young man grinned once again. "You're sure the counterbreakers didn't pull anything?"

"Nah," Zip said. "I'm just that good."

"Yeah, you are," Jitters agreed, and Moss was happy to see her happy. It was a weight off his conscience. "Seriously, kid; bum bum dum dum," Jitters imitated fanfare. "What you did was remarkable."

"Thank you," Zip said, his skin turning the color of a tomato.

"Come on," Jitters said.

She pulled them around to the back of the truck as the lock was cut and the heavy metal handle was lifted and spun, swinging the door open.

Moss's heart broke as he saw all the people chained together. Sunken eyes stared at them as the woman who had opened the door began speaking to them in Cantonese, presumably assuring them of their safety. Red Eyes pushed past Moss with a jug of water in each hand.

The people were all gaunt, filthy and terrified. The smell of sweat, fecal matter, disease and decay poured from the back of the box. Moss couldn't shift his gaze without seeing ribs, bruises, scabs and patchy hair. The cruelty of man was staring him in the face. He wanted to scream, to hurt those who had done this. He wanted to shoot Buck again.

"Hey," Jitters said, breaking his mind free and pushing bolt cutters against his chest. He grabbed the heavy metal implement and heaved himself into the container. He had to move carefully to avoid stepping on the people on the floor. He didn't know if they were alive or dead or somewhere in between. A finger moved as his boot brushed over it and his heart broke so painfully that he wanted to turn and run, to flee from all the pain of the world.

Shaking his head, he reminded himself of the good they were trying to do and lifted the bolt cutters. One confused child screamed but was reassured by some of the adults. Moss began to close the cutters. It took two hard squeezes, twice, to break a chain. Many were rusted through, leaving orange-brown streaks on the wrists and bodies of the poor souls.

Once he had begun he could not stop. He broke chain after chain. Some of the people embraced him, leaving wet stains on his clothes; others ran straight out the back, gasping for air; still more whispered thanks in hoarse voices before immediately grabbing cups of water. Zip was standing at the back, helping people down. As a little boy headed out, looking desperately for a parent, Zip wrapped him up in his arms, speaking softly to him as he carried the boy over to where blankets were being handed out.

"Moss," Sandra interrupted as he continued to work. "You gotta go."

"Right," he said, turning and handing the bolt cutters back to Red Eyes, who tucked them under an arm.

Moss felt a hand tug his and he turned, expecting to see one of the freed thanking him, but it was Jitters. She looked at him with sad joy.

"Ptchhh," she said, mimicking an explosion and moving her hands away from her temples with flair. "You are nothing like what I expected and everything you need to be."

Moss shook his head. "This was all Zip Thud," he said, not willing to take any credit for the job the kid did.

Jitters smiled as the last few people made their way out of the container. "Exactly," she said and when Moss gave her a puzzled look, she added, "A true leader gives credit to those who deserve it."

Moss felt himself blush. Jitters held out a shaking hand with fresh black nail polish. "I look forward to working with you."

"Me too, you," Moss said, shaking the hand. "Still sorry I fucked up your op."

"We can call it even," she said as she dropped out of the box, nodding at Sandra before going to help the others.

"Quite a thing," Sandra said, patting Moss on the back before turning him around and shoving him gently toward an exposed metal staircase at the back of the room.

"I got intel too," Moss told her, explaining everything Buck had told him.

"Them bonus points'll go a long way," Sandra said. "I'll tell Half and they'll sort it."

"Good," Moss said, and he paused, listening to their boots against the metal. "Felt good to do good."

"I know. Gotta keep in mind though, we are always doin' good. May not be this kind of good, the tangible good, but the big shit is big shit. Remember that."

Moss sighed. He wasn't in the mood for a lecture. Sometimes he just wanted her to hear him. "I remember," he said, but his words betrayed his annoyance.

His grandmother paused at the top of the stairs, turning to Moss instead of pushing open the door. "Don't get me wrong, this *was* a hell of a thing. You and the kid saved a lot of lives and got us in good with another crew — to say nothing of what you did earlier: killing that prick and establishing a new narrative. You did great today and I'm as proud of you as I've ever been."

Moss smiled.

"But we have work to do," she added. "Lots more. We are close. We may actually be able to get Carcer out of here, disrupt and eventually destroy them."

"But it's about more than that," Moss snapped. "Getting Persimmon elected will be good for the city. Getting Carcer out is only the first step, and it sometimes feels like it's the only part you care about."

Her eyes narrowed. She hated back talk but then she seemed lost for a moment. "You know what they did to me."

"Yes, and that's why I want to fight Carcer, but it's only one domino."

"I know, and don't you presume to lecture me," she said. "You may think you're some big shot 'cause you ran a couple of successful missions, but I'm still the one who makes the calls. As long as I draw breath, I'm the leader here and I decide what direction we go."

"Some leader," Moss said in a stage whisper, grunting like an annoyed teenager.

Sandra just laughed at him. "You'll get your shot soon enough, Little Britches, but right now you are showing how far you are from being ready to lead."

"Speaking truth to power is a sign of leadership," Moss said, proud that he was speaking his mind.

"Your truth ain't The Truth," Sandra said, cocking her head in superiority.

"Fine. But, really, grandma, I'm starting to see some shit that worries me."

"You and me both," Sandra said and pushed the bar to open the door.

Anders was waiting beside the stolen Carcer dropship he and Judy had been modifying. Rather than decking it out in personalized touches or giving it a sleek paint job, the two had agreed that all the mods needed to be about function, not form. The rectangular ship with pointed nose and angular cockpit had the usual four rotating thrusters at the bottom and smaller ones all around the tops and sides to allow for more nuanced motion. A door opened on the side and a cargo ramp could be dropped from the back.

The midsized ship was painted a dark grey over the Carcer black so it would blend in with fog and buildings. The interior was where some good work had been done. The

175

strapped seats, meant to hold either officers or prisoners, had been hard metal before but were now coated with a soft foam that contoured to the body. The small screen that once showed nothing but the Carcer Channel, a propaganda network for employees, had been replaced with a holoprojected screen and the heavy door that separated driver from passenger was clipped open.

A small fridge had even been soldered to the floor and filled with sandwiches and beers. Steampuck offered Moss a drink as he stepped into the ship without turning to say goodbye to Sandra. He was pissed and had nothing he wanted to say to her in that moment.

Sandra closed the door behind Moss, and he pulled the handle before the automatic locking mechanism activated. He sat across from Puck and strapped himself in as Anders gave a thumbs up from the front seat. Puck handed over the beer and Moss welcomed it, gulping the whole thing down before belching and feeling the bubbles burn the back of his nose.

"Never anticipated a return to Cape City," Puck said. He wore, by his standards, a subtle outfit: a crushed crimson velvet jacket with black lapels over a frilled black silk shirt and gray pants tucked into leather boots. Moss thought he must have bought it since moving to B.A. because the entire ensemble had LED lights in the trim.

Moss pointed to the lights. "Guess you're CyberPuck now?"

"How dare you," Puck said, chuckling and putting his hand dramatically to his heart. "Couldn't be helped, despite my protestations. Denizens of this city have a great deal to learn about fashion."

"It's nice to see you enter the modern day a bit," Moss said with a smile. It was a jarring change of pace to go from talking to a kid who had spent his whole life online to speaking with a man who would only read paper books if he could help it.

"I enter it but grudgingly," Puck said.

"I know," Moss said and looked the man in the eyes. "How are you holding up?"

"Happy." He smiled, but there was the eternal sadness behind the smile that he had carried since the death of his sister. "I spoke to you of a desire to do more. I have found great pride in crafting a narrative for revolution, but my greatest role seems to be in front of me."

"You feel confident that you can become this man?" Moss asked.

Puck cleared his throat. "Todd Davis, here, and I work for the evil Carcer Corporation," Puck said in a high-pitched American accent. A few words were ever so slightly off but he sounded good for the most part.

"Don't know what the man sounds like, but the accent was pretty good," Moss said, bowing his head slightly.

"Cheers," Puck said. "Most people won't think much of the voice as long as the face matches, and we both know that Synthanee's work is the best in the world."

Moss had used the woman's false faces once before and they had fooled everyone.

"I've been curious about something since we met her," Moss said, and Puck raised an eyebrow. "Why don't more people do what she does? The genetic copying? Seems like a good business and people would pay a huge amount for the services."

"Precisely the point," Puck said, tapping his nose with a gloved finger before grinning broadly. The man loved to educate. "After the national government fell in the U.S. and the current city-states were establishing themselves, many a war

177

was fought for control of the territories between the cities. While this land is toxic to those of us who breathe, it is valuable to companies who wish to grow food or gather resources or the like.

"These wars were fought both on battlefields and in board rooms. One such instance saw a different kind of war unfold, the kind that scares the megas worse than violence," he said, looking expectantly at Moss.

"Loss of control?"

"Precisely. D2E was the second largest entertainment company in the world at the time and they did exactly what we are planning to do. They had several members of the board of the largest company killed and replaced with their own people wearing these perfect genetic masks. By the time the remaining board members realized what had happened, a sale had already been brokered and their mouse logo was replaced by D2E's Gopher.

"This was the nightmare scenario for the other companies, and they all decided that anyone doing this type of work would be shut down; and if any companies were caught doing it, the others would team up against them. Or so the rumor goes."

"Wow," Moss said. "Makes sense."

"Certainly," Puck said. "Also explains why people like Synthanee are rare commodities."

"So why do it?" Moss asked, genuinely interested. "Why risk your life to do something like this?"

"A question, I believe, for the artist herself."

Moss nodded. "And how did you get the sample to make the mask?"

"Hard though it may be for you to believe, missions are run in your absence and without your participation."

Moss snorted. "Why does everyone seem to think I'm some cocky prick? I just meant how did you pull it off —not that it couldn't happen without me."

"Struck a nerve, did I?" Puck asked.

"Sorry," Moss said, and as he blinked, he felt the weight of his eyelids becoming heavier. "I'm tired and today has been a lot."

"Of that, I have no doubt," Puck tipped his top hat. "Suffice it to say, we outwitted the corporate buffoon with clever trickery."

Moss smiled, unsure if it was the beer, the flight or the fact that he had been up for more than a day, but the exhaustion was now enveloping him. "You got to play dress up?"

Puck chuckled. "Even better. I got to dress up your paramour."

Moss nodded, barely hearing Puck anymore. "You'll have to tell me more about that…" he trailed off, and when he opened his eyes to finish the sentence, the ship was glowing with the light of day and Puck was fast asleep in the seat across from him.

They were cruising now, and Moss unstrapped himself, standing to stretch. His body cracked and he rubbed his face. He knew the drowsiness would hang on a while longer.

"Guessing you don't have a coffee pot on this ship?" Moss whispered as he made his way to the cockpit, flopping down in the copilot's chair beside Anders.

Anders looked at the exhausted Moss and pointed under the chair. Moss reached down and felt a warm thermos.

"You might be the best person on the earth," Moss said, pulling the warm metal up and unscrewing the top. The aroma filled his nose as the steam poured upward.

"Don't know about that, but it's a pilot's job to predict the needs of his passengers," Anders said.

Moss poured some coffee into the cap, blowing on the dark liquid as he looked out the window to the cloud layer far below. "You've spent a bit of time at The Conservation, yeah?"

Anders turned, extending an open hand and nodding. "I have," he said as he pulled a little metal mug with an image of a stegosaurus off its hanging place on one of the operating levers.

Filling his cup, he asked, "Why? You miss it?"

Moss hadn't considered that part of it. "Honestly, I do. I know we were there for only a couple hours, but it made quite an impression on me."

"You and me both," Anders said in his rich, deep voice. "But why do you ask?"

"I'm starting to think about what comes next," Moss said. "We kick the megas out, what then? I want to rebuild this planet, but I don't even know what that looks like. I was raised in a fucking plastic beehive. I have no idea what the world should be."

Anders smiled thoughtfully. "Administrator Chester would know what to do, how to help you heal the world. All the people like him, all the places in their network would work with you. It is what they have been waiting for. They have saved samples and seeds, kept records of what plants and animals lived where. They are your people; they have the answers."

That made Moss happier than he had expected. Knowing there was something more than just destroying the companies, some hope for the world, made him feel like everything they were doing truly had purpose. It wasn't just avenging the planet but helping to start it anew. He took another sip of coffee, thinking about the beauty of The Conservation and all the work they did.

"You know what I wonder though," he said.

"I don't know."

"Don't know what I have been wondering?"

Anders shook his head. "I *do* know what you have been wondering; I don't know the answer."

Moss laughed. "Oh, yeah?"

"Yeah," Anders said, turning and smiling at Moss. "You want to know where they get the money to do all that."

"Oh," Moss said, realizing that Anders had him dead to rights.

"And I don't know," Anders said. "I've asked Chester, but he won't give it up. Even asked his daughter, but Amy doesn't know. She just said there is always enough when they need it."

"Guess it's heartening to know that someone out there is on our side," Moss said.

"More and more people are on our side," Anders told him. "You should see the boards. People are going mad about Duke Doland. Even with the election coming up, petition for a recall is already e-signed by half a million people. That's in less than a day."

Moss felt full. He had been so focused that he had not taken a moment to ask about what was happening in the greater world. "That's amazing."

"It is," Anders said, and they both stayed quiet for a moment before he turned and looked Moss right in the eyes. The man had a knack for cutting to the root of things and Moss knew it was about to happen again.

"Isn't there something else you want to ask me?"

CHAPTER 17

Moss looked at Anders, waiting for him to speak again.

Anders stared back at him wordlessly.

"You spend a lot of time with my grandmother," Moss began, and Anders smirked.

"There it is," he said, raising his eyebrows.

Moss dropped his head, embarrassed that he was so easy to predict. "How," he began, a bit at a loss for words. "I dunno, how has she seemed?"

"That's not what you want to know," Anders smiled.

Moss let out a deep sigh, releasing a world's worth of tension. "Fine," he said but he didn't push. He didn't care to push. If Anders had something he wanted to say or to feel clever about, Moss would let him say it.

Anders stayed quiet for a long time too but eventually relented. "You want to know if Carcer broke her. You want to know if she can come back from all she's seen and all she's been through and lead us."

Hearing it out like that, he knew Anders was right. That was the question. That was what he needed to know.

"Yes," he murmured.

"I don't know," Anders said. "We've all seen that vacant look people get. And I've known people who've known trauma; I've known hurt so bad I never thought I would come back. That I *could* come back. I know you've felt the pain too, but not like us. Not the way that blinds a person to everything else. The kind of pain that makes you forget there is anything but pain. Sandra, your grandmother rather, has known nothing but pain for half your life. And while she was being brutalized, she lost her son, daughter-in-law and the love of her life.

"She's blinded by a well-deserved rage and won't quit until the people who hurt her know her suffering. She's single-minded like a dog on a scent. She's your greatest weapon in the fight against Carcer, but may pose the biggest threat to us.

"But also, the woman loves you. She may not tell you and she may bust your balls to smithereens, but that woman worships the ground you walk on. Amidst all the other noise, remember that."

Moss did. He knew it always. He worried that he knew it but was happy for it as well.

"Thanks," Moss said, and he turned to Anders, eyes full and mind as confused as ever. "You," he began but didn't finish. He just let it hang.

"Yeah," Anders said. "Her name was Layla. Thought I was doing right by her, thought I was making the smart decisions. Turns out money isn't what kids need and my desire to 'set her up for life' cost her that life. But it's why I know, how I understand how Sandra feels when she looks at you."

Moss nodded. He wanted to ask more questions, but this was the most he had ever gotten out of Anders about his past and he didn't want to push his luck. "But is she like you?"

Anders blinked, surprised for the first time in the conversation. He sipped at his drink and leaned back thoughtfully. "She just may be," he admitted.

Moss frowned and Anders looked at him again, saying, "But if anything can set her free, it's you."

"Morning, gents," Puck said from the doorway.

Moss groaned. "How long have you been listening?"

"Rather longer than you would have liked, I expect," he said honestly.

"So now you know," Anders said.

Puck cocked his head. "Knew already," he said, bursting with pride inappropriate for the moment. "You carry the weight of loss more obviously than the scars on your back."

Anders nodded.

"Why, too, I suspect, that you collect those little treasures and send them with runners in the night."

"You been watching me?" Anders said, his voice now hard and cold. He was a very private person and clearly did not like that someone knew his business.

"I watch everything," Puck said. "And you'll get no judgement from me. For my loss, I welcomed death and would have had it if not for Moss. You, it seems, have turned your pain into something healthy. Like the seed fallen from a burning tree, sprouting life anew. A more enviable trait I cannot imagine."

Nonplussed, Anders just shook his head. "One hell of a weird guy you are, Steampuck."

He smiled and twirled his moustache. "Would it surprise you to learn that you are far from the first person to tell me that?"

Anders let out a shallow laugh. "No. The opposite."

"Don't suppose you have a cup of tea up here as well?" Puck asked, seeming to know the answer already.

"No," Anders said. "I have a thermos of tea."

He reached under his own seat and pulled out another cylinder. Puck looked as though he was going to burst into

185

joyous song. He clutched his hands to his chest and said, "The bards will sing of your greatness."

Anders looked to Moss. "He have an off switch?"

"Not that I've found," he said with a laugh, then turned to Puck with deadly seriousness. "*Do* you have an off switch?"

Puck simply smiled, pulled a handkerchief from his pocket, and placed it on his lap as he unscrewed the cap, poured himself a spot of tea and sipped it. "No," he stated. "I do not."

They made small talk for a while longer before Anders told them it was time and ordered them to retake their seats. The two men made their way toward the rear of the ship and sat side by side.

"Excited to be going home?" Moss asked as they descended toward Cape City.

"Not even at all," Puck said with a flat expression.

The ship began to rattle and shake as it dropped back toward the earth. Flames licked the sides and Moss felt his stomach hit his throat. He instantly wanted to vomit and gripped his legs, pressing his fingers deep into his flesh.

He felt a hand on his and saw that Puck was smiling at him. The small kindness made him feel just enough better to make it through the cloud cover. Smoke and steam billowed before clearing to reveal the city rushing up to meet them. They passed through the flighted traffic and towering buildings toward Synthanee's workshop.

"Well, shit," Anders called back.

Moss's heart sank. He should have known better than to expect two things in a row to go right. As the ship veered down the street, Moss saw what Anders meant. The familiar building with its bank vault door was surrounded by armed men and women in khaki outfits. Moss remembered The Safaris as a local gang of guns-for-hire. They must have been hired by one of the nearby companies after they found out about her work.

Moss heard a metal whirring and looked up to see a minigun lowering from a nook in the ceiling. Robotic arms lowered it into position and pointed it toward the rear of the ship. Behind the handles was another metal bar with semicircular metal rim buckles.

"Strap in," Anders called back, looking Moss dead in the eyes over his shoulder.

Moss looked at Puck who shook his head. "Mass murder is more up your street."

Moss pulled on gloves he always kept folded in his pocket. The ship was still moving as Moss began to open the buckles with great difficulty. Gripping the seat, he stood, sliding back and forth and trying to keep from falling as the ship swung again.

In a brief moment of smooth air, Moss hurled himself toward the pole of the gunner's aerie, grabbing onto it as his feet betrayed him and he was left clinging to the straps. He pulled himself to his feet and moved around, pressing his back against the worn green padding and pulling the buckles together across his chest. They were designed for a larger person and hardly held him in place.

Moss gave Anders a thumbs up and pulled down the power cable, screwing it into the weapon. The ramp at the rear of the ship began to open and wind whipped through the space, sending everything that wasn't strapped down flying. The sounds of the thrusters and wind made it impossible to hear anything. Moss blinked hard, trying to keep his eyes open in the blasting air and wishing he had a helmet or glasses.

The brightly-colored buildings were dull in the gray of the foggy afternoon. They were still high in the sky, but the heads of the gangers on the ground began to turn upward. Moss watched as a man in a leopard-skin hat, clearly the leader, pointed toward the ship. Guns started to aim Moss's way and he felt his thumb twitch and the six barrels began to spin. A deafening buzz filled the space as one hundred rounds per second sprayed from the weapon. Shells rained out the back of the ship to the street below.

Moss had only practiced shooting the weapon once and never while flying, so his aim was off. Buildings and walls were chewed up and the Safaris all ducked behind whatever cover they could. The leader, trying to look tough and yell orders, was shredded as Moss turned the gun on him. His blood sprayed the streets before Moss stopped firing.

The remaining thugs ran as fast as they could up the street and down alleys as Anders set the ship down, the heat of the thrusters igniting garbage and sending it flying. Moss felt the ship go idle and he unstrapped himself, plucked a Trogon assault rifle off the wall and jumped down.

Anders kept the ship running and Puck was hot on Moss's heels. The two charged toward the open vault door. Moss saw a blur of khaki make its way toward Puck, who twirled his beautiful walking stick topped with a bronze lion head, audibly cracking the attacker's jaw. Before Moss had time to blink, the hidden blade from inside the stick released and plunged through the chest of the Safari.

They moved into the anteroom to discover the second door had been blasted open. Debris was everywhere and dust particles still hung heavy in the air. Pressing forward, they heard yelling up ahead and Moss raised his weapon as more Safaris turned. He hardly ever used traditional firearms, but in the low glow of the large vats growing false human parts, the smart bullets in the rifle were as convenient as they were expensive.

He fired in short bursts, making short work of the invaders.

"Synthanee!" Puck called, causing a few more Safaris to dart out and take wide potshots before being gunned down. The wafting smoke glowed eerily as bioprinted faces stared down at them with empty sockets. Jars of eyes, fingernails and hair were stacked along the walls. Tubes and cords were draped from the ceiling and snaked along the floor.

"Synthanee!" Puck tried again, sounding more desperate this time.

They heard heavy, rapid footfalls. Puck aimed the blunderbuss he unslung from his back as Vince, Synthanee's drudge, appeared from the darkness holding a pistol.

"Welcome back, fuckface," the machine said with an American east coast accent. Two red points of light glowed from its face; it had a new tattoo of a baobab tree on the grown skin that Synthanee had affixed to its chassis.

"Where is she?" Puck asked, stepping towards Vince.

"In the back," the drudge said. "She's fucked up, man."

Puck pushed past him and Moss followed right behind. They moved toward the rear of the building to another blown-out chunk of wall. Synthanee sat in a plush chair in her lab. The explosion had knocked everything over and the room smelled of chemicals and gunpowder.

Synthanee was clutching her side and her chair sat in a puddle of blood.

"Too late, I'm afraid," she wheezed as Puck skidded to a stop beside her, clamping his hands over hers.

"No, no, old friend," he assured her. "We will take you to a doctor presently."

189

Moss could see she would not survive. There was too much blood on the ground, her face had lost too much color and her eyes were already elsewhere.

"I know more about the human body than ten surgeons," she said weakly. "I am to die today. Within minutes. I can tell."

Puck began to sob, and Moss felt the pain of more death wash over him. He had met the woman only once before, but she was another link in a seemingly endless chain of loss.

"It is okay," she told him, her accent thicker now as her consciousness faded. They heard more gunshots and figured Vince was fighting off the Safaris Moss had scared off the street. "I get to see Vince again. The real one."

Synthanee reached into her pocket, fished out a key now slick with blood, and handed it to Puck. She coughed and gasped. "Vat nine," she told him. "Go."

He stood slowly, miserably. "See you on the other side, old friend."

"On the other side," Synthanee parroted as Puck turned to get his synthetic mask.

"You know who did this?" Moss asked. "Who sent them?"

"Does it matter?" she asked.

"I suppose it doesn't."

More gunshots. She beckoned him closer with a curling finger. "Tell Sandra I'm sorry."

Moss furrowed his brows. "For what?"

"She asked me to send it secretly, but I know she trusts you," Synthanee whispered conspiratorially.

Moss nodded. "She does."

"It's in a case in my desk drawer," she said, and her head dropped heavily before she caught herself and corrected. But she was dying.

"Don't worry about that now," Moss said, watching as her eyes seemed to scan for something in the distance. Something she couldn't find. Would never find.

"You keep up this fight," she told him.

"We will," Moss assured her. "But don't worry about that. Is there anyone you want us to contact? Anything you want us to do?"

"Vince knows my wishes," she told him. "I don't think I ever told you how I met him," she said and exhaled for the last time.

Moss felt sick. It shouldn't have been him with her for her last moment, but he knew Puck couldn't handle it and didn't know what Vince was programmed to feel about it. He closed her eyes and looked at her for a moment. Her death was another reminder of what the companies would do to protect themselves. But she wasn't the only victim. The Safaris shouldn't have died for this either. They didn't believe in causes; they were simply desperate people out for some cash — and for that, they died too.

Moss rose from his crouch beside Synthanee and walked over to her desk. Large and stainless steel, it had been knocked over in the corner of the room. Moss clambered over some rubble and pulled at the drawer mounted on its left. Papers and loose items fell out . . . and then he saw it. A face pressed between two panes of specialized flat glass, encased in a thermal control ring.

Moss just shook his head. He instantly recognized the face and knew what was in his grandmother's mind. He grabbed the face, tucking it into his belt line along his back, and turned with a nod of farewell to Synthanee as he left the office.

Back in the creation lab, Puck was using tongs to transfer the face of the Carcer manager to a small, specialized transfer jar. Vince was watching him, saying, "Be careful. You need to be careful with that. Is it helping that I'm telling you to be careful? Or do you think it's annoying? I don't think it is."

Puck was distracted by suffering and too focused on the work to pay the drudge any mind.

"Vince," Moss said, and the machine turned to him.

"Dead?" he asked.

Moss nodded.

"That's too bad," he said more as a fact than anything else.

"You were not programmed to feel sadness?" Moss asked bluntly.

The machine shook its head. "Not that, actually. Guy I was based on just weren't the get-sad type, so I ain't either."

"I suppose I could have guessed that," Moss said with a small chuckle.

"Nah," Vince said. "You seem a little simple."

That made Moss laugh. Amidst all the pain and confusion, there was nothing else to do when called stupid by a robot.

"What will you do now?" Moss asked, making sure that Vince planned to see Synthanee's wishes met.

"Once you two get out, I blow the lab and bury Synth," he said. "She has a particular spot off the Garden Route."

"Sounds nice," Moss said as Puck screwed the top on the jar, activating a light within that illuminated the face floating in liquid.

"Presume you will deactivate after that?" Puck asked, sounding hopeful.

"Nah, fuck that," Vince said. "Once I see her buried, I think I'll kill every dumb fuck in knee socks," he said, gesturing to one of the dead Safaris.

"Poses an interesting moral dilemma," Puck said thoughtfully.

Moss threw the assault rifle at Vince, who caught it with mechanical precision.

"No, it doesn't," he said without considering the irony. Let's go home, Puck."

CHAPTER 18

Stepping into the light, Moss looked around the street, the carnage. Wild lines of bullet holes like creeping vines covered the street. The Sarfari leader had been dragged away. Nearby windows had been shuttered. The Leaking Brain, a hip little bar next door, was utterly destroyed. Shell casings crunched underfoot as Puck and Moss made their way back to the ship.

Both men were quiet and contemplative as they stepped onto the ship.

"Get what you came for?" Anders asked as he set down a push broom. Puck held the jar up without his usual flourish. "Great, I'll let Sandra know."

The two nodded silently and Puck loaded the jar into a secure locker at the rear of the ship just below the wall-mounted weapons. Once again, they sat side by side.

Anders looked at them and his normally stoic face registered concern. "Anything else before we head back?"

Puck shook his head.

Moss was about to as well but then thought of something and asked, "Do we have breathers?"

Flying low, it didn't take Anders long to find what Moss wanted and he set them down nearby. As he unstrapped and pulled a helmet with built-in purifier over his head, Moss looked at Puck and asked with his eyes if the man wanted to join. When he shook his head, Moss stepped over to him and held out a hand. Puck nodded and stood, removing his hat and putting on a helmet as well. Following Moss down the ramp, Puck still looked distant.

They walked quietly through the brush. The sun was setting over the savanna and the grass rippled in a golden shimmer under a cool wind. Anders had set them down just behind a little hill and Moss led the way upward toward a lone acacia tree at the crest. Looking down below, there was a large watering hole and Moss stared in amazement at the site.

A troupe of elephants with their young splashed at the bank, hosing their backs with their trunks. Off to the side, zebras startled themselves as they lapped water. Baboons played and groomed in the distance where the tree line met the opening to the hole. Countless types of beautiful bright birds flitted from tree to tree and a hippo emerged from the center bellowing out what sounded like a laugh.

Moss couldn't even begin to count the animals or identify all the species, but it was just like what he had seen in nature documentaries from the past. It didn't seem like it should be real. Nearly all the land outside B.A. City was used space, but out here there was wilderness. Proper wilderness. All these animals lived out their lives as they would have before the age of man.

He smiled at the idea that he could help restore any of this to the planet.

"Remarkable," Puck said.

"Like nothing I've ever seen."

"Living in the city, smuggling antiques, I forgot that all this existed," Puck admitted, sounding disappointed. "Just beyond a wall was all this and yet..." he trailed off.

Moss couldn't help but laugh. "Puck, I would never have felt natural sunlight on my skin if it weren't for my parents being revolutionaries."

"One hell of a thought, that," Puck said with a weak chuckle. "I forget how different a world you knew."

"Two people of different backgrounds united by a cause," Moss observed.

"Not counting the pirate from outer space guarding our ship," Puck noted. They watched the wildlife as they spoke. Five oxpeckers appeared and landed on the back of a large elephant, picking the bugs.

"Right," Moss said.

"Though, you know," Puck said softly, "this was never really my fight. My sister blamed the megas for what they did to Mum and Dad, and I went along for the ride. Mortal peril is not precisely what I had envisioned for my life."

"What would you have done?"

Puck turned with an eyebrow raised.

Moss chuckled. "There is still time. I think there are three community theatres in our district alone."

"My greatest performance is upcoming and is of an indeterminate duration," Puck reminded him.

"You worried?"

"To pretend to be the man at the head of the world's largest private military force who agrees to leave behind one of their most lucrative contracts?" he said sarcastically. "No, why should that make me nervous?"

Moss chuckled. "Anyone wants to fuck with you, you will have a lot of people with guns in your employ..."

"It's not those from without whom I fear," he said, watching as a flock of crowned cranes took flight in a flurry of movement, sending antelope scattering before returning to drink.

"Right," Moss said, thinking about the reality of infiltrating Carcer and being left to fend for oneself. It was a terrifying prospect. "So why do it? If this isn't your fight?"

The slightest of smiles crossed Puck's lips as the setting run reflected brilliantly on the visor of his helmet. "To honor her memory. So badly did she want to heal the world, keep children from growing up as we did, I want to pick up where she left off."

"I understand," Moss said. "It's how I got into this, too. I got sucked into my parents' fight."

"But you carry the torch for them now of your own accord."

"Yeah, I believe in what we are doing." Neither spoke for a long moment. "I mean, look at this. Look at the natural splendor here. We could get this back. There are better ways to strike a balance. The companies now just subjugate both man and nature. And for what? More money? To rule the world from their literal gold tower?"

"Little on the nose, that," Puck added with a hearty chuckle.

Moss shrugged. "Don't have to be subtle when you own the planet."

"They don't own this," Puck said with a sweeping gesture toward the animals.

"They don't own this," Moss repeated. "Thank you, Puck. Thank you for joining us and for what you are about to do. It is a terrible risk, and I will never be able to repay you for jumping into the viper's den."

Puck clapped a hand on Moss's shoulder. "At least you are dressing me as a viper," he said, sounding more like himself.

Moss wanted to ask about Synthanee and how Puck was feeling after being there, but he could tell that the man was trying to focus on what was before him rather than behind, so he left it alone for now.

"We should head back to the ship," Moss suggested.

Puck held up a hand. "You are right, in part," he said, pointing to a spot at the base of the tree casting a long shadow down the hillside. "I will head back but you: take a moment. Enjoy this. From here, things only get all the more complicated."

"Sure, but. . ." Moss began but Puck pressed down on his shoulder until Moss sat, the earth warm against his fingers.

"Take the moment," Puck insisted, and Moss simply nodded in response. He turned back, leaned against the tree, and watched the animals.

"She's dead?" Sandra asked, sounding more angry than sympathetic. Only Moss knew the truth behind that response.

"Yes," Puck said miserably as the rest of the crew began to gather around the table. "But," he said, pulling the jar from under his jacket, "we got what we needed."

"That's what matters," she said. Moss studied her eyes, watching the wheels of her mind turn.

"Things have been moving fast out here," Judy put in. "The mayor's office scrambled to put up another candidate, but our trolls have been working hard to smear their whole office since you killed Double D Three. Looks like we could actually win this thing. And, as an aside, Persimmon really liked you two."

"Of course," Gibbs smiled, spreading his arms wide. "I'm charming as fuck."

"Get over yourself," Ynna mocked.

Gibbs cocked an eyebrow at her. "Charmed your pants off."

She rolled her eyes. "Still don't know how that shit happened."

"Come here and I'll show you," he said suggestively from across the table, eliciting groans from the rest of the group.

Except Belle who smiled and said, "That's sweet."

"With the Carcer lockdown, Persimmon is gaining a lot of mileage by running on a platform of getting Carcer out of here," Judy continued as though nothing had been said in the interim.

"That means we have two orders of business," Sandra explained. "We gotta get Fancy Pants here to replace Todd Davis and then we have to kill Warden Ninety-Nine."

"Just that?" Moss asked with a little smirk. The gravity of what they were about to attempt was so large that everyone couldn't help but laugh.

"We are going to have a lot of balls in the air all at once," Ynna said. "We think that election day is the best time to do this. I'm going to help Puck infiltrate Carcer. Sandra, Moss and whoever else you think you'll need can go after Ninety-Nine. We will all meet here after to pop champagne."

"We won't get this opportunity again," Patchwork put in. "Getting the intel that Todd Davis was going to be named the next President of Carcer was really hard."

"Many Bothans died to bring us this information," Gibbs quoted, but Ynna's face fell flat.

"Dude," she said solemnly. "We *did* lose a couple of people."

"Oh, shit," Gibbs said. "Sorry."

Ynna laughed and stuck her tongue out. "Are you ever not going to fall for that?"

Patchwork cleared his throat. "Actually, Ynna..." he trailed off.

Ynna examined his face to see if he was joking. When he didn't break, she quietly said, "Oh."

A big grin crossed Patchwork's face. "You two really do deserve each other," he said with a guffaw.

Sandra dropped her head and started rubbing her temples. "We need a few more old folks in this crew."

Judy shook their head. "Don't have to be old to find this exhausting."

"To that, I will agree," Puck said.

"In the meantime," Sandra said, redirecting the conversation. "Gonna be all hands on deck making this election go our way."

"And getting ready for the wedding," Ynna added.

Belle squealed.

"Patchwork can give you all marching orders in the morning," Sandra concluded. "Get some rest and we can get rolling on the electioneering tomorrow."

"Movie night!" Gibbs called and nods were seen around the room. Even Judy cracked a smile.

"Rain check for me," Moss said, feeling the exhaustion in every bone in his body. Though he had passed out on the ship, it had been far from restful. He needed proper sleep.

"Boo, you whore," Gibbs said as the rest of them started to grab drinks and snacks. Then he laughed. "Just like old times."

"What are we watching?" Zip asked.

Gibbs began to answer, explaining the choice and its cultural relevance, but Moss wasn't listening. He was already walking down the hallway to his room. He felt fingers lace though his.

Issy was smiling up at him as he turned.

"Don't want to watch the movie?" he asked.

Rolling her eyes, she said, "Every night is movie night around here. But I hardly get to see you."

He nodded, feeling like he hadn't seen her for a month.

They made their way into his room and he flopped down onto the mattress with Issy by his side. He was happy he had quickly hidden the mask from the lab before meeting with everyone.

They lay a moment, staring up at the cracked popcorn ceiling.

"Been nonstop for you," she observed.

He sighed. "Not sure how many people can say they were in Africa this morning."

"It isn't even just that," she said. "First you and Gibbs met with the hot chick, Persimmon, and The Tailor. Then the Duke Doland thing *and* the docks with Zip. All that just before getting in a firefight in Cape City. Shit, do you even remember how you got that bruise on your face?"

He laughed. "Only now that you say something about it."

She rolled onto her side and kissed him lightly, but his face radiated pain. He hadn't thought about it or even felt it since, but now that they were calm and the adrenaline was gone, his whole body hurt.

He looked at Issy then, examining her face as she looked back in his eyes. In moments like this, in every moment like this, he felt the same way. "You are the most beautiful person in the world," he told her.

"Oh, shush," she said, but she couldn't stop the blush response.

"So," he said with a little smile. "Will you be my date to a wedding? I'm the best man and everything."

She gasped in mock awe. "No way! I'm a bridesmaid!"

"Really?" Moss asked, actually a little surprised.

Issy's face fell. "Yeah," she said quietly. "I'm pretty sure all of Ynna's girlfriends are either dead or in prison."

Moss knew that was true but didn't say anything.

"When I asked about her family," Issy added, "she clammed up pretty quickly. For as much as she talks, it takes a bit for her to open up."

Moss nodded. "She's seen a lot of hurt."

"It shows," Issy noted. "Think that might be part of why she likes Gibby."

"I think you are right," Moss said. "You know, he said she doesn't really like all his movie quotes and shit, but I think that childlike enthusiasm is part of what attracts her to him. She had to grow up so fast, there is something about the way he clings to immaturity that she likes."

"You may be on to something there," Issy agreed, considering the words. "Their lives were so different from ours, you know?"

"Who?" Moss asked.

"Ynna, Zip, to say nothing of Anders," she said. "We thought we knew what was what, and man, we didn't know *anything*. I thought that I was tough joining BurbSec." She laughed at herself. "I didn't know the first thing about tough."

She dropped her right hand on Moss's chest. "When I left that rooftop after you and Ynna and Gibbs had come for me,

I was so lost. I had only ever considered one thing for my whole life: BurbSec at Burb 2152. Then, one day, it was all gone. Dad had escaped and I met him in an apartment above Masala Dosa that he had rented the very day he learned that your family were more than just… well, you know.

"I discovered that he had been siphoning money and converting it in some underground currency exchange so our family wouldn't be broke in the outside world. I learned that everything I had ever known was a massive lie and that my life would never be the same."

She looked at him with a sheepish expression. "Though I guess I learned that part when you shot me."

"I'm . . ." Moss began to apologize but she covered his mouth with her hand.

"This is not about that. My point is that we were just so blind, blind to everything," she said. "It just puts the company we keep in perspective."

Moving her hand, Moss said, "It is hard to fathom. I mean, my family was taken from me before my very eyes, but ThutoCo went through the trouble of breaking into my brain and erasing my memory of it all. Ynna had to watch her mother get shot and has to live with that memory."

"Do you wish you could remember?" Issy asked thoughtfully. "More than just the little flashes of memories?"

"I've thought about that," Moss said. "I always feel like my answer should be yes. I feel like it is important that I remember, but if I'm honest…"

She nodded. "Ignorance is bliss."

"Yes. Is that wrong?"

"No," she told him. "Nothing about how you feel can be wrong."

He liked that. "Thank you," he said, and he really meant it. He felt as if he had been carrying the weight of that for a long time. "I'm lucky, too," he added. "Because of the program, I still get to see my dad, even if it is just a false reality."

"More real than most people get," she noted, tapping his chest with a finger.

"I know," he said. "I thought about that in Africa. Synthanee had created this drudge copy of an old friend of hers. The idea was similar to what my dad was doing, what ThutoCo has corrupted.

"These copies of people's personalities. At first, I thought they could help others the way it has helped me, but I don't know anymore. As we speak, a programmed AI based on a real person who is dead is murdering real people to avenge a person who is dead. Pretty sure that's not the world we want."

"Probably not," Issy agreed. "What kind of a world do you want to live in?"

"Been asking myself that more and more," Moss said. "I've come to realize that we are so focused on the problem — the megas controlling our lives and destroying everything — that we have lost sight of the solution. Or rather we haven't even considered the solution. That's what's next for me. Once Carcer is out and Mix LeBeau is in office, I am going to start thinking more about what we do to heal this city and this world. How we help all the disenfranchised people of this planet."

Issy didn't speak for a long time, so long that Moss nearly fell asleep. "You are a good man, Moss," she finally said. The words struck him like a lightning bolt of joy. It was exactly what he needed to hear in the moment he needed to hear it. He turned to his side and kissed her lightly on the lips.

"I love you, Issy," he told her.

"I love you, too," she said with a smile. "Want to have sex?"

A laugh came from deep within him and she smiled like a Cheshire cat for having caught him so off -guard.

"Yes," he said, but as he tried to move, he realized he didn't have the strength for it.

She could tell and chuckled. "How about I sneak back in tomorrow morning?"

"Actually," he said, rolling onto his side so they were face to face, "I want to know more about when you got to the city. I want to know more about what your life was like. I should have asked sooner."

"You have had a lot on your mind."

He shook his head. "No excuse. I really want to know."

She smiled. "Okay," she said and began to tell him everything.

CHAPTER 19

The next few weeks were nonstop activity.

When the major companies realized that Persimmon was gaining traction, they began to throw huge amounts of money into the campaign. Rather than simply boosting Duke Doland's replacement, they also tried everything they could to ruin LeBeau's reputation.

The people of the city seemed to be waking up and seeing through the lies. Carcer's stranglehold only made things worse. As they kicked down doors and drove tanks through the city, the people didn't feel safe or protected but scared; and intimidation did not make for satisfied voters.

Patchwork and Zip coordinated online campaigns to keep people talking and hating on the establishment while the rest of the crew ran small jobs against Carcer in the name of LeBeau, who was quickly becoming a hero of the people. They didn't meet or even communicate but the coordinated effort was working.

For the first time, it felt as if they had the companies on their heels, playing catch up and on the defensive. And while it should have made them happy, these people who were used to always being the little guy, felt worried. There was an unease that something was going to go wrong at any moment. But as election day approached, the polls were still in their favor.

Desperate, the companies tried to bribe citizens to vote their way; but Zip hacked the system of anyone who took a payout and quickly the internet deemed the whole thing a scam.

D2E was covering the election full time on several stations, and you could get the election coverage in whatever flavor you liked and met your particular belief system. The news was on in the safehouse twenty-four hours a day. They were never without a constant stream of input.

At the same time, Ynna and Gibbs were readying for their wedding. It was a surreal thing for everyone. Going dress shopping, picking out a menu and deciding on guests while Carcer officers patrolled the street and every company on Earth was trying to find them.

But Gibbs and Ynna were happy. They seemed to be floating on air all the time. Even Sandra started to lighten up and the tension in the house calmed. Moss didn't mention the mask to anyone; he didn't want to. He would eventually have to confront his grandmother, but he couldn't bear to spoil the mood in the house.

On the morning of election day, Moss stepped into the kitchen to find Belle making breakfast in just an apron, the way Zip liked it.

"Morning," he said, rubbing his eyes.

"Heya," Belle said. Zip had deactivated whatever setting made her act groggy, so she was as chipper in the morning as during the day. Things like that often made Moss wonder how he would set a partner, what modes would most please his sensibilities. These questions always made him return to the idea that he liked the unpredictability of a real person, because even when he thought he knew someone, they could surprise him. He could even surprise himself.

The highest-end relief aides had the option for randomization algorithms that existed within certain parameters to mimic this human element of surprise, but Zip said a person could still tell. He explained that for large portions of the robosexual community, being able to tell was part of the attraction; but, of course, it took all kinds.

"I brewed a French roast," Belle told him, lifting a pot.

"Yeah," he said. "I heard you grinding the beans."

"Oh, that wake you?" she asked as she asked most mornings.

He nodded. "Yes."

"Oh, sorry about that," she said, and Moss just rolled his eyes. Belle's programming could not be altered by anyone but Zip Thud, who had made it clear that he enjoyed the small power of it. "Are you excited for the election?" she asked, handing him a cup of coffee.

"I'm more excited for this all to be over," he admitted. "Today is going to be a complicated day."

"You are right about that," Belle agreed, and the oven timer went off. She pulled out a tray of delicious smelling flakes she had made herself.

The smell alone made Moss's stomach call out. "What is that?"

Belle beamed with pride. "Avocado and goat cheese infused sugar flakes. I got the recipe from that fancy cereal place up the street. Tastes way better than it sounds."

Moss wasn't interested in a discussion about the nature of taste in an android, so he simply said, "Fancy cereal is so in right now."

"I know, right? What will they think of next?" Belle joked.

Moss thought a moment. "Where did you get avocado and goat cheese?"

"Oh," she said happily. "My little Zip just hacks me a delivery drone from time to time for ingredients. Not like B.A. Mart cares or even notices."

"Suppose not," Moss agreed. "Didn't occur to him to offer this service to the rest of us?"

"Um, excuse me," Belle said, all sass now. "He *does* share with the other kids; you are just not around enough to notice. You think Gibbs makes all those dinners with what? Stuff he grows himself? You see a cow on the roof? Maybe some chickens?"

Moss held his hands up defensively and smiled. "Fair enough," he said. "You're right that I may not pay enough attention. Sorry."

"Damned skippy you are sorry," Belle said with a dainty laugh. "Can I make you something while the cereal cools?"

"No. Thank you, though," Moss said, holding up the steaming beverage. "I'm good for now."

"Okay," she said, smoothing the apron and causing a breast to pop out. She was not bothered but Moss averted his eyes out of instinct. Quietly, she said, "May I ask you something?"

He looked back up, meeting her gaze, knowing this was serious. "Of course."

"Is Zip fitting in okay?" she asked with the genuine concern of a loving partner.

"Oh, Belle," Moss said. "Yes, he is. He has been a wonderful addition — you both have. It has been great to have some kind new souls in the group. If anything, we are really lucky to have you guys."

Belle blushed and smiled. "Thank you for saying that. I guess I kinda figured, especially after the dock raid, but I did not know for sure, you know?"

"I do," Moss answered. "Can I tell you something?"

Belle smiled. "Shoot."

"I never thought I would even be asked a question like that. I was never cool or anything like that. I just had the two friends, and we were all considered lame, so to have someone ask me if they are fitting in is bizarre to me."

"I have a hard time picturing that," she said. "I mean, I can conceptualize it exactly, as you would imagine, but when Issy talks about the three of you back in the burbs, it does not seem possible. These three rebel leaders all just little peons working for the man — it is crazy."

"If I'm honest, they feel like different people," Moss said. "If me then were to meet me now, I can't even imagine what he would think."

"What would you tell him?" Belle asked. "If you could go back in time."

Moss let out a sad chuckle. "So many things," he muttered. "Tell Rosetta to stay back, or Stan to duck. Keep Burn closer to the door. Hold back Irene. Don't shoot Issy..." he trailed off as he contemplated all of the mistakes he had made.

"Instead of not shooting her, you could trust her," Issy said as she walked into the room and put a hand on Moss's shoulder. Nodding, he handed the cup to her.

"That is what I meant," he said.

Issy nodded and squeezed his shoulder. "I know."

"You two are so cute I could die," Belle said. "Not quite as cute as Gibbs and Ynna and not anywhere near Zip and me, but like in an old-married-couple sort of way."

"Thanks." Issy laughed before she looked onto the stove top. She bounced over to the tray. "Are you making that recipe you got from Cereal Ciller?"

"Yeah girl," Belle cheered and they high-fived. Moss smiled. He liked to see Issy getting along with everyone.

This crew, this group of very different people from very different worlds, really was a great team. Ynna and Gibbs walked in, followed shortly by Patchwork, Judy and Anders.

"Polls open in a few hours," Patchwork said as though they weren't all fully aware.

"Today is the day," Judy added, sounding as ready as Moss felt for this part to be over.

"Then it's all wedding planning all the time," Belle said.

Anders laughed as he began to do pull-ups on one of the door frames. "A week out; you guys must have everything planned at this point?"

"We do," Gibbs assured everyone.

"Who is this 'we' I'm hearing about?" Ynna asked, cocking her head. "A fucking upturned broom could have contributed as much as you have."

"Not true!" he cried in mock offense. "I made one contribution."

Ynna laughed out loud. "Saying 'let's have a spaghetti-western-themed wedding' does not count as a contribution."

Gibbs nodded in agreement. "I suppose not," he said. "But let's be real: the best thing that I could have done for this wedding was get out of your way."

"Said every groom ever," Judy scoffed, but Moss could see the hurt behind their eyes.

"Thank you, Jude," Ynna said.

"Why thank them?" Gibbs asked with his mouth hanging open. "I was the one who said it first."

"Put some fucking clothes on slut-bot," Sandra sneered as she entered the room and, as always, they all fell silent. Belle scampered away, looking as if she was going to cry.

"No need for that," Moss said. He and his grandmother had been cool to each other recently. Neither had wanted to clear the air, so they had left things unsaid and everything had been slightly uncomfortable.

"Yeah, freakin' Debbie Downer," Gibbs muttered under his breath.

"How about Debbie-who-is-gonna-take-down-Carcer?" she said, deadly serious..

"That's a way less funny character," Ynna said flatly. She had been avoiding Sandra as much as she could, telling Moss that things were mostly fine so long as they stayed apart. Ynna was in too good a mood these days to let Sandra's attitude ruin it.

"Everyone clear on their jobs today?" Sandra asked, looking around the room.

She was met by silent nods before everyone went about making themselves breakfast.

"Can we talk?" she asked Moss.

"Of course," he said, following her down the hallway and to the rotting stairs that led to the floor she had commandeered.

Her suite looked the most like a real, livable space. She had put Judy to work early on to help fix up the rooms, patch the walls, rewire the lights and pull up the carpet. Unless a

213

person looked closely, they would be hard pressed to know that it was in the middle of a dilapidated, abandoned building in a far corner of the city.

She had explained to Moss that after over a decade in a cell, she needed to ride out her life in a clean, well-manicured place. For a woman who had spent her formative years in military barracks, this desire surprised Moss but it made a certain sense. There were few adornments, including a large clock, a refrigerator and little bar, and a seating area with the two best remaining chairs in the building. A closed door hid Sandra's bedroom. No one but her had been in there.

She gestured for him to sit and stepped over to the bar. He had been expecting this. She was always one for a little pep talk before a mission and this one was like none they had run before. This would set in motion a tectonic shift in B.A. City life, corporate control and global politics.

After pouring two drinks into square, etched glasses, she walked over and sat opposite him. Setting his drink on a stack of ammo boxes used as a side table, she sighed but didn't speak. He scooped up the glass and took a swig. With each passing day, he was getting more and more accustomed to the hard stuff.

"You ready for today?" he asked her finally.

She nodded. "You?"

"I am," he said, and he believed it. After feeling as if they had been planning forever, he felt ready for their big move.

"Good," she said, her eyes piercing him. The way she watched him in the dim light of two small lamps made him uneasy. He wondered if she knew he had the mask. But she had called this meeting and he would not budge. She took a sip and said, "You've never run a mission like this."

"That's true.".

"You wishin' you could use your program?" she asked pointedly.

He was not expecting that question. "No," he told her truthfully, running a hand down his face. "It got too scary. And anyway, I don't need it."

"I agree." She raised one foot to set on the opposite knee. "Miss your dad?"

"Yeah," he admitted. "Even though it wasn't real, it was nice to have."

"Who even knows what's real anymore," Sandra said, sounding her age.

Moss couldn't help but take the bait. "You don't have to be so mean to Belle."

"Gonna bust my balls if I call the toaster an assshole?"

"The toaster wasn't given human emotions." Moss shook his head. This talk was not what he was expecting. She usually tried to bond when she knew their relationship was rifting, but this time she wasn't. He didn't know why, but he knew it would have to be him.

"How are you feeling?" he asked. "No bullshit."

He looked up at her and could see the surprise. Even wrapped in wrinkled lids, her eyes were sharp.

"I'm excited for today. I have wanted this for so long. I want to hurt Carcer like they hurt me, stop them from being able to hurt others. Stop them from tearing families apart and run the world with a wad of money in one hand and a gun in the other."

"Today is just one part of it," Moss reminded her.

"I know. And I know you worry about me, but you have to remember that I do everything I do for the greater good."

"I know." He wanted to add that he wasn't sure she knew what the greater good was anymore. He didn't say it. He didn't say so many things. He was tired and didn't want to fight

215

with her before going into the breach beside her. He wanted her to have a clear head and to have his back. There was a time that he would never have doubted his grandmother but now, he wasn't so sure. Even that doubt made him feel guilty.

"Listen, Moss," she said, her voice cracking slightly. "Whatever happens tonight, we are about to change the world."

"We pull this off, it really will be the first step in some big things," he said with a little smile.

"We will," she assured him and stood, finishing her drink.

Standing as well, Moss recognized there was so much being left unsaid. He knew that if something happened later, he would regret not speaking up, but all he could muster was the one thing that was most important. "I love you."

She smiled a genuine smile. "I love you, too," she said and wrapped her slight, strong arms around him. But even the embrace felt different; strained. He knew her mind was already working on the next part of the day, but he took solace in the fact that at least they had spoken.

"Let's go light the spark of revolution," she said as she made her way back toward the staircase, but she stopped and turned when Moss laughed.

"But that's just it," he couldn't stop himself from saying. "It's not all about the spark. We should want more than to see these things burn."

"And you need to get it out of your head that things like that are mutually exclusive," she said in such a pitying way as to make Moss feel like a child. "The most fertile ground is made of ash."

PART 3

CHAPTER 20

"Twice in one week," Moss noted as he and his grandmother entered the sewers.

"Dreams really do come true," she said, the words dripping with sarcasm.

Moss chuckled. Dressed in black with his Dermidos under cargo pants and vest, he had all the gear he needed. Multiple weapons were holstered all over his body, but he would only use his Kingfisher if given the option. A large metal gas tank was heavy on his back and its shoulder straps were buckled across his chest. He had to heave himself into the open grate.

Seti had arranged for a transport and Moss saw what looked like a small, gray maintenance jet ski hovering in the dark tunnel. A bright headlamp pointed into the blackness and the sound of wet echoed off the walls. Even the air was damp. Moss had expected it to smell like shit, but it reeked of mold and rust.

He sat down behind his grandmother on the maintenance vehicle. He was more nervous than he predicted as the little engine revved and Sandra took off down the weaving web of tunnels. The sewer system had been greatly expanded after so many people were forced into the city. What had been a vast network was now a sprawling subterranean city unto itself. The city's citizens were always in need of more water and restrooms, but even providing the limited amount available was a massive undertaking. It was how the water company justified charging so much for each drop.

The endless sameness of the tunnels was only differentiated by cracks, loose tiles or burned-out bulbs. Sandra was using the navigation Patchwork was feeding her but not the autodrive. She would never let a machine drive for her if she could help it. It made the speed and movement all the more harrowing for Moss, who would have preferred the precision of a computer.

They twisted and turned for what felt like an interminable time before eventually humming to a stop in another dark patch of tunnel. Killing the engine, Sandra stepped off and looked at her grandson, nodding in the direction they were heading. Both wore advanced lenscreens that Ynna had boosted from a truck the week before. They set their optics to night vision and moved down the tunnel, peering around a corner at a pair of Carcer guards. They were linked into a tracking system that would alert the security office if their heart rates stopped so Sandra and Moss knew they couldn't kill them. Patchwork was working to intercept a call if it turned out the company checked on guards whose heart rates even changed.

As they were devising the plan, Ynna had said, "We need to think of every eventuality." In that moment, Moss had once again realized what an asset she was. How she thought of every little thing. That she was more like Burn than even Sandra was.

Now, Sandra communicated to Patchwork on his computer back at the house. She raised her weapon at one of the guards as Moss aimed at the other and she counted down with her fingers. They fired at once, the blue bolts flashing an instant before sending the guards into lumps on the ground.

The two darted forward and began undressing one of the guards, taking the armor for Moss.

"I really should just keep a Carcer uniform," Moss joked.

Sandra looked at him and winked. "Won't need it again after today."

"Here's hoping," Moss said, placing the tank from his back delicately on the cement lip of the tunnel. It wasn't explosive but it still made him nervous to carry it around. The guards were not quite the right size, and the black plate armor was too tight on him, but they were hoping no one would notice until it was too late. Sandra was already wearing a Carcer Maintenance Crew suit that Judy had stored away since their days at Carcer.

Everyone had been shocked that they still owned it, that they had taken it from safehouse to safehouse. Judy had not said anything about it, but Moss couldn't help but ask in a private moment. Judy didn't answer for a long time, but they finally looked up at Moss with wet eyes and said, "It's what I was wearing when I met Stan."

Moss nodded, feeling the tears coming on too. Judy and Stan had the love that every person desires and Moss knew the pain Judy felt every time they spoke of their former love. As contentious as their relationship sometimes was, Moss now thought of Judy as a sibling he never had. He had wrapped them up and the two stayed silent for a long time.

To see his grandmother in the outfit now was strange, knowing its history. Sandra plucked an ID badge from the chest of a fallen guard and stepped to the heavy barred door leading to the underbelly of The Night Crystal, Carcer Corporation's

B.A. City headquarters. The walled-in complex was the size of a small town with its own internal economy. Like many of the larger companies, Carcer didn't want its employees out wandering the streets unless dispatched there. Instead, they were paid in their own digital corporate currency spent in stores within the fortress.

Since Carcer was a military contractor, the design of the entire complex was modeled after an army base with barracks, mess halls, motor pools and prisons. The layout was perfectly square with straight, well-labeled streets. At its center was the headquarters and the building after which the entire complex was named.

The Night Crystal was a pyramid of black-tinted glass around whose base more diagonal pyramids slashed out into the sky like a crown of blades. It was designed to look militaristic and imposing and did the job well. Many of the smaller satellite fortresses around the city were designed to look similarly imposing, reminding the local population that Carcer was always watching. This was all the more true recently.

Rumor had it that the name had come from locals making a grim joke as it was being constructed. The architect had been so delighted that he had declared it the name of the building and it had stuck. Moss didn't know how much of it was true; he only knew it was one of the most secure buildings on Earth and he was hoping to even the odds.

He and Sandra continued through the door and into the white maintenance tunnels. They moved down the narrow passages, constantly on the lookout for unexpected patrols; the human element was the only thing they expected to throw a wrench in their plans. Yellow lines pointed the way. Fluorescent lights buzzed while the pipes coating the walls and ceiling like metal bark vibrated with pressure.

Moss felt it shouldn't have been so easy for them to break in, to have access to the building like this. But as he had discovered before, the Carcer Corporation suffered from the overwhelming inefficiency of bloat. The company had grown too large too quickly and suffered as a result. That didn't mean it would be easy to get into the building proper nor that they would survive once they did, but at least this part was easy.

Sandra held up a hand and he heard, *Ping me and replace cam hall west.* She raised her weapon, and as soon as Patchwork told her he had done as she asked, they rounded the corner. The guard was down before Moss even laid eyes on her. Sandra found the nearest door leading to a valve room and dragged the body inside.

"Shouldn't make it easy on them," she grunted as she pulled the body. Moss knew better than to offer help. She was strong enough to do it herself and didn't like being offered assistance even if a second pair of hands would help.

"Still know where we are going?" Moss asked.

Sandra simply nodded and kept moving. She was more determined than Moss had ever seen her, and he had never seen her as anything other than determined. Her eyes were focused; her mind was on the target. She knew what she wanted to do, what she needed to do.

All his doubts about her would be resolved soon. They were close to having the revenge she so desperately wanted. Moss was scared to find out what would happen next but it was far too late to reconsider the mission.

"Hey!" he heard from behind him and fired a bolt from his Kingfisher without looking back. He turned but Sandra shook her head.

"We're close now," she said, poking her head around one last corner. She turned to look at him, and for the first time in what felt like a long time, seemed to actually see him. "Thank you for this."

The comment took him aback. She had been so guarded for so long, so distant and disconnected. The timing felt wrong, but the moment was welcome.

"I know how important this is," he said. He meant it, not just for her but for the world. Getting Carcer out of the city was vital. Loosening its foothold on the world was important work. But more than that, he knew how important it was to her. He was happy to help her with this, even if he feared what it would do to her and how far it had driven her.

"It is," she said and put her hand on his shoulder. If their embrace earlier had felt forced, this felt genuine. "I know things have been strained but they'll be better now."

He didn't know if that was true. She was hurt and lost, and the doubt overwhelmed his hope. "I know," he said, and wondered if she could see the lie.

She turned back to peer down the hallway, moving toward the heavy metal door painted red with a hazardous gas sign on one side, a flammable warning plaque on the other and danger spray-painted in bold letters on the front. Holoprojected caution tape scrolled in front of the door in case all the other indicators weren't enough.

Sandra ran the stolen keycard over the lock and it flashed red. Judy had warned them that security officer keycards probably wouldn't work. Grimacing, Sandra pulled the two charges Judy had constructed and placed them against the hinges. As they magnetized to the metal, small telescoping shields encased the charges before they detonated simultaneously, blasting the door open. It swung inward as Moss and Sandra pulled on their gas masks.

The ventilation room was illuminated in red to indicate the inherent danger of working within. Moss and Sandra stepped around the busted door and followed a staircase deep into a maze of pipes, fans and metal boxes with lights. When they reached the bottom of the stairs, Moss pulled the tank off his back as the lenscreen cameras began to scan the room. Grid lines ran through Moss's vision as the program Patchwork created began to work.

Patch had consulted with Judy so they could get it just right. Before too long, two figures made up of green pixels appeared in the room. The augmented reality people began to move, going through the process that Moss and Sandra were to imitate.

"Ooh, rather than just walking him through it, you'll just show him with the lenses?" Issy had asked with a little smirk. "That's probably smart; he's more of a learn-by-doing type," she said in a playfully mocking tone.

"That's what I figured," Patchwork said with a wink.

"Make fun all you want," Moss put in, folding his arms across his chest. "I *am* a learn-by-doing type."

Issy scrunched her face in mock condescension. "And look how far you've gotten," she said, patting him on the head like a dog.

Moss leaned into the joke, holding up his hands like paws and panting.

"Don't be fooled," Gibbs said, taking his feet down from the table. "That comment wasn't even about you."

Patchwork gave him a questioning look.

"It was about how good a student she was," Gibbs winked. "It wasn't an insult; it was a back door brag."

Issy rolled her eyes. "A thing can be two things," she said, sticking her tongue out at Gibbs the way she had when they were kids. Moss had smiled then as he did even at the memory of the moment. For as many things as had changed in his life and as different and dangerous as it had become, he had Gibbs and Issy by his side. The two people who had been his family when his parents had been killed. The two people who had carried him through his life, lifting him when he was down and carrying him when he couldn't go on.

He smiled as his grandmother slapped the back of his head. "Where you at?"

"Sorry," he sputtered.

"No time for daydreaming," she snarled. "We are underneath an army."

"Right," he said. "For now."

That made her smile.

The AR image of Sandra picked a large wrench off a rusting metal rack mounted on the wall. Instead of using it to open some huge pipe, the image clamped it on a padlock. Sandra did as the image did. Moss followed his own, helping his grandmother pull on the lock. Judy had warned them about what would come next.

The lock was strong and could not be broken with the weight of two small people, but the two thin slivers of metal the lock was threaded through bent and buckled before ripping off the box. As they fell to the ground, the wrench pinwheeling away to the far wall, Moss couldn't help but laugh.

"Get the world's strongest lock but use it to secure weak metal," he said as he got up and dusted himself off. "Can't think of a more perfect metaphor for Carcer."

"I can think of better ones," Sandra said as she stood quickly, her body cracking and popping as she did so. The room was loud with all the machinery and flowing water and gas, and being able to hear her body creak over the din reminded him just how old she was. She was so strong of personality and physicality that he sometimes forgot that she was in her seventies.

Swinging the panel open, they watched as their virtual thems flipped a switch labeled with little more than a piece of masking tape with illegible chicken scratches. Once the switch was flipped, they heard the grinding and scraping sounds of heavy machinery unused to working. Valves closed and they turned as their avatars moved. Sandra's went to one of the pipes and began to open screws while Moss's began screwing a hose with a latch onto the tank.

The humans followed suit and Moss was relieved to be physically following the instructions rather than being talked through them. If this was to be an option again, he would take it.

His hands moved in smooth, sure motions as he affixed the cap then lifted the tank carefully toward his grandmother. She was prying open a panel and the screws had come out with ease, but the pipe had been painted over several times and the metal flap was painted shut. Once it was finally open, she pulled the previous accelerator free and nodded at Moss. He placed the tank in the pipe and attached his accelerator to the newly vacant spot.

He nervously put his hand on the valve and began to unscrew it, but he felt a force from his side as he was pushed to the ground. The wind was knocked out of him as he heard gunshots. A bullet hit a pipe and the room began to fill with an unknown gas. Sandra fired her energy weapon and Moss heard a scream.

"We have to hurry!" she yelled, and he moved quickly back to the tank to continue his work. Once finished, he gave

Sandra a thumbs up and she ,moved back to the panel with Moss right behind her.

"You can do the honors," he said, and as she raised her hand to the switch, he saw the blood.

"Wouldn't have it any other way," she said happily, flipping the switch.

They didn't hear the screams, didn't hear the frantic pounding on windows and doors as the Carcer operatives' lungs filled with the toxic gas. All they heard was a slight change in pressure from some of the pipes.

CHAPTER 21

"Ain't nothing." Sandra answered the question Moss wasn't asking.

They were running now and Sandra was pressing a hand against her side. Despite her assurances, she was leaving a trail of blood spots like breadcrumbs to grandmother's house. It made Moss nervous. He didn't know how badly she was hurt and knew she wouldn't tell him, but the little grunt she let out with every step spoke volumes.

They knew the way. This was the part they had studied to prepare for. Running toward the staircase from SUB 02 to the surface, they passed a couple of crumpled human forms who had been stopped in their tracks by the gas. They had died so fast they had hardly reacted: their hands were not clutching at their necks and their eyes weren't bulging. They apparently had collapsed on the spot.

Moss had long ago given up feeling sympathy for these people. He used to have guilt about hurting or killing people who he had deemed to be 'just doing a job.' Over time, he had come to believe that by taking a job as an instrument of evil, they were not only complicit in the evil but active participants. They weren't just desperate people trying to make ends meet; they were part of the plague that was killing society and destroying what semblance was left of human decency.

Up and up they went until they burst into the lobby of The Night Crystal. As with the exterior, the structure's interior was designed to look imposing. Massive obsidian statues sat atop black pillars illuminated by single beams of bright lights. Holoprojected screens lined the walls, displaying faces of valuable bounties and bodycam videos of successful apprehensions. A large round desk station was set in the center of the room with a touch-screen surface for visitors.

People lay everywhere around the room. Moss tried to wipe down the fogged-up plate on the front of his mask so he would not trip over a body as they moved. He wondered how many people in the complex were now dead and it unnerved him to think how happy his grandmother must have been to see them all. Warden Ninety-Nine's words in the bathroom echoed in his mind.

He heard the wail of a siren as they neared the tall glass entrance doors. It grew louder as they neared, and Sandra looked back at Moss before her eyes drifted outside where scattered Carcer troops were converging on their location. They had known some stragglers would be walking between buildings during the initial attack, but more soldiers were moving toward them than they had anticipated.

Sandra pointed just beyond the doors at two gigantic statues on huge square bases. They stood on either side of the entrance and were both of women pointing guns outward toward the base. One was dressed in Victorian Era clothes like what Irene had worn and the other depicted an American Western gunslinger. Moss and his grandmother sprinted out, taking positions behind the two statues.

Once again, Sandra began to count down with her fingers. Moss readied his weapons. They were a long way from where Warden Ninety-Nine was likely to be and would now have to fight their way there.

As one they peeked around the corners of the granite bases and opened fire. Taken by surprise, two of the guards were killed instantly, but the others scattered behind cover. Long rows of steps gave Moss and Sandra the high ground and they used it to pick off officers as they peeked out from cover.

Moss was feeling confident until Carcer stopped returning fire and he realized they were regrouping and coming up with an actual plan. As much as the team loved to mock Carcer and its corporate mistakes, the soldiers did spend most of their lives training and were well-armed and equipped.

For a while, they heard nothing but the sound of the siren before Moss saw a grenade come bouncing between the statues. He only had time to cover his face as it went off. Blinding light and deafening sound burst out before he felt the base of the statue raining down chunks on him as the officers let forth a volley of fire. Pinned down, deaf and half-blind, Moss felt momentarily paralyzed.

Then he gripped his weapon. He knew a swarm would move toward him during the covering fire. He took deep breaths, waiting for the storm of bullets, cloud of smoke and rain of stone to clear. When it did, he turned to try and see his grandmother, but there was too much dust and dirt in the air between them.

He popped his head out just for a second and saw six bodies, clad in black with guns raised, headed his way. He ducked back just in time as he saw the muzzle flash but still heard nothing. He pulled a digimine from his jacket and tossed it toward the attackers. It landed and peppered the Carcer officers with directed shrapnel.

It wasn't enough to penetrate their armor, but it had the desired effect of creating confusion. Moss shouldered his body around the corner and opened fire on the six officers. They were distracted by the bits of metal that had shredded their armor.

One lucky break was that a man was clutching his neck. A stray piece from the mine had hit the jugular.

Three were down before the others regrouped and turned their rifles on Moss. He hid again as the world around him exploded in bullet fire. He tried to call out to his grandmother but could hardly hear his own voice over the ringing in his ears. Sliding his back along the smoothed stone and sliding over a plaque, he moved to the other side of the base. He took a deep breath before rounding the corner.

He and two men approaching him fired simultaneously, but Moss had the advantage by moving before pressing himself to the ground. Both officers fell but Moss watched in horror as many more took positions behind barricades at the bottom of the steps. Ducking, he held his position a moment, waiting to see if the three coming up the middle were going to come at him.

When they didn't, he knew they were waiting for him.

The counterbreakers had clearly been able to stop Patchwork's hack. Moss heard armies of drones beginning to take off from the nearby base. At the same time, he smiled to hear the buzzing of their own drones, ready to take on the black Carcer ones. Suddenly, the sky erupted in light as a massive battle was joined. While their numbers were fewer, Zip was working with the drone's AI and had the advantage over Carcer's automated drones. Shells fell like metal rain. Smoking metal carcasses began to fall, and Moss used the confusion to dash out and shoot the three waiting officers.

But so many more were taking up positions and Moss ran through the cover of the smoke to the opposing statue. His grandmother was nowhere to be found. All that was left was a trail of blood leading around the corner of the statue's base.

"Shit," he coughed. He ran forward, following the blood. He saw the trail go down toward the barricade. She

234

would have to have been knocked out to have been taken by the Carcer officers. Dread built within him as he feared he was now alone. He felt exposed and gritted his teeth as he considered his options. He couldn't take on this whole place by himself. There were too many soldiers and he still needed to find Ninety-Nine.

Hearing a commotion, he watched as Sandra seemed to appear out of nowhere beside the barricaded officers. His eyes went wide as she grabbed one, pressing his own weapon against his chin, exploding the contents of his head into the sky. She spun him before he could fall, using his body to shield herself from the incoming fire and pressing his finger against the trigger.

Two more officers fell in line with the first and she snagged the weapon from his hand before charging the remaining officers. They fired wild shots and should easily have been able to hit her from that distance, but they were so surprised they were unable to aim with any precision.

Moss couldn't believe his eyes. He knew his grandmother was a badass and had seen it proven many times, but this was something else. She kicked one man's gun into the air in such a way that it seemed to spin in slow motion. Throwing the pistol at the final officer and knocking him to the ground, she caught the second weapon and spun it. A blast of bullets shredded the man before he even understood what was happening. She sprang past him and jammed the rifle's barrel in the face of the final man.

As he began jogging down the stairs to join his grandmother, he heard her demand, "Where is Ninety-Nine?"

"I – I don't know," the man said, hands raised and face contorted with terror.

"Where is he!" Sandra thundered, as if all the pain of all the years of torture were escaping her lips.

235

"I don't know!" the man screamed before his words were silenced with lead.

Moss jogged up. "Shit, Grandma, that was like an action movie."

When she turned, she blinked hard several time as though she was trying to refocus on the world. When her eyes locked, she snarled, "Meanwhile, you're over there with the bucket of popcorn."

Moss just shook his head. The emotional whiplash she was putting him through was getting old and he was tired. He had nearly been killed and it still wasn't enough. He opened his mouth to speak as more drones flew by, no doubt heading to take down more emerging officers.

"We end this," Warden Ninety-Nine said. "Now!"

He strode out from around the corner of a tent barrack Moss was not surprised to see t that he man wore the mechanized armor Carcer reserved for 'enhanced militaristic operations.' The armor was twice as tall as the warden, with a bulletproof glass windshield, thick impenetrable metal casing and massive guns that attached along the machine's forearms.

The ground shook as the mech strode forward, the Warden's voice amplified through the speakers. "I don't know what you thought you could do here, but The Night Crystal is where you die," he said with self-assured finality. "No long speeches, no heroic final fight, just death," he said and raised the arms, the targeting systems no doubt working to eviscerate Moss and Sandra.

The machine stopped moving.

All the faith they had left in Patchwork and Zip now paid off.

No bullets fired. Nothing happened. Then the cockpit of the armor hissed and began to swing up. Ninety-Nine looked more angry than scared.

"Fucking theatrics," he groaned, pulling the straps off his shoulders and sliding up and out of the armor. Moss and Sandra walked toward the large man as he climbed down the ladder soldered onto the side of the armor.

"He's mine," Sandra told Moss as they stood before one another as in an old west gunfight. But no one drew arms. They all knew this had to be sorted out with bare hands. It was how they all wanted it. Ninety-Nine had a hunger in his eyes — a desire to end this rebellion himself. The CEO of the company wanted to prove he was still strong enough to solve his problems with his hands.

Sandra wanted revenge. Her narrow eyes fixed on the man who controlled the company that had captured her.

Moss just wanted to be done with the man who seemed to show up everywhere. Who was always one step ahead, who had shot Ynna and captured Moss himself. He was ready to tip this domino and watch all the other pieces fall into place. The citizens could breathe freely, the Scubas could return to the city with their secrets, the mayor's office could effect real change and the AIC would cower in fear. All these things required the death of Warden Ninety-Nine.

Stepping forward, the large man unhooked a telescoping baton from his belt and slammed it into his hand, locking the metal stick with a threatening clang. Moss moved forward too, but his grandmother pressed a hand to his chest.

"It's all revenge with you," Warden Ninety-Nine snarled. "Though I suppose I should thank you. I got this job because of you."

Sandra spat on the ground. "Alice Carcer's death was a gift to the world, as yours'll be."

Warden Ninety-Nine looked at Moss with a bemused expression on his face. "This is the leader of your movement?" he asked in true disgust. "You believe she is going to lead the world into some bright future? She is a murderer out for revenge."

"Don't buy his shit," Sandra snorted to Moss out of the side of her mouth. She and the Warden confronted each other like two vipers ready to strike.

"You didn't tell him?" Warden Ninety-Nine chuckled now and Moss watched his grandmother twitch nearly imperceptibly. "She not only got me this promotion, but also the last one."

Sandra pulled her long nanoblade from her belt and struck at him. She was fast and strong, but not nearly as strong as the Warden. He sidestepped the blow with ease, and she moved again to thrust the blade in his side; but he hit her hand with the baton, causing her to drop the blade and withdraw.

Moss had never seen his grandmother like this. He had seen her vicious but never out of control. She crouched, appearing ready to strike again, but Warden Ninety-Nine had the upper hand. He was calm and smiling with foregone conclusion, as if he had already killed them both.

"You see, Mister Moss," he continued, "I was just a lowly guard until your grandmother here gave me a piece of intel that I leveraged into a promotion."

"Shut up!" she shrieked and, grabbing the knife, charged him again. He once again moved out of her way and allowed her to fall past him, landing hard on the concrete.

"It was one thing when she told me that Grimy would turn but it was quite another when I got him on our payroll," he announced to Moss. "For all her tough talk of loyalty that I am sure she spouts, she's just another Carcer operative."

Moss shook his head. "My grandmother may be many things," he said as he moved toward the man. "But 'Carcer operative' is not one of them. Bragging that you beat some hidden truth out of her does not anger me toward her. Only you."

Moss knew his grandmother was too upset to fight properly and he was done with Warden Ninety-Nine. After all these years, he needed to end it here and now. No more near misses. He would leave here having killed the man, or having died trying.

Just as in that bathroom, he knew that Warden Ninety-Nine was a superior fighter and that he would have to be smart to get the better of him.

"I'll admit," the Warden said as he closed in on Moss, "I expected the revelation to affect you more."

He seemed genuinely disappointed, and even in the heat of the moment Moss couldn't help but wonder what the man was actually like. Or if he even had a life to speak of outside of Carcer.

"A fucking scumbag being promoted for torturing someone is hardly a revelation," Moss said.

Something seemed to snap in the Warden. Something about the comment pushed him over the edge. He charged. Moss saw it in time and told his cybernetic legs to spring out of the way, but it happened too fast.

Moss felt the hand around his throat, the fingers closing in. The loss of oxygen registered quickly. In movies, it took a long time to choke someone to death, but Moss felt his body's desperation for oxygen immediately.

"I am not some scumbag," Warden Ninety-Nine spat in Moss's face. "I do this for the good of the world. For all those people who need protection. For the people who can't stick up for themselves. For my li—" but he was cut off.

Moss felt the warm blood spray his face. Felt the grip loosen and felt his desperate lungs fill with air.

He watched as Warden Ninety-Nine fell to his knees, clutching his slit throat. He burbled and gurgled.

"The fuck you say to him that got him all hot and bothered?" Sandra panted, smiling down at the blade in her hand coated in the Warden's blood. "Near forgot I existed."

Moss nodded, blinking hard and realizing they had done it.

Just like that.

"Wasn't actually what I was going for," he wheezed through pain. His throat would hurt for a long time to come.

"Don't matter," Sandra smiled. "It worked. We got him."

Moss looked at the body of Warden Ninety-Nine. He was really dead. The domino had fallen. "If we see him again, we will know it is just a recreation," Moss noted, rubbing his neck.

"Nah," Sandra said. "Won't give 'em the chance."

She grabbed a handful of black hair, pulled his head upward, and grinning, began to slice through his neck.

CHAPTER 22

"And then he was dead," Moss said with a strange finality.

"This fucking monster with whom we have been at war for so long was just dead. It happened so quickly. It felt like there should have been more — some grand finale — but there wasn't. Instead, he began to pummel me and she," Moss hooked a thumb over to his grandmother standing off by the edge of the rooftop, "just cut his head off."

Ynna chuckled. "Yeah, it was like that with Alice Carcer too. It just happens quickly."

"They may be big deals, but they are all just people," Gibbs observed. "And people can be killed."

"Non-people can be killed too," Belle noted.

"Right," Gibbs nodded.

"How was your mission?" Moss asked, putting his feet up on the little table and taking a swig of his beer. They were back on the rooftop of the building Mix LeBeau had set aside for people who had escaped from ThutoCo after Moss exposed them. The building was one of the few places in the city that felt truly safe.

Though they were surrounded by buildings full of corporate peons, this one place was well-protected. It was where Gibbs and Ynna had planned to get married. It was an open space with a small faux grass patch at its center. Fire pits were spread around with little seating areas. The uncharacteristic heat of the last month was continuing and everyone was happy and drinking.

For the first time in a long time, things really seemed to be looking up. All their operations had gone off without a hitch and now they were taking a moment to enjoy one another's company and revel in their various successes, swapping stories and having a good time.

"Our mission was a little less straightforward," Ynna said, taking a glug of whisky.

"You can say that again," Gibbs put in, sucking whatever sweet-smelling drink he was enjoying through a little straw.

"Anyone going to tell me or is it just all preamble here?" Moss said, rolling his eyes. Issy came over and sat next to Moss on the couch, leaning her back against the arm rest and draping her legs across Moss's lap.

He smiled, sucking in a lungful of warm air. Polluted as it was, it felt like free air. Very little had changed, but something about knowing that Warden Ninety-Nine was dead made the world feel better, safer.

"Okay, so here it is," she began now that almost everyone was listening. Zip and Patchwork were on one couch with Belle while Gibbs and Ynna sat across from them with Moss and Issy on a third sofa . A holoprojected blue fire danced in the pit between them and an ivy-covered canopy shielded them from the sun. "We thought it was going to be pretty straightforward, but things went belly up pretty quickly."

"It wasn't so much that they went 'belly up,' as much as. . ." Gibbs began, but Ynna clamped a hand over his mouth.

He continued to talk into her palm as though nothing had happened, and everyone chuckled.

"My story," Ynna said. "So, we went to find this Carcer bigwig. We had costumes all picked out and a cover story and everything. We went into the lobby and made straight for the front desk. One thing we didn't account for was that it would be a friggin' drudge working the counter. We tried all of our workarounds and clever plans, but the dumb fucking machine wouldn't let us pass." She turned and added, "No offense, Belle."

"Why would that offend me?" she asked and Ynna grinned. Zip's lips pursed.

"Anywaaaay," Ynna continued with a self-amused smirk on her face. "We realized we weren't getting anywhere with the robot, so we ended up having to steal a car that we took to the roof, used the window washer's thingamabob to ride down, break the glass to get into the hallway and *then* got to use our disguises to get into the room with the guy."

"Why—" Moss began but Ynna cut him off, doing a low-voiced dumb-guy impression.

"Why didn't you just use drone packs," she mocked. "Because we didn't bring them and didn't want to run back here and grab them and then run back to the job."

"Okay, okay," Moss laughed, holding up his hand defensively.

"What happened when you got into the room?" Issy asked with a clever smile.

Ynna snatched an olive out of a dish on the table and threw it at Issy, who laughed. "I see what you are doing," Ynna said. "So, we got into the room using our awesome disguises."

"Are you going to keep saying they were awesome, or do you plan to tell us about them at some point?" Patchwork said.

"I'm happy you asked," Ynna said.

"Knowing you, I can only assume you were half-naked," Judy said as they strode up.

"Don't you start too, Jude," Ynna said.

Gibbs laughed and pointed to Judy. "But you are, of course, right."

"That aside," Ynna pressed. "When we got into the room, the dude had some ninja-ass muscle and we had to go hand to hand. 'We' being a relative term." She narrowed her eyes theatrically at Gibbs.

He chuckled and looked at everyone else. "It's true. Puck and I were useless."

"At least Puck tried to hit that one with his cane," Ynna said.

"Okay, okay, *I* was useless," Gibbs corrected.

Ynna began chopping at the air, spilling some of her drink. "So, after I kick all their asses, Carcerman is left to deal with. Of course, he doesn't want to die and starts offering us deals and secrets, anything we want to spare his life."

"Meanwhile, asshole oversaw Carcer City Three on the east coast for years," Gibbs added.

"Right," Ynna said. "More than happy to commit atrocities day and night but as soon as it's his ass on the line, 'oh, I have kids,' and all that."

"Not that we turned down the secrets." Gibbs winked at Moss, who smiled and nodded.

"Fuck no we didn't," Ynna cheered. "We got all that intel back to Seti and then did what needed to be done."

"How did Puck look?" Moss asked nervously.

Ynna grinned. "You know, that mask shit really worked. He looked just like the guy and, credit where credit is due, his impression was spot the fuck on."

"It really was," Gibbs agreed. "Steampuck may have missed a calling to the theatre."

"He'll get his chance now," Moss said.

That quieted everyone for a moment. "It's pretty badass, really," Ynna said. "What Puck is doing. Always kind of thought of him as soft, but infiltrating Carcer like that, just after the death of the current head, it's ballsy." She cupped the air.

"Talking about me again?" Anders joked as he strode over, smiling down at the resting crew. "I have spent the whole day shuttling crews around the city to take down Carcer sites, and all the while you lot are sat here like a bunch of lumps."

"Hey," Ynna said, pointing a finger. "We got our man in at the top of Carcer!"

"And we killed Warden Ninety-Nine!" Moss added. "We deserve a break."

Anders smiled. "I suppose you do."

He grabbed a sweating beer off the lip of the firepit and opened it with his teeth, causing Issy to wince. Moss remembered the first time they had seen someone do it at one of the first parties they had all been invited to. Gibbs had spent the whole night getting shot down by one girl after another. Meanwhile, Moss and Issy had stood in a corner, sipping their drinks as everyone became increasingly sloshed. They had spent the whole night talking. Issy had been coaching Moss on how to talk to girls and about what they liked, and it hadn't been until years later that he realized she was actually giving him advice on how to seduce her.

"None of you guys are even watching that screen," Anders said, hooking a thumb at the election results being streamed onto a massive holoscreen. He was right; they really hadn't been watching. They all knew how important the election was, but they had also all done something rather remarkable and wanted to enjoy the moment.

Anders tapped Moss on the shoulder and he scooched down the couch to make room. Issy adjusted herself so she was now sitting half on his lap. Everyone began to speak about the election and their various days and Moss stared into space for a moment, thinking about all that had changed for him. He was tired but happy. Things were beginning to feel like they could work out.

He understood there was more fighting ahead of them, but they were winning for the first time ever. Smiling, he took another sip of his drink.

"Think LeBeau can do it?" Anders quietly asked Moss.

"I do," Moss said. "And I think they will do great things with the office."

"Happy to hear that," Anders said. "The winds of change are blowing," he said with a smile and Moss knew that he was thinking about that little girl at The Conservation and all the others like her.

"That they are," he agreed, smiling at his friend.

Anders lowered his voice. "How's she doing?" He nodded toward Sandra.

Moss shook his head slowly and looked in Anders's eyes. "Hard to say. She was practically giddy as we were leaving the Night Crystal but as we got away, she became quiet — almost morose. More than usual."

Anders nodded. "She's not young and I'm sure she's wondering if her work is done now."

"We've talked about that, and there is something to what you are saying," Moss said. "She has been — well, is, really, so focused on revenge. It has consumed her, driven her. And now I wonder if there is a void."

"Only in part," Anders said, his voice full of implications. "There is much more of Carcer. Even if LeBeau wins tonight and we manage to get Carcer out and Puck can begin working against the company from the inside, there is still a huge amount of work remaining. She shouldn't, and probably won't, feel like this is over. May just take some time."

"Plus all this," Moss said, gesturing around, his drink spilling a little. He realized he might be more drunk than he thought. "We need her leadership."

Anders paused a moment as though considering if he should tell Moss something. "You know, I have become somewhat close to Sandy over the last year and the leadership stuff is more complicated than you may understand. I told you how much she loves you and wants to see you succeed, but you also must understand there is a desire to protect you as well. Protect you from what she has been through, from everything she has seen and experienced.

"Listening to her speak, I can see that she is of two minds. One, she knows she is going to have to let you learn and grow and be the man she wants you to become. Two, she wants to teach you for as long as she can so that you are ready."

Moss exhaled slowly, taking it all in. He thought he was talking and thinking about his grandmother too much, but was also heartened to know how seriously she was taking his growth. He knew he was becoming a leader, but he also knew that he wasn't the only one.

Looking across the firepit, he watched as Ynna laughed and joked with Gibbs and Patchwork. The whole crew believed in her and she had earned it. She hadn't been given some chip

247

made by her parents; she had worked hard and done what needed to be done to get where she was. He knew that in some ways, she would always be the leader of this team. He might be the figurehead, but she would be the brains of the operation.

"What about Ynna?" Moss asked.

Anders ran one massive hand down his face. "Sounds to me like Ynna and Sandra have always had a mother-daughter thing. They fight, but they seem to have deep feelings for each other. Burn loved Ynna like a daughter too. It's a complicated thing they all have going. But Sandra doesn't feel about Ynna the way she does about you. I can sense it in the way she —"

Moss felt a warm spray on his face. It seemed to happen in slow motion.

As Anders spoke, half of his face erupted, ripping open from one side.

"Layla," seemed to echo in Moss's ear with the sound of the gunshot. Anders's body poured blood as Moss turned. Everyone was moving, looking for weapons or just trying to understand what had happened.

Moss saw the gun in Belle's hand but didn't comprehend what it meant. Her eyes were glazed with a robotic sheen, and she began speaking in a slow, threatening Chinese dialect that Moss did not know. As Belle's head snapped toward Moss, he leapt to his feet, trying to put himself between the gun and Issy. The metallic smell of blood filled his nose as the barrel of the weapon pointed squarely at his chest.

He closed his eyes but heard a scream as Ynna brought Patchwork's samurai sword down on the machine's wrist. But Belle was fast; her other arm wrapped around Ynna's throat before the human had time to react.

Moss leapt over the firepit, snatching the sword from Ynna's hand and driving it up through Belle's head. The machine shut down and Ynna collapsed, gasping for air.

"No!" Zip Thud screamed, running over to the destroyed love of his life.

Moss looked back at the couch and at Anders's destroyed body. The bullet had shredded his face. Moss wanted to throw up. Gibbs was consoling Ynna and Zip was sobbing over Belle's destroyed body as it leaked whatever synthetic material was acting as blood.

"How the fuck did that happen?" Sandra asked, striding over. The color drained from her face as she looked down at Anders's body. "Dammit."

"I — I don't know," Moss muttered. His mind was reeling. It had all happened so fast. His ears were ringing and his mind was dull.

"Xuegeng Technologies," Zip whispered through his sniffles. He seemed like such a little kid then. "They must have counterhacked me."

Moss heard the shot before he even had time to think. Watching Zip's chest explode was too much for him. He turned and tackled his grandmother to the ground, the gun clattering along the rooftop.

She looked at him with venom in her eyes. "Get off me."

He didn't speak and she snarled, "Once again I did what needed doing."

Moss couldn't believe he was hearing her words. Zip was just a young man. He may have been hacked, but he didn't deserve to die. The crew began to gather around Moss and his grandmother.

"I am protecting you!" she thundered. "He put us all at risk. Who knows what they know now."

Eyes flashed between the dead bodies and the two panting people on the ground. Everyone appeared to be in shock. Too much had happened too quickly. Sandra shoved Moss and pulled herself to her feet.

"I saved your lives," she announced. "Again!"

She gave one last look at Anders, her fallen soldier, and stomped away.

No one spoke. Standing, Moss wiped the drying blood from his face.

A cheer went up from around the city. All the buildings were frantic with activity and the streets below were a cacophonous din. Like zombies, they all turned to the screen to see the announcement.

"Persimmon LeBeau named Mayor Elect of B.A. City."

CHAPTER 23

"**Y**ou look great," Moss told Gibbs.

The black tuxedo did look good. Gibbs had said he wanted to look like James Bond and he had pulled it off.

"Thanks, man," Gibbs said. "I can't believe it."

"*You* can't believe it?" Moss laughed. "How do you think I feel? I watched you get shot down for years and years and now you are getting married."

"If all those girls knew what they were missing," Gibbs said with a smile as he looked at himself in the mirror. They were getting ready in an apartment Mayor LeBeau had set aside for them in the building under their protection. In spite of the fresh memories it now held, they were still getting married on the roof.

"I wish any of our parents were alive to see this," Gibbs observed quietly, a small misery in his words.

"Guessing Ynna's dad isn't coming," Moss joked as he pulled a small piece of lint from his friend's shoulder.

Gibbs laughed. "Better to be dead than to be that kind of person," he observed. "No, he is definitely not coming."

"Guess that's for the best," Moss said. He stepped in front of Gibbs and looked into his eyes. "Listen, I know I've said it, but I am so happy for you, so proud of you and so happy

251

that you came with me that night. If you hadn't forced your presence on me, I would be dead a hundred times over. You and Ynna have both saved my life and I love you both and I am so happy for you both."

They hugged, their suits crunching together softly, and Moss could feel Gibbs begin to cry into his shoulder. Moss figured he understood. They had all been emotional wrecks for the past few weeks. To lose Anders, Belle and Zip Thud like that had torn everyone's hearts out. Even Sandra, who everyone was still enraged at for killing Zip, was miserable about Anders. Missions had been impossible and everyone seemed happy to distract themselves with the wedding, even if the pain was always lingering just under the surface.

"I know, man," Moss soothed but Gibbs pulled away, his eyes as red and pained as Moss had ever seen them.

"No," Gibbs said. "You don't."

Moss cocked an eyebrow, but he had a knot in his stomach. Gibbs never looked like this unless something was very wrong. Moss wiggled his fingers nervously as Gibbs tried to find the words.

"So, Ynna and I have been talking and . . ." He paused, and Moss's heart felt as if it was trying to escape his chest. "We think that after the wedding, we are going to take some time for us, you know?"

There it was.

He had seen it coming; he had even asked Issy if she could sense it too. He had known they were fed up. Gibbs was never meant for this life and Ynna had not been the same since Zip died. Moss was so lost in his thoughts that he didn't speak; he just watched suspended dirt dance in the light streaming in from a window.

"Look, look, listen," Gibbs stammered. Now he would justify himself. "Things are good now. We got the mayorship, Puck was made the freakin' head of Carcer, you got the hunters in place, the Scubas are going to be able to move back and give you that intel and the off-worlders are beginning to supply us."

"I know, but . . ." Moss began weakly.

"But nothing," Gibbs said. "For the first time, things are actually okay. We think it's a good time to take a step back, take a breather. You don't need us."

That broke Moss. "Of course I need you!" Moss yelled before covering his mouth as the words reverberated through the door. "I need you both," he whispered, his hands shaking. The idea of being without Gibbs was terrifying. He had been through so much, but the one constant in his life was that he had his friend by his side. He didn't care if it was selfish; he just didn't want to be without them.

"You don't," Gibbs said, his voice quavering too. "You have Issy now and your grandmother."

"That's it, isn't it?" Moss asked, a little angry now. "This is all about her, what she has done?"

Gibbs didn't answer for a moment and then said, "In part, yes. It's not just what she has done but what she keeps doing. You know Ynna believes in this cause more than anyone, but she needs to get away from Sandra. They are not good for each other and it's come to a crisis point. You know she really liked Zip and that was the last straw."

"I get it," Moss admitted.

"And we both love you too much to ask you to choose sides; it shouldn't have to be like that. You should be with your family," Gibbs said, putting a hand on Moss's shoulder.

Moss considered the words. "Okay," he said miserably. "If you guys need some time away, I won't try to stop you or convince you not to go. You need to do what you need to do."

"Thanks," Gibbs said. "We are going to stay in the city after our honeymoon, so it's not like we won't see each other."

"Sure," Moss said, but he doubted the words. If they didn't want to see Sandra anymore, they were not going to want to pop by for a visit. He would see them from time to time, but it would be awkward, and they would make small talk for a bit before parting and saying, "We shouldn't take so long before seeing each other again."

His heart was ripped out. The deaths they had all just experienced and now the loss of two of his closest friends were too much for Moss. He was supposed to be some hero of the revolution, a person who was going to change the face of the world. Instead, he felt like a sad kid whose best friend was moving away.

Gibbs wrapped Moss in his arms again. "This was why Ynna told me to wait until after the wedding."

"She's always right," Moss said, and he realized that losing Ynna was going to be as bad for the crew as losing Gibbs was going to be for him. She did so much. He had come to understand that it was she who made most of the arrangements, set things up with Seti and got things moving. Without her, Moss was not sure how this whole operation could continue. He supposed he would have to do it, along with trying to keep Sandra from killing anyone else.

She had not been the same since that day either. She always spoke of the loss of soldiers and how a leader had to be prepared for it and have an ability to move on. But she was taking Anders's death hard. She didn't care that she had killed Zip — she truly believed that needed to be done — but she and the pilot had become close. She stalked around the house, barking orders and lecturing the crew on their responsibilities.

Moss sometimes wondered how much of his grandmother was left. How much had been left after they killed Ninety-Nine, or even after her years in Carcer City. He tried to think back, remember being a child, having her visit them in their hex. Like seeing through murky water, he recalled her lying on the floor with him, playing with figurines. He couldn't imagine the woman he knew now playing or even smiling anymore. His grandmother had been transformed.

But maybe that was how a person had to be to survive. How she got through the war, how she lasted for so long in C City. As much as Moss didn't want to admit it, he had changed too, and not just for the better. He had become stronger of will and a better leader, but he had also become more vicious and more willing to do what he needed to do. Or felt he needed to do. He had not compromised his ideals but he had changed them to fit his circumstances.

He wondered if, given enough time, he would become his grandmother. If he would do anything he needed to do for what he thought was right. He didn't know the answer anymore. Wiping a tear from his face, he said to Gibbs, "Ready to get married?"

The rooftop was beautifully decorated. Rows of wood frame chairs topped with white pillows lined a grass aisle leading to an archway of lush green vines. Lines of twinkling white lights were strung all around. Protective drones buzzed in the distance, but smaller drones wafted just overhead raining a slow drizzle of white flower petals on the assembled crowd as well as a soft sheen of scented water. The surroundings were so lovely that it was easy to forget all the surrounding skyscrapers and flashing holoprojected ads.

Moss looked at Gibbs. His eyes were fixed on the back row of chairs, waiting for his bride. His friend was lost in his joy. Moss had never seen him so happy. Everything they had done and been through, all the tough decisions and brutal losses were gone in this moment. All that existed was this moment. Looking to the front row, Moss's eyes met Issy's. She was beaming too, and a tear of joy already streaked her face. She wore a bright yellow dress that perfectly complemented her skin tone, and Moss knew there was no more beautiful woman on the earth.

She smiled at him, and just as it was for Gibbs, there was nothing else in the world but his love. It didn't feel wrong that he was happy; it just felt good for that brief moment. For obvious reasons, Steampuck couldn't be there but the hologram of him streaming from his office at Carcer began playing the wedding processional on a violin.

Everyone stood. Moss grinned as he saw Ynna. The woman who he had always known as a total badass looked absolutely stunning and, more than anything, happy. Truly happy. Moss's heart cried out in joy for them.

Ynna had dyed her hair deep purple and pulled it partially up into flowing curls that cascaded down her face. Her white dress was all lace on top and smooth satin flaring from the hips to the floor. A large bow was tied at the base of her back, and she had done one thing that she had always sworn to Moss that she wouldn't: she had her cybernetic hand replaced with a shiny new model. The chrome sparkled in the fading light.

She began walking down the aisle with a large man in a fine suit by her side. The man Ynna had only introduced as Hector was intimidating. Though he had been amiable and talkative, Moss could sense an inherent power in the man. It was the same thing he had felt with Burn or with his grandmother and the same thing he hoped to someday possess himself. He didn't know what he would have to do to obtain that commanding presence, but he knew it would help him.

Hector let her go at the base of the little platform where Gibbs and Moss were waiting and Ynna stepped up across from Gibbs. Moss watched as the couple he would least have expected to ever get married grinned at each other like schoolchildren.

The officiant cleared their throat and everyone sat, the sounds of creaking chairs and shifting bodies fading into silence.

"When these two asked me to perform this wedding, my first thought was, 'isn't literally anyone else better for this job?'" Judy said to amused chuckles from the audience.

Moss knew how true those words were. Judy was eternally pained by the loss of their love and even struggled to see love in front of them.

They continued, "But they reminded me of something. Ynna told me that I was the one person she knew who had experienced true love. Love like the one we are here today to celebrate.

"Ynna and Gibbs," they said with an uncharactcristically warm smile. Judy looked lovely in a black and white striped suit, their hair slicked to the side with a white plumeria set just above their forehead. "When I met you two, I didn't like you," they said with a smirk, and another chuckle came from the assembled guests. "And I don't know how much you liked each other. The little princess turned cyber-badass, and the pretend badass and actual weenie may not seem like a perfect match to some. But everyone who knows them knows how good they are together.

"They not only share interests but *passions*," Judy said, emotion showing on their face. Moss wanted to reach out and hug them. It had been kind of Judy to do this despite how hard it would be for them. "They make one another better and raise each other up. Where one is weak, the other is strong. Together, they become better, fuller people. They have that strange and secret thing that you only know if you know. It does not matter if they *seem* different because they are the same where it counts.

"It is a blessing to find love in this world and even more of a blessing to be able to celebrate it. All of us here know the struggle, the toil and the pain. Once in a while, we should know the joy and celebration as well. It is a good time in this world, an optimistic time, and the perfect time to celebrate the love these two share. They have, of-fucking-course, elected to write their own vows."

Moss looked out at all the smiling faces. Seeing grins and happy tears put him ill at ease. It felt as if every time they were happy, something terrible happened. But seeing Issy's smiling face made him feel safe. Like he was home.

"Ynna," Gibbs said, his eyes already welling. "Even though you scared me to death, I was in love with you from the moment I met you. And it wasn't just because you are hot," he said with a perfectly Gibbsian smile as Moss shook his head. "It was that you also knew video games!"

Laughter from the audience followed. "But then we got to know each other and you opened up to me." He winked ever so subtly at her, and she rolled her eyes. This small, shared moment broke Moss's heart once again. He couldn't stand to be without them. "And as I got to know you better, I realized how amazing you really are. You don't just kick ass and know everything, but you are also kind and thoughtful. Behind every mean name you call us is a hint of love. Behind every joke you make, there is spark.

"You are a warrior and a leader, but you are also a hero and kind soul. You inspire everyone you meet, and you work to make this world a better place when it has given you no reason to do so.

"You took in two bubs and taught them the world, and you took one of them and taught him how to be himself. You have made me the man I always pretended to be, and I will work for the rest of my life to earn that. I love you … even though you still scare me to death."

As he folded the little scrap of paper in a trembling hand, she looked at him with wet, joyous eyes.

"Gibbs," she said, having to choke down emotion to speak. "When you first stumbled into my life, I thought I would have to protect you. And I did," she said, laughing at her own joke. Everyone joined in, especially Moss. "I still don't know how you survived, but somehow we ended up meeting and my life was forever changed. I never thought some ginger bub could make me feel happy and safe, but you do.

"I never thought someone who knows nothing about women could help me understand myself, but you do. And I never thought someone who had only ever eaten bagged food could get me addicted to his chicken parm, but somehow, you have."

Gibbs was weeping now as he looked into Ynna's eye, now glowing orange with the setting sun.

"You are a good man with a good heart who helped me to open doors I thought were shut forever. You are there when I can't stand to look at anyone, especially myself, and you are there when I need someone — even if I am too proud to admit it.

"Despite all odds, I love you and I want to spend the rest of my life with you," she said genuinely, tears rolling down her face.

"You got Ynna to be sappy," Judy joked. "You really have changed her."

Ynna reached out and pushed Judy playfully on the shoulder. They continued, "No turning back now. Samuel Gibson III, do you take this woman to be your wife?"

"I do," he said softly, happily.

"And Marina Ann Hawkins, do you take this man to be your husband?"

"I can't believe I'm going to say this but, I do," Ynna said with a smile that showed every one of her teeth.

"Then, by the power vested in me by literally nobody, I pronounce you man and wife," Judy announced to a cacophonous cheer. "You may kiss your bub."

CHAPTER 24

"No rings?" Mr. Greene asked as he swayed to keep his daughter asleep on his shoulder. Moss's mentor from ThutoCo was living a happy, peaceful life, but had insisted on coming to the wedding. He had only met Gibbs a handful of times, but it was enough to want to be here.

"Ynna said they got them but that she didn't want it to be part of the ceremony," Moss told him.

Mr. Greene nodded. "Brian was the same at our wedding; he had to have everything his way," he laughed, lost in the memory for a moment. "Think you'll marry Issy?"

Moss sighed. "I hope so," he said. "But I have a few irons in the fire."

"We regret the things we don't do more than the things we do," he observed.

"Yeah, I've heard that one before too," he said. "It's just . . ." Moss paused, considering his words. Even though it had been years and everything about their lives had changed, he still looked up to Mr. Greene and still felt nervous when speaking to him. He always felt like he was talking to his boss. "Look, I'm not trying to make excuses or anything, but we are on the precipice of something huge and I feel like I should focus on it as much as I can."

"Love isn't a distraction," Mr. Greene told him. "Look at those two," he said, pointing to Gibbs and Ynna on the dance floor, laughing and moving together. "They are both better precisely because they embraced their feelings. You have deep scars because your parents were killed and the company that raised you erased your memories," he said so bluntly that it was like a slap upside the head. "And that's perfectly fair, but don't let it paralyze you."

Moss couldn't help but notice how similar his advice was to his father's. He began asking the question before it even formed in his mind.

"Did you know my dad?"

Mr. Greene's daughter burbled on his shoulder and he bounced even more rhythmically. "We met once at a party early in my managerial career," he said. "I had a famous name but hadn't proven myself yet and your dad was already a titan. His research was groundbreaking. He was one of those guys that everyone wanted to talk to, to meet or to shake hands with."

Moss snorted a laugh. "He was never that person to me."

"Naturally," Mr. Greene agreed. "And he wasn't that person at the party either. As I inched my way over to listen to him addressing the assembled crowd, you know what he was talking about?"

"His research," Moss said flatly.

"No," Mr. Greene said with a smile. "He was saying how his three-year-old son would wake up early, and rather than crawling into bed with his parents and waking them up, would cross his room and pick up a book — even though he couldn't read yet. All he did the whole night was brag about you."

It was like another gut punch. Moss knew it should make him happy, but it just made him so sad that he didn't have his father in his life. That he didn't have his mother. That he was about to lose the two people closest to him.

Mr. Greene seemed to pick up on Moss's energy and continued. "It's part of the reason I pushed to have you in my division when your parents died and you were old enough. I wanted to know this kid who had so inspired such an inspirational man. It was also why I was so hard on you when you were apathetic and why I was always trying to push you. Some good it did me."

Moss chuckled. "I guess I needed the right job."

"That you did," Mr. Greene agreed. "And you have it now."

Moss shrugged and turned to look at the dance floor, where all the finely-dressed people with their drinks moved to the music.

"No, really, Moss," Mr. Greene said, recapturing his attention. "You have come such a long way since you were the little kid I was trying to get to excel. You have found your calling. You are a natural leader, strong and decisive."

"Thank you," Moss said, feeling far from the person his mentor considered him.

"It's true, Moss," Mr. Greene assured him. "You are stronger than you know, and I believe you will change the world."

"Thank you," Moss said. "But enough about me. Tell me about her."

"Thank you," Mr. Greene said with sincere joy. "That's as long as I want to go without talking about Millie."

He talked for the better part of twenty minutes and Moss listened and smiled, glad his former boss was so happy now. Issy waved him over from the dance floor.

"Duty calls," Mr. Greene told him and pushed him toward the mass of bodies. Moss laughed and moved toward Issy. He had almost reached her when he felt a tug on his arm and saw the telescoping metal eyes of Seti.

"The Scubas are in. They have been talking, and it's big" she said as she continued to dance with Judy. Moss was intrigued but looked past her to Issy. "Nothing that can't wait until morning though," Seti added with a little smile.

"Thanks," he said, giving her shoulder a squeeze before sidling up beside Issy.

She draped her arms around him and he pulled her close. She stank of booze and sweat and joy. Smiling up at him, she said, "I love you."

"I love you, too," he said. She smiled so happily that Moss felt he could fly off the roof at that very moment.

"I love them too," she said, pointing at the happy couple. "Fucking Gibbs is married before us; can you believe it?"

Moss laughed. "No, no I can't."

"We'd better be next," she slurred, narrowing her eyes and pointing a finger.

"You got it," Moss said, his heart racing. He knew she was drunk but also that she meant it. And he meant it too. He did want to marry her. It didn't matter that the institution was meaningless now; it only mattered that he wanted to pledge himself to her.

"Good," she smiled, using his shoulder as support as she swayed. "I really am so happy for them."

"Me too," Moss said, masking his sadness over Gibbs's recent revelation.

"I think Ynna gets to join our little lifelong crew now," Issy said. "The tripod becomes a quadpod."

Moss smiled, looking over his shoulder at them. "I like the sound of that."

"Get your hands off me!" Moss heard and he was sucked out of the moment as he watched his grandmother stumbling away from the bar with a bottle in her hand.

He sighed so deeply that it sounded as if his soul was trying to escape.

"Go," Issy said but her annoyance and disappointment were obvious.

He stormed over to his grandmother, who had moved to her favorite spot on the roof where there was a gap in the handrail and she could look out over the city.

"You have to make a scene? Here? Now?" Moss hissed.

She turned red eyes on him. "I ain't some child," she said, her words slurring together.

"Grandma," he whispered, the word a plea.

"Don't you pull that on me, boy," she said and took another swig.

"I'm not trying to pull anything on you," he murmured. He could hear the exhaustion in his own words.

"Think you know best," she said. "You don't know shit."

Moss gritted his teeth. She saw him as some weak child, and even though he didn't always believe it himself, he knew he was actually the person Mr. Greene saw.

"I know you ordered a GenMask of Persimmon LeBeau," he snarled.

She turned and smiled at him like a shark. "And what of it?"

"What of it?" he parroted. "What was your plan? To have a good person elected and then replace them?"

"Yes," Sandra said flatly.

It was the answer he most dreaded. From the moment he saw the mask in Africa, it was the thing he feared. "That's fucked up," was all he could manage.

"War is fucked up," Sandra said, and there was no denying that truth.

Moss shook his head. "Yes, but how you win it is important. Can't you see that anymore? If we kill our allies, we don't deserve to win."

"Foolishness," Sandra said.

"No," Moss said, "it isn't."

He watched as his grandmother swayed on her booted feet in a dress that looked ancient despite having only been worn once or twice before. She was still such a powerful force, but she was also so lost. She had given them all so much but also taken so much.

He had to ask the thing that he had been wondering since they killed Ninety-Nine. "With Carcer gone, do you feel like your fight is over?" Moss asked softly. "Honestly."

Sandra looked over the vast city for a long moment. "No," she said, sounding a bit calmer. "And yes."

Moss nodded and she kept talking but didn't turn, the lights of the skyscrapers reflecting in her eyes. "I needed this. Needed to kill that man and start this ball rolling. But it doesn't feel done to me. And I don't mean because we have more companies to fight, but because Carcer still exists on Earth."

She paused for a long time as Moss studied the face of the only blood family member he had. "But also," she said, and though she was standing right beside him, she seemed as far away as the moon that looked down on them. "I'm tired, Moss. I was never meant to live this long. Should have been Burn. He was always the good one. He would have taught you right."

"You have taught me," Moss argued. "So much."

266

"Don't just mean you," she said. "All of you."

"Oh," Moss said.

"Right," Sandra said. "I lost them the moment I killed that kid, the moment I did what had to be done. I told 'em, I explained it to them, but it don't matter. They will see that in the future, but they can't see it now: they were weak for wanting to protect him." Her ire was up again and she took another swig. "They were fools!"

She spat off the edge of the building. It felt like the edge of the world. She was the version of herself that she seemed to default to these days. The version of her that Carcer had made.

"They don't understand that I do these things because no one else will, and if they don't toughen up, they will die."

Moss felt a tear roll down his cheek. "They are tough. I am tough. But we have to be more than tough, more than vengeful. We are the hope for this world, and we have to lead by example. We need to work together, to be a family."

"I am your *only* family," Sandra corrected.

"No," Moss said, thinking about all the people he loved, singing and dancing nearby.

He knew who his family was.

He put a firm hand on his grandmother's back, took a deep breath and looked out into the lights of the city before closing his eyes.

THE END

EPILOGUE

Arthur Smith was exhausted. He had warned both the mayor and Warden Ninety-Nine what would happen if they tried to lock down the city but neither had listened to him and now one was dead and the other had been supplanted and his son had been killed. Now Arthur had to ingratiate himself to another head of Carcer. It was sickening.

The President of ThutoCo sighed as he stepped into the foyer of the Night Crystal. It looked like a war zone. Shattered glass crunched underfoot, bullet holes pockmarked the walls, drones buzzed overhead as they scanned and analyzed the scene and rows of body bags lined nearly every wall.

"Fucking terrorists," Arthur heard from over his shoulder. He turned to see Todd Davis standing beside him. He did not know the man except by reputation and was not sure why he had been named next in line of succession at the Carcer Corporation.

"Sorry for all the loss your company has seen," Arthur said, sounding sincere.

Todd nodded. "It's not your fault but I appreciate the sentiment."

Arthur smiled subtly. Maybe this man wouldn't be so bad. He was the first person at Carcer not to blame Arthur for everything Moss and his henchmen did.

"Is there someplace we can talk?" Arthur asked.

Todd nodded, watching as a drudge carried another bag past them. "Certainly," he said, "follow me."

He led Arthur to a bank of elevators and stepped to the centermost one, letting a scanner run over his face. The gold-plated doors slid aside and the two men stepped in before being rocketed to the top of the building. When the door opened again, it did so right into the office that overlooked the city on the far side. The ceiling was sloped and the walls were covered in military artifacts and taxidermized animals. A naked blond girl in a collar was kneeling in the corner and Todd stepped over to the bar.

"Drink?" he offered.

Arthur nodded, taking a seat on the alligator skin couch at the center of the room.

"So, Mister Smith, what is it that I can do for you?" Todd asked as he handed the man a drink and sat across from him, crossing his legs delicately.

"Well," he said, trying to assess what the best tactic would be with the man. "I assume you have been approached by the mayor's office?"

"I have," Todd agreed, sipping at the cognac.

Arthur didn't speak, hoping the other man would. Todd was a bit older, graying hair falling around his face in a false disheveled appearance that company heads liked to foster. He was clean shaven and wore the black suit that seemed to be required of a senior manager at Carcer.

"May I ask the content of the conversation?" Arthur asked in as amenable a tone as he could muster.

Todd smiled but Arthur instantly saw the look behind the look. The man had been promoted for a reason. The little look was all it took for Arthur to know. "Mister Smith," he said with an equally false tone. "This is our first meeting and these are our first words. I am not foolish enough to think that you are here simply to welcome me but I also know that you are not foolish enough to think that I am just going to give you information. I would be happy to continue the tradition of friendship between our companies but you will have to do better than that."

Warden Ninety-Nine had been a blunt instrument but this man was much more like Alice Carcer- clever, cunning and intelligent. Arthur would complain but he enjoyed going tête-à-tête with people like this. It was what he trained his whole life to do. He was supposed to be doing it back in Cape City, at his family's company, but he was here instead. "Certainly," he said, taking a long sip before pulling two cigars out from the case in his jacket pocket. "From Cuba," he said. "Did you know that entire island is tobacco and sugar? I think just three humans live there; all the rest are our drudges."

He nipped the tips and handed one across to Todd. "If it means that I get cigars like these, let there be no people left," the man said with a grin.

Arthur winked at him as he lit Todd's cigar. "A man after my own heart," he said suggestively, testing to see how much Todd actually knew. But once again, the man did not speak. He was playing things close to the vest.

"I asked about LeBeau because they ran a campaign about your company," Arthur said.

Todd nodded. "That they did."

Arthur knew he wasn't going to get anything else so he continued. "I do not think it would be in the best interests of the city for your company to pull out."

Todd smiled at him, letting the smoke pour from his lips slowly. "And why is that?" he asked finally.

Arthur felt his blood begin to boil. "You cannot be serious," he said, anger getting the better of him. "This city must be one of your biggest contracts. It would be foolhardy to give all that away."

"Ah, yes," Todd said. "I know why it would benefit my company to stay, but I am curious why it helps you."

"Because," Arthur said. "Because the streets will go mad. Security is paramount at a time like this."

"No," Todd said. "I don't think that is it."

Did this man know something he wasn't saying? Had Alice Carcer left information for her successors? Or was he just fishing?

"What do you think it has to do with?"

Todd smiled, firing streams of smoke from his nostrils. "I think this has to do with the Scubas and I think that if you want to be friends, it's time you took a leap of faith."

Arthur had to make his choice quickly. He was enraged that the man knew his secrets but would rather trust him further than risk the world finding out. "Yes," he admitted. "It is the Scubas. They know something that we do not want the world finding out. Something that could damage us forever."

"And that is?" the man asked with an eyebrow raised.

"If I tell you, will you assure me that the Carcer Corporation will stay in B.A. City?" Arthur offered.

Todd smiled. "Certainly."

"Those people, those religious freaks know that we were able to cure the prophet root disease years ago," he said, trying to get a read on the man's face but it was blank- a mask of serenity. "They know that we contaminate pockets and places to ensure the news feeds get footage of the infected and people cower inside the cities. They know that we no longer need the misters and that the planet is largely habitable again."

Todd smiled, a broad, genuine smile. "Thank you for trusting me."

"Thank you for returning the favor," Arthur said, breathing a sigh of relief. He was never able to talk openly about these things. These massive secrets. He was only able to make vague allusions to them and it was nice to speak the words for once. Moments like this were why he helped set up the Amalgamated Interests Council. Why he thought it was important for all the major companies to work as one.

"Well," Todd said, standing and extending a hand. "It was nice to meet you."

"Likewise," Arthur said with a smile, shaking the man's hand.

The shake lasted too long and he tried to pull away. He didn't like touching people to begin with and this was something he couldn't abide.

Then he felt it. Burning on his face.

It happened so fast. The cigar struck his cheek and exploded just before the balled fist made contact. He was knocked to his knees. he hadn't felt pain like that since he was a boy, since the last time he had disappointed his father.

They were still holding hands and Todd pulled him up. Arthur tried to swing but the man was too fast.

"We are not your puppets," the man growled and struck him again.

Arthur yelped in pain. He had misread everything.

Carcer was done with them.

Everything was falling apart.

"Get out of my office," Todd said, pushing Arthur toward the elevator.

He wanted to fight back but his head was swimming and his face hurt in a way he had forgotten existed.

"I'll kill you for this," Arthur threatened.

The man stomped over and kicked Arthur on his retreating ass, sending him toppling forward. "The weak make threats," the man said, towering over him. Arthur crawled toward the elevator, reaching up and pressing the button. The waiting elevator opened in an instant.

"You'll regret this," he hissed, feeling warm blood in his mouth.

Todd smiled at him. This knowing smile that made Arthur want to spit.

He looked as though he was going to say one more thing but Arthur scrambled into the elevator. After the door closed, he was alone with his thoughts and with his rage. Pulling himself to his feet, he saw the blood, the bruises and the imprint of the cigar.

Bring my car around, he demanded.

He would have his revenge. On Carcer. On Moss. On the whole world.

It was time. Time to put his plan into motion.

NOTE TO THE READER

Thanks for reading *Augmented States: A Cyberpunk Saga (Book 5)*. If you enjoyed the book, please leave a review; it is incredibly helpful to new authors. Reviews are one of the ways in which people can discover new work and help me to create more of it. Thanks again for reading.

For free content, a glossary of terms, cosplay, concept art and much more, visit Thutoworld.com

AUTHOR BIO

Matthew A. Goodwin has been writing about spaceships, dragons, and adventures since he was twelve years old. His passion for fantasy began when he discovered a box set of the Hobbit radio drama on cassette tape in his school's library at the age of seven. He fell in love with fantasy worlds and soon discovered D&D and Warhammer miniatures.

Not wanting to be limited by worlds designed by others, he created Thutopia (now called the Thuton Empire), a fantasy world of his own, which he still writes about to this day.

Like many kids with an affinity for fantasy, a love of science fiction soon followed. He loved sweeping space operas and gritty cyberpunk stories which asked questions about man's relationship to technology. That led him to write his first published work, *Into Neon: A Cyberpunk Saga*, which takes place in a larger science fiction universe.

He has a passion for travel and wildlife, and when he is not off trying to see the world, he lives in San Francisco with his wife and son.

Made in the USA
Las Vegas, NV
18 December 2022

63218747R00173